Out
of the
Ashes

Keren Hughes

ISBN 978-1-912768-49-3

Published 2019

Published by Black Velvet Seductions Publishing

Out of the Ashes Copyright 2019 Keren Hughes
Cover design Copyright 2019 Jessica Greeley
Cover photograph Copyright 2019 Keren Hughes
Illustration Copyright 2019 Jodie Harrold

www.blackvelvetseductions.com

Dedication

Jodie, you are the most amazing, inspiring young woman I've ever had the privilege of knowing. You always push me to do better, to be better, to achieve my dreams. You don't let me give up and you always tell me "You Will" and I know that with your love and support, I really will.

Thank you for being my rock. You're like tanzanite in a world full of diamonds; rare and precious ~xoxo~

Acknowledgements

To my nan; thank you for always being my inspiration. I love you from the bottom of my heart. It feels strange living in a world where you're no longer here. You left me before this book could come out, but you knew about it and you were so proud of me. I wish you'd gotten to at least see the cover, alas you did not. But I poured a lot into this book because of you. Thank you for always being my biggest cheerleader. I owe so much to you. A debt I'll never be able to repay. You were my mom, my rock, my everything. I still feel your love surrounding me every day. You are my North star. I love you.

To my son, Calum; thank you for always being you. You're funny, witty, smart and I love the bones of you. You are the very best part of me. Being your mom is the best thing I could ever do. Thank you for cheering me on in my writing all the time. I am humbled every time you say you're proud of me. Love you, kiddo <3

To Jodie, in short, for always telling me "you will." You don't say maybe, there isn't a 'possibility'. To you, it's always a done deal. Your belief in me has inspired me and pushed me to grow. You are the daughter I never had, you're one of the people I love most in this world. You always believe in me 110%. I love you for that. I can't wait to celebrate OoTA's release with you. Thank you for loving Nate and Nix as much as I do.

To Ric, my boss-man; thank you for always taking a chance on my writing. For every contract I've signed with you. I've not only gained a publisher; I've gained a friend. Thank you for everything.

To Jessica Greeley, thank you for making my gorgeous photo into an even more amazing cover.

To Tiffany Robinson, thank you for being my perfect Nix. And to Robert W for being my Nate. You guys rock this cover! You embody my characters and I couldn't have asked for a more perfect couple on my cover.

To Wander Aguiar for capturing the perfect essence of my Nate and Nix. This shit is amazing, as you always are. It was a dream to have a Wander shot for a cover. Now that dream has come true. You are an inspiration.

To Donna Payne-Latham, thank you for helping me select the perfect image for my characters. This cover wouldn't be the same without you.

To readers, bloggers and everyone else; thank you for choosing to read my books. Without amazing readers, authors wouldn't be able to do what we love most. We'd have stories in our heads but no-one to tell them to.
Thank you for your continued support. It means the world to me every time someone takes a chance on my books.
Whether you've been here since my journey began in 2013 or only just picked up a book by me, thank you for everything. You rock!
I hope you all enjoy Stone and Joss as much as I enjoyed creating them.

Keren xoxo

Prologue

The ink is dry. The decree absolute makes it final. The smile on my face says it all. Stanley Eugene Mason is out of my life once and for all. I changed my name by deed poll the moment the divorce papers got served. I no longer want any association with that man and that includes his name.

Going by my maiden name now makes me smile every time I think about it.

What's in a name? It's just letters, right? But his boring name was also a reflection of his personality. He'd told me when we met that his name was Lee. Even he'd been loath to tell me his full name.

I pawned my engagement ring and my wedding band, not because I needed the money, but because I didn't know what else to do with them. It turned out that they weren't worth much. Typical of my entire marriage. Turns out I wasn't even worth a real diamond. The jeweller looked up at me over her horn-rimmed glasses and flashed me a sad smile as she told me it was a cubic zirconia.

I'm not a materialistic person by any means. But doesn't every woman think she's worth a decent engagement ring? It's meant to symbolise the love between the couple. Instead this symbolised my cheap-ass ex who had only forked out for a gold-plated ring with a stone worth little more than if it had been a prize inside a Kinder Egg.

My wedding band had been bland. Just a plain, gold-plated band. I wasn't even worth nine-carat gold, which isn't exactly expensive.

"Lee" had a friend who worked in the jewellery business and said he'd asked for only the best for the woman he loved. But that ended up being a lie, just like our marriage vows.

Lord help the woman he's with now. I actually feel sorry for her. Not only is she lumbered with a man so boring he could be compared to watching paint dry, she's with someone as cheap as those knock-off designer suits he wears.

I look at my beautiful house and smile. I finally have something that belongs only to me. Something he couldn't take in the divorce because I didn't sign on the dotted line until the divorce was final.

Two months ago, I moved into this place with only a few meagre belongings to my name. I didn't want anything more when I walked away from the marriage than when I had entered it. I took only what was my own. I gladly let him have everything else, even though the grounds for divorce was that he'd cheated on me and that made me entitled to more than I got.

Miss Perfect Tits, as I affectionately call her, is the latest in a long line of women he saw behind my back. What they all saw in him, I really don't know. Any trace of what I saw in him disappeared the moment I found him in bed with some blonde with an inflated chest. He'd thought I was at work. Like that was an excuse to bring some whore to our marital bed. So yeah, I'd let him take everything, especially the bed.

Now here I am, alone and starting over. But it doesn't scare me the way I thought it would. Instead I'm delighted to have my own space. I have room to breathe, unlike when I was being suffocated by my marriage. When I left, the day I'd found him with Miss Bottle Blonde, I looked around at the beautiful house we called home and it no longer looked like somewhere I remembered. When you leave someone, you can't erase your memories and you can't burn the whole place down. But you can move on. It was onwards and upwards for me from then on.

Here, in this new place I call home, I am no longer surrounded by things that remind me of my delightful ex-husband. There's no wedding photo on the mantelpiece, happy smiling faces beaming at everyone. There are no belongings that we bought together, things that I had once thought meant something to us both. No, I left all that shit behind for him to do with as he pleased. I no longer want anything that is tainted with memories I'm trying my hardest to forget.

It's funny how "things" hold memories. Gifts you bought one another, items you picked out for your first home together. All of those things and more. They were contaminated the moment I saw Miss Bottle Blonde grinding her hips and moaning as her orgasm coated his cock.

Jeez, what a thought. Now I look back and wonder if *I* ever really had an orgasm with him. Did I always fake it? Even the memories in my head became contaminated, an infection spread through them, tainting them all one by one.

At least here I am free to discover what truly makes me tick. I may not be able to forget my marriage, but I'm telling myself it was a learning curve. I remember all the good, the bad and the ugly because I don't want my future to be the same old crap as my past. I want more for myself than a boring man, with a boring name and a tendency to fuck anything that moves.

"Lee" was a good man. He treated me like I was the only woman alive. He made me feel special. But once Stanley showed his true colours, Lee became but a distant memory.

I'm sitting at the kitchen island, drinking an iced coffee I grabbed from Starbucks on my way home. I almost want to frame my decree absolute, but instead I tuck it away in a drawer full of paperwork. I want to make something of my life now. I don't know what, but having a blank canvas gives me the ability to be whoever I want to be, do whatever I want to do. So, I better get to thinking.

Grams left me this house in her will, along with an inheritance. So, I'm going to make a fresh start in a house I loved as I grew up. Where do I start?

Chapter One

Jenna

I'm nervously anticipating something I've wanted to do for years but have never had the courage to go through with. In fact, my ex, Stanley, was adamant that he wouldn't allow me to go through with it, he even threatened divorce if I did. That goes to show how much of a prick he was. I just wish I'd learned that lesson sooner.

Why am I so nervous? I should be excited; there's something freeing about being a single, independent woman, allowed to do whatever the hell she wants with her own body. What was I thinking when I decided to come alone? I should have had my friend, and assistant at the florist shop I own, Brogan come with me and hold my hand. I've always been a bit scared of needles, and here I am waiting to get not only a navel piercing, but a tattoo as well. I take a couple of deep breaths and mentally shake myself. No one can tell me what to do anymore; this is my life and I am going to get on with it the way I see fit.

"Jenna, Nate will see you now," the receptionist with quirky rainbow-coloured hair says.

I stand and follow her to a room down a small corridor. She opens the door for me and steps back.

"Take a seat. Nate will only be a minute," she says with a bright smile as I enter the room.

I look around as she leaves and closes the door behind her. There's art on the walls and it's as eclectic in style as the rest of Blank Canvas. There are some gorgeous drawings that look like tattoos Nate or someone working here may have done before, and then there are canvases dotted around that depict a mishmash of things.

Realising I need to pee, I walk to the door and open it a crack, looking up and down the corridor to see if there's anyone around who can point me in the right direction. It's empty, so I walk to the far end, knowing that the toilets weren't anywhere in between the reception and the room the spunky young girl showed me to.

Seeing the toilets set at the very back of the shop, I enter and lock the door. Making sure to wash my hands, I check my makeup and hair in the mirror before walking back to the room for my tattoo.

Once I'm back in the corridor, I realise I didn't count how many rooms were between mine and the toilet. Damn! I'm sure Nate is waiting impatiently for me to return. I open the door to my left and it takes my mind a moment to register what I have walked into.

There's a man in a chair, and he's got to have the biggest cock I have ever seen in my life—not hard when you consider Stanley was nothing but a little prick, pun fully intended—and he's having it pierced. Not once, not twice, I can't even count how many piercings line this guy's privates. I feel my face blush red with embarrassment at having walked in on this guy, and, in that moment, he looks at me. He throws me a casual smirk before focusing his attention back on the blue-haired woman doing the piercing.

I can't even begin to imagine how much the actual piercing hurts, but what worries me most is how it must feel for the woman in his life. Or guy, I guess. I don't know his sexual orientation. But damn if it doesn't give me phantom pains between my legs. I feel my private parts clench in silent protest. I could never sleep with a guy who had that many piercings. Yes, I slept with a guy before Stanley who had a ring in the end of his cock, but that was different. It was one piercing, not multiple.

"It's called a Jacob's Ladder," a deep, sensual voice whispers in my ear, causing me to simultaneously break out in goosebumps and jump out of my skin.

I can't take my eyes off the piercing going on in front of me, but that voice has me curious as to what its owner looks like. Mentally shaking myself, I pull my eyes away and turn to the guy behind me. I'm met with the most stunning blue-green gaze and I find I want to get lost in those eyes. They twinkle with mirth. I mean, he did just catch me staring at a guy's cock. I may have even been drooling for all I know.

"I'm Nate, your tattooist," he says in that sinfully seductive voice.

"Jenna."

My voice betrays me by squeaking out my name in an unladylike way. Not the best way to impress the guy. Not that I should want to impress him, but damn if looking him over doesn't make my ovaries want to spontaneously combust. He is the hottest guy I ever remember laying eyes on.

"Well, Jenna, it would appear you are in the wrong room; follow me," he says as he turns on his heel and walks off towards the door to his room.

I follow him, making sure to quietly close the door behind me as I make a hasty retreat.

Once I am back in the room I started off in, I breathe a sigh of relief, but it's short-lived.

"Don't worry; it happens all the time. Walking into the wrong room, that is. Plus, I'm sure the guy didn't mind being watched. And he *did* know you were watching. I saw him smirk at you. Don't mind him though; he's harmless. He's always in here getting a new piercing or tattoo."

So much for not having to mention it. I feel myself heat as I blush for the second time in a short space of time. Nate smiles as the colour tinges my skin. His eyes are twinkling again, and I can't help feeling hypnotised. He really is handsome. Now I have the time to look him over properly, I can see he's at least six feet tall, has sleeves of tattoos down both arms, and damn if those arms don't look like they could squeeze me deliciously. His dark brown hair is tousled, and it looks like he's been raking a hand through it. Probably while waiting for me to hurry my ass up.

"Sit down. I won't bite," he says and chuckles at me as I walk to the leather chair in front of him.

Looking at his hands, I see yet more ink and I find myself wondering if I'll be able to sit still throughout this tattoo. I didn't know the guy who would have his hands on me would be this hot. Damn it, why does he have to have the most panty-melting smile known to man...or woman?!

I sit down, and Nate begins to pour ink into little pots beside him. I've never been into a tattoo shop before, I don't know what I expected, but it certainly wasn't whatever this is. The sparks I can feel coming off him. That's not natural. I never felt any sparks with my ex. My friends talk about sexual chemistry and, although I'm by far no virgin, I have never felt a chemistry like this. It's like an electrical storm, gathering energy all around me, zapping me with high-wattage currents. I have to clench my legs to quell the feelings there. I hope Nate doesn't notice. But what I wouldn't give to have him feel the same way.

He's a virtual stranger, albeit a handsome one. Why am I lusting after someone who I know nothing about, except his name and the fact that he has a sinfully sexy voice and a body carved of marble—or what I can see of it, at least.

His arms are muscular and tattooed. He has so many tattoos it's hard to focus on just one. But his ink isn't what I'm attracted to—well, it might be in part—it's him as a whole. He's nothing to me, but he makes me feel like a giddy teenager with her first crush.

Looking up at me, he flashes me a megawatt grin and I see he has a perfect "Hollywood" smile. There's something more though. It's in his eyes. I can't name it. Is it lust? What I feel can't be mutual, surely?!

"Ready?" Nate asks, startling me.

"Umm…" I ponder it for a moment before nodding.

"Then let's get this stencil in place so you can be sure you like the positioning."

"Oh, umm…"

I thought he was ready to begin tattooing me already. I've totally forgotten about the design. To tell the truth, I'd probably let him tattoo whatever the hell he liked on me.

Taking my sweater off, I reveal the tank top I'm wearing underneath. Noticing where Nate's gaze is, I quickly realise I pulled up the tank as well as the sweater, baring my skin to him. I'm almost embarrassed, because not many men have seen so much of me. But considering a few moments ago when my face must have betrayed my embarrassment at seeing the guy with all the piercings, I'm sure I couldn't blush much harder.

His hands are soft as he applies the stencil, pressing all over to make sure the ink is left on my skin. I find myself imagining what those hands would feel like if he was touching me somewhere lower.

"This is big for a first tattoo; you're braver than some who come in here," Nate says as he steps back to check the design looks right. "Check it out in the mirror and, if you're happy, we'll begin."

Admiring the beauty of the piece on my right shoulder, I smile. This tattoo represents my freedom and my rebirth into the woman I was meant to be but, wasn't ever allowed to be. I can just see it when

Nate has finished—the fiery oranges, the bold yellows and reds that will replace the simple lines of the initial drawing. I smile, and Nate flashes me a salacious grin as he sits down next to me.

"Shall we begin?" he asks as he pulls on a pair of latex gloves.

I momentarily feel deflated, knowing that his skin won't be pressed against mine. Smiling, I adjust my sitting position a little and get comfortable. This is going to take around four hours according to the person I spoke to when I booked myself in. I was nervous then, but now I know that it's Nate that will be doing the tattoo, I feel better. I feel shy and yet somehow relaxed in his company. He seems to have an aura of peace around him. That seems kind of at odds with how imposing and beautiful he is but seems to fit perfectly at the same time.

As the needle is pressed to my skin, I suck in a sharp breath, bracing myself for the pain. But when it doesn't come, I relax and enjoy the feeling in a way I didn't know was possible.

Nate looks happy, like this is something he was born to do. And maybe he was. I know nothing about him. Not that I would mind getting to know him better, in more ways than one.

"So, Nate, how long have you worked here?" I find myself asking, wanting to know more about the alluring man with his hands on me.

"I've been here for about eight years now. I found this place empty and knew without a doubt it was perfect for my vision. I started working at Tattoo Envy when I was eighteen and just an apprentice. I honed my craft until I felt I was ready to open my own place when I was around twenty-eight. To be honest, I would have started out on my own before then, but I really loved the staff that had become like a family to me. I didn't want to leave them. But they urged me to spread my wings and that's when I started Blank Canvas. I had learned the business side of things from Hannah, the woman that owned Tattoo Envy, and so I had all the necessary skills to start this place. I just didn't know if it would take off. I'm glad it did though."

I hadn't been expecting him to divulge so much information and, as he realised this himself, he apologised for oversharing. Smiling at him, I told him apologies weren't necessary.

"Is there a story behind this?" he asks as he nods his head at where the wings are starting to really take shape.

"You know what they say about rising from the ashes," I start. "Well, I guess it's true. I'm making my fresh start. I should have done it a long time ago, but I didn't possess the courage. Or at least I didn't think I did. This tattoo represents me being stronger than I ever knew. I guess you could say the ashes and flames of the design represent Lee, my ex-husband. And the phoenix is me, rising from the past to a beautiful new future."

There, I'd overshared in reciprocation. Though I didn't admit Lee's real name wasn't in fact Lee, or Douchebag, or Cheating Asshole, or Serial Shagger. No, I'd kept that information to myself. Stanley Eugene "Douchebag" Mason was a part of my past I'd rather not discuss with the hot, muscular, tattooed guy with his hands on me. He's not a therapist after all, just your run of the mill tattooist. Though I'm not sure anything about Nate could be classed as "run of the mill".

"I know the feeling. And to think I almost married her. Thank goodness for small mercies."

His statement has me curious, but his gaze collides with mine and all the air leaves my lungs in a rush. There's something like hunger in his gaze as his eyes roam over me. I cannot get entangled with any man, much less this incredibly hot specimen. I'll end up hurt and my heart can't take any more right now. I can sure dream about the hot guy who took my virginity though—ink virginity, that is.

My best friend, Brogan, has told me I have what she calls "virgin skin". I laughed at the notion, but I guess it's true.

"I did marry mine," I reply after a pause. "I was young and naïve. There's no chance of me making that mistake again. Hurt me once, shame on you. Hurt me twice, shame on me too. I couldn't stick around for him to hurt me again. There are only so many chances you can give a person and, while I'm a believer in second chances, I don't believe in twenty-second chances, you know?!"

Nate looks at me with something akin to pity in his gaze, but all traces of that vanish when he looks me square in the eye.

"I'm sorry he hurt you. I may not know who he is or what he did, but I do know if I had a woman like you, I wouldn't want to hurt her for the world."

My blood begins to sing in my veins and my heart beats faster at the sincere tone in his voice. If I didn't know better, I'd make a play for him, let him know I was his to do with as he pleased. But sadly, I know better. I know that so many relationships end in bitter resentment. And I'm too old to want to "hook up" as the kids call it these days. I'm not interested in one-night stands or anything casual. But sadly, I'm also not interested in trying for anything more serious either.

Brogan would tell me to go for it. To make a move, be bold and just see where it takes me. But then, she's a fair bit younger than me and hasn't been married, let alone found her husband in bed with another woman. She says you never get anywhere in life if you don't take a risk here and there. But I'd rather stay risk free and pain free too.

Nate and I make small talk as he continues with my tattoo. I close my eyes every so often as he brushes my skin, and it causes me to stifle a moan. He flirts with me, but I'm guessing that's one way of getting repeat custom from women. Flirt and they'll fall all over themselves for you. Well, not me. Although mental images assault me and tempt me with their soft allure.

When Nate clears his throat, it's clear I was too lost in those mental images to notice he had finished the tattoo.

"Oh, Nate," I gasp as I gaze down at my shoulder. It's no longer bare. Now there is a stunning phoenix rising from the flames. I can't wait for it to be healed, so I can walk around proudly with this reminder on my skin. I am the phoenix, and I fully intend to rise from everything Lee turned to ash.

"Stand up and get a better look in the mirror, then I'll wrap it for you before giving you the aftercare instructions."

I do as he says and look at the glorious ink in the mirror. I was right—the fiery oranges, bold yellows and reds, they mix to make the most amazing artwork I have ever seen. The graceful bird rises from the ashes and flames around her as she soars above it all. I gasp in astonishment and appreciation.

"Beautiful," I murmur.

"Truly stunning," Nate replies, and I get an inkling he's talking about more than just his artwork as his gaze looks appreciatively over me.

Goosebumps break out on my skin again as he comes to wrap the tattoo for me. It feels like the first time he's touched my body, and yet it feels intimate and familiar at the same time. I really must get these kinds of thoughts out of my head.

"If you want to follow me, I'll take you to Steph, the lady who's going to do your piercing," Nate says as he walks towards the door.

He stops short of opening the door and turns to face me. I stumble as I didn't realise he was going to stop. With strong arms, Nate catches me before I face-plant the floor like a total idiot. Instead of letting me go, he looks down at me and roots me to the spot with just one look. His strong hands hold my hips, and his handsome, strong jaw dips towards me. I have only a moment to register what he's asking without words. I nod infinitesimally and brace myself as his soft full lips close over mine.

My senses are on overload as Nate's kiss sets me on fire. He licks at the seam of my mouth, seeking access to kiss me more deeply. For once, I go with my heart instead of my head, and I open my mouth to allow him to explore with his tongue. Our tongues dance together, and Nate's hands play with the hem of the tank top I'm wearing, making me shiver in the most delicious way. Maybe I didn't imagine the chemistry after all. A feeling I've never experienced before works its way up my spine as I allow him to take all I have to give in this one kiss—a kiss that sets a trail ablaze, searing its way across my heart and soul.

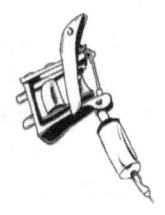

Chapter Two

Nate

Fuck! I don't know what I was thinking. Kissing a customer could get me in all sorts of hot water. I have a feeling she wouldn't report me for sexual harassment, but that feeling is more one of hope rather than based on actual facts.

She kissed me just as fervently as I kissed her. Those soft, full lips felt amazing as she opened her mouth to let me explore. Little tingles of electricity ran up and down my spine. The only thing that stopped me kissing her was Steph knocking on the door. She'd come to see how far along with the tattoo we were, as she had to pierce Jenna's navel at some point.

Jenna followed Steph down the corridor, and I was left to my own devices. I had another client booked in but needed a few minutes to gather myself first.

The women round here see me as a bad boy. A total player. Whilst that isn't true, I haven't done much to try and dispel the rumours. It doesn't hurt me to have them thinking whatever they like about me. I'm not looking for love, so it doesn't really affect me. Or it didn't. Until today. It's not like I'm wanting to run off and marry Jenna, but fuck if I didn't want her. My cock had been straining to be freed from the moment her lips seared mine in a kiss so passionate, so hungry it was like she was on death row and I was her last meal.

It took ten minutes for me to finally calm down enough to start my next client's tattoo. Ten minutes of scrubbing my hands over my face, tugging my hair, pacing the length of my room. Ten minutes of wanting to rip open the door, race down the corridor to Steph's room and see if they were done. I don't know what would have happened if I had done that. She'd looked like a rabbit caught in headlights. She was skittish. After a kiss so deep my soul felt it, she was nervous enough to run behind Steph the second the door was open.

Something told me that as much as she'd wanted that kiss, she had also done everything possible to keep it from happening. Well, not quite *every*thing as it had happened. But I knew she'd thought about it and was at war with herself over it. I don't know how I knew; I just had a feeling that was the case.

I'd let her run off without so much as a glance over her shoulder, and I hadn't gone after her. But now I'm regretting that decision because she's gone, and I have no way of contacting her. I don't even know her surname. There's no way to look her up. I looked through the shop's diary to see if she'd left a mobile number, but she hadn't. That was unusual as our receptionist normally asks for one from every client. But I didn't bother to question it. I just felt deflated as I walked back to my room to clean everything down before we closed.

Spraying the leather seat she'd been sitting on makes me think of her. I close my eyes and see her there. Such a gorgeous creamy expanse of skin. I only wished I hadn't been wearing gloves so that I could have touched her properly. Damn hygiene rules! But no matter whether the gloves stopped me feeling her skin, they didn't stop me from feeling the electricity that buzzed through my veins with every stroke I made. I feel it hum in my veins as I stand here with my eyes closed.

My grandfather would kick my ass and tell me to hunt her down, no matter what it took. He would no doubt say that any girl that makes you feel that way is one worth pursuing. He and my grandmother had such a beautiful relationship and had no problem with public displays of affection. They taught me what real love looks like. My grandmother's death hit him hard. It hit both of us hard, but my grandfather has become a shell of his former self since she passed. He seems hollow and haunted every time I visit now. The smile he had permanently etched on his face when she was alive no longer touches his eyes and makes them sparkle. He's lost that vitality. It makes me sad to think about how much he's lost.

My grandmother was one of the most amazing women I have ever known. She and Gramps took me in when my parents died many years ago. They had been the best parental figures I could wish for after my real parents. I don't have many memories of my mum and dad these days, just some old photos and stuff that was kept in the attic for me. My grandmother had made a memory box full of things from my childhood and as many things of my parents as she could. It's painful to look through it, but it's a welcome pain. It means I can still feel.

It hit me like an articulated lorry when my parents died. My life had been turned inside out, upside down and left in chaos. My grandparents took me in and were there for me when I had nightmares or wet the bed. They were the ones that soothed all my aches and pains, but I can't do the same thing for Gramps now, and that kills me.

I finish cleaning down my room and turn out the light. I'll pay Gramps a visit tonight. I'll even swing by and grab him takeaway from his favourite restaurant. He'll be happy to have real food compared to the slop they feed him at the home. Or at least that's what he calls it. I'm sure it's fine really, but he always moans that, no matter what he has to eat, it all tastes like the same crap. His words, not mine.

Closing the door behind me, I walk down the corridor to the front of the shop. Star, our receptionist, is just logging off her computer as I come up behind the counter.

"Hey, boss," she says in that effervescent way of hers.

"Hey, Star."

"You all finished up? Seems like everyone else has gone for the evening."

"Yep. Just off to The Steakhouse to grab Gramps a T-bone."

"That's so sweet. You have a good night, boss," she says as she grabs her coat and slips into it.

"You too, Star. See you tomorrow."

I walk to the parking lot after locking up. My shiny black Miata MX-5 is waiting for me. I hop in and start the engine. She purrs like a kitten and I smile as I remember the last time I took Gramps out in her. He said that it was a good job my grandma wasn't alive when I bought her, else she would have had a heart attack. She would've preferred me to drive something more "safe looking" according to Gramps. I told him that she was perfectly safe, and I had taken him on a ride out to prove my point. He'd fallen in love with my baby but said Grandma would have had kittens if I'd taken her out in it.

Laughing at the memory, I pull out of the car park and head for The Steakhouse. Prime T-bone steak with fat chips, mushrooms, and onion rings, with horseradish sauce, that was the order of the day. Gramps would cheer up a bit if I provided him with his contraband—you're not supposed to smuggle food in to the patients at the home, but what they don't know won't hurt them.

The question is, do I tell him about Jenna and wait for him to impart me with a pearl of wisdom? It might do him good to think his grandson is interested in a woman after all this time. My ex put me off women for the longest time and although my reputation precedes me and labels me a player that couldn't be further from the truth. There actually hasn't been anybody since her. My heart wasn't in the right place for anything with anyone. My grandma had died at around the same time, so I wasn't in the right frame of mind for finding love when my Gramps had lost the love of his life. And she was his life. They had done everything together. They'd been together since they were sixteen and had a good, long life together before she passed. Lillian Peterson had been the life and soul of the party. Everybody naturally gravitated towards her. There was just something about her that everyone loved. My gramps especially.

He said the day he'd met her was the day he knew he was going to marry her. She'd come into his life like a gift from god. Gramps believed she'd been put in his path for a reason and they'd gone on to marry, then had a baby a couple of years later. He was their only child and I was their only grandchild. I had no other family to speak of which is why they'd been the ones to take me in when my parents died, even though they weren't getting any younger and having an eight-year-old running them ragged must have been hard at times. But they never complained. They showered me with love and affection on a daily basis. Loving them had been so easy. The two of them were so special to me. Which is one of the reasons I had gone off the rails when my grandma died.

Heading into The Steakhouse, the owner sees me and walks to greet me.

"Nate, the usual is it?" he asks as he walks with me to the counter.

"Yep. I'm off to see the old man and I'm assuming that the food he was given this evening wasn't up to his standards and he probably refused to eat it, the stubborn old git."

Devin laughs as the guy behind the takeaway counter comes to take my order.

"He's stubborn alright. Please pass on my regards. It's been a while since we saw him. Do you think you'll be able to sneak him out of there anytime soon to come and have a proper meal with us?"

"I'm not sure, Dev. It's like trying to break out of prison. You'd think they'd let me take him out, being his grandson and all. But they say he needs twenty-four seven care and they seem to think he'd wander off if it was just the two of us."

"That he might, lad. Dementia is a hard thing to deal with. I'm sure they don't mean any offence in thinking you can't look after him. They just mean that it's possible he'll get confused and end up giving you the slip."

Devin must see the hard look in my eyes because he holds his palms up and gives me a small smile.

"I didn't mean any offence, Nate. Your gramps, he's a great guy. But the dementia does things to his mind, you know this. I'm not saying you wouldn't keep careful watch over him. But what if you did something as simple as went to the toilet? You couldn't take him with you. You'd be gone for all of sixty seconds maybe. But that's enough time for him to wander off."

"I guess. Sorry, Dev. I just get a bit … well, a bit touchy when it comes to him. Call me overprotective and sensitive. Okay, looking at me you wouldn't think I'm so soft at heart. I look like a hard-ass guy who couldn't give a fuck. But that couldn't be further from the truth. I love the bones of my gramps. I would give anything to take him out of the home, even if only for an hour. I'd drive us around, and he wouldn't have chance to give me the slip. I'd take him cruising around the city he loves so much. But no. Rules are rules. Hence why I'm sneaking him this contraband tonight. They can stick that particular rule where the sun doesn't shine!"

The server hands me the bag of containers and I hand over the cash. Devin walks me to the door, apologising again for any offence caused and I tell him to forget about it.

Climbing into my car, I set the takeaway bag on the passenger seat and bring the engine to life. I drive out of the car park and onto the main road, the one that leads me to Haven Lodge Residential Home.

***

Gramps is sitting in his chair facing out of the window when I arrive. He startles when he sees me in the reflection.

"Daniel, how good to see you son. You wouldn't believe the day I've had, and I haven't seen your mother all day. I don't know where she's got to."

"It's Nate, Gramps. I brought you a steak."

A look ghosts across his face and I wish I'd played along and said I was my dad. Sometimes it's easier, and I don't like the thought of bursting his bubble. But sometimes I just want him to remember it's me.

"Oh, Nathaniel, sorry, I thought you were your father. A steak, you say? It better be a T-bone!"

His face lights up as I place the bag on the table and begin to unpack its contents. I grab plates from the cupboard and cutlery from the drawer. He's not supposed to have them in here, but I keep them hidden from the staff. Or at least I think I do. They haven't said anything about them, yet.

"Damn, Nathaniel. I forgot how good a steak tastes," he says around a mouthful of medium-well steak.

"It's good, right, Gramps?" I reply as I tuck into my own.

We don't talk much as we devour our meals. Gramps's eyes are set alight as he enjoys every morsel. Comfortable silence has settled around us and I don't know what to say for fear of setting him off this late in the evening. It only takes the slightest thing sometimes, and you never know when those times are going to be. I guess Devin was right about taking him out of the home, even for an hour. So much has the possibility of going wrong. That doesn't mean I have to like their rules, but I know that Gramps isn't going to get better. Eventually, the dementia will get worse, and instead of having days where he remembers who I am, I'll be lost to him forever. So, I intend to make the very most of however long we have before that happens. And even when it does happen, I'll still come to visit. Even if it means pretending to be my dad. As much as that will hurt me to imitate my dead father.

"I met a girl," I say as I watch for his reaction.

His eyes twinkle and he smiles a mile wide. Boy I've missed that smile. It's been too long.

"Tell me more, boy. Don't miss out a single detail. I want to know everything," he says, coercing me into spilling the beans about Jenna, even if there's not that much to tell.

***

As I leave Haven Lodge, I smile to myself. Gramps was as much like his old self as he could've been, other than initially mistaking me for my father. I don't have many memories of my parents, only photographs and the stories Gramps tells in his lucid times.

I know I look like my father though. I see it every time I look at my parents' wedding photo. I have his eyes, my mum's nose … It's like looking in a mirror only now I'm looking at a ghost.

Gramps told me he thought I should do everything I could to track this girl down. He said that for all I know, she could be "the one". I didn't tell him I don't believe in "the one". I didn't want to ruin the mood. But our conversation did light a fire in me. I want to find out more about this girl, this woman. Jenna. How the hell do I go about finding out though? We didn't have a number listed for her, and the only thing I know is that she lives locally. I decide to ask Steph at work in the morning, just to see if she gleaned any information from her that would aid my search. I can trust Steph. She's the only one of my employees that knows the real me. She knows I'm not the player everyone else takes me for.

Resolving myself to wait until morning rather than whipping out my phone and texting Steph to ask—because then I really might seem stalker-ish—I get into my car and make the short drive home.

The house is cloaked in darkness as usual. Nobody home to keep a light on. Nobody to come home to and talk about my day. Not that I'd want to talk about today, per se, but maybe what Gramps said rubbed off on me a little. Maybe I would rather come home to someone rather than the cold reality of being single. I told him that just because I'm alone doesn't mean I'm lonely, but he scoffed at me and told me to stop being so bullheaded.

Grabbing myself a beer out of the fridge, I flick the cap off the bottle and settle in on the big sofa. Turning on the television, I channel hop until something takes my interest. Nothing does, so I look up my recordings. I just need something to distract me for an hour or so before I go to bed.

Deciding to rewatch the latest season of Game of Thrones from the start, I press play on the first episode, "Dragonstone".

An hour later and the house is cloaked in darkness once more as I ascend the stairs. Once in my room, I switch on my bedside lamp before going into my en suite. I turn on the water in my fancy shower. I'm not even sure what all the buttons and nozzles do, but I decided to splurge on a decent shower when the studio started making me some decent money.

Once my clothes are discarded in the laundry basket, I look at myself in the mirror on the cabinet above the sink. My two-day-old scruff needs a shave, but I can't be bothered. It can stand to go another day.

Standing in the shower, underneath the most powerful jets, I make quick work of washing and then stand there for a few moments longer, letting the water pummel my aching muscles. The memory of Jenna's lips and their powerful hold over me springs to mind. Her soft, full lips felt like heaven. My blood burned through my veins as her touch set me on fire. It's been a long time since anybody made me feel so alive. What to do next is the question. Maybe she'll get another tattoo. Maybe she felt the connection I felt and will come back to seek me out. But I get the hollow feeling that she won't. During the kiss, all I felt was a searing connection, binding us together. But afterwards, she walked away with Steph and I didn't see her again. Surely if she'd felt anything she felt was worth exploring further, she would have come back to my room.

Dragging my ass to bed, I towel off quickly, dump the used towel in the basket and then climb under the covers. I can't wait for sleep to claim me. Maybe I'll dream of Jenna. And maybe that will be a good thing. Or maybe it won't. After all, what good can a dream do except haunt me at night?

Chapter Three

Jenna

I wake from a dream where Nate claimed my body as well as my lips. He was a passionate lover and I had been willing to submit to him and allow him to dominate my body as well as my mind.

Showering away the remnants of my dream, I smile to myself as I dry off. I look in the mirror and see the beautiful ink that adorns the top of my arm. The ink is just the start of my rebirth from the miserable old Jenna. I need to inject some fun into my life, and I know just where to start.

Calling to make an appointment, I smile as the receptionist books me in. I have new ink, a new navel piercing—what's next? My hair, of course. The blonde that Lee loved so much—and insisted I keep—can go to hell. Don't get me wrong, I'm not doing anything wild, I'm just removing traces of the woman Lee claimed to love.

Looking in the mirror, all I can see is the bleach blonde hair of a bimbo. I hadn't wanted to dye it, but Lee insisted that he didn't much like brunettes; blondes were more his "type". Why I ever allowed that man to make my choices for me, I will never know. I thought it was love, but now I know it was more like my stupidity. So now, I'm going back to the chocolate brunette I used to be. I was so much more confident before Lee. I let him keep me as some downtrodden little woman, someone who did as she was told because she wanted to keep her husband happy. I was a fool. There's no denying it anymore.

***

Walking out of the salon with my head held high, I feel a confidence seeping back into my veins. A woman capable of making her own choices and never letting another man dictate to her, that's what I am now.

I walk past the window of Blank Canvas and smile as I see Star raise her hand to me. I give her a little wave back and carry on to my next appointment of the day—a job interview. One for my side business anyway. By day, I am the owner of Venus in Rhapsody, a florist here in the centre of town. But my other business is in graphic design. It's a relatively new thing for me. I started with pen and paper, just drawing, doodling, dreaming. But when Lee and I split, I decided to do something more with my art qualifications. Don't get me wrong, I love being a florist and owning my own store, but my art was something I was passionate about when I was younger, dedicated enough to it to study it at college and university. But Lee didn't think art was a vocation. It wasn't something I could do full-time and make a living at. Now I know he was wrong. Morgan & Co Design has been keeping me busy on an evening after the store is closed.

My best friend, Brogan, encouraged me. She kept dropping not so subtle hints for me to really do something I am good at. So, rebranding small businesses is what I do with my evenings. Naming businesses was never my strong point though, so I just used my surname and added the "& Co" to it to make it sound like a bigger business than it really is.

The job interview I'm going for is for a slightly bigger business than I normally take on. It's a small chain-store deal. Marcus Dudley, the proprietor, saw my business card somewhere and gave me a call to ask me to bring in my portfolio. If he wants to retain my services, then I'll have to ask Brogan to cover some more shifts at the store to cover for my absence. I've got a feeling I'm going to need to be on call for this guy anytime he likes. Evenings alone just won't do.

***

The interview with Marcus Dudley went better than expected and he hired me on the spot. The trouble with that is, he really does want me on call, day and night. I called Brogan and after squealing loudly down my ear, she congratulated me and agreed to manage Venus in Rhapsody in my absence. Hopefully this job won't take up too much time, but it's a great thing to be able to add to my C.V. Rebranding a chain store is something people will look at and instantly feel better about the standard of my work—I hope.

Marcus expects me to have it done in a timely manner and has agreed to take me on a tour around one of his stores, so I can get a feel for what it is they do and what he wants from me. I'm happy—giddily so, having just landed something so huge—but also nervous as hell. This could lead to something more, a brighter future for my designs, but if I get it wrong, it could be the biggest disaster of my life. Of course, I'll be presenting Marcus with a couple of design concepts—a sort of backup plan in case one is a flop—but what if he hates all my ideas? There's no time for worrying though as I'm due at the pub to work my evening shift.

The Siren Song is a bustling pub just on the outskirts of town. I've always liked the atmosphere and it was a job to take my mind off the crap I was going through with my divorce. Lee was being obstinate about the smallest things and I just needed human interaction because he'd driven away all of my friends over the years. It also happens to be the place I connected with Brogan.

Working behind the bar, Brogan was a natural with the customers and pulled a good pint. I poached her for my florist shop when I opened it and I'd agreed to cover some of what would have been her shifts, in an agreement with Riley, the landlord and owner of the pub. He knew she was looking for more than just pulling pints, and he knew that I was after a job that connected me with people more than just my own customers. So, it was actually a win all-round.

Entering the pub, I see it's getting busier thanks to most people having knocked off work by now and wanting to let off some steam on a Friday night.

Brogan is on shift tonight too, after closing the store for me, so I'll no doubt have a laugh tonight. Just what I need.

***

As I knew she would, Brogan quizzed me about Nate in our spare moments between customers. She admired my ink and I flashed her my new piercing. Brogan is one of those people that think ink is an addiction; she says they're like Pringles—"once you pop, you can't stop"—and although I thought of that as a weird analogy, it's typical Brogan.

She has ink adorning both of her arms, full sleeves on both of them. I admire her confidence as she struts around, swishing her hair, flirting with customers… I find myself wishing I was a little more like her. More carefree.

Reliving the kiss has been bittersweet. It's a nice memory to have, but it's something that if revisited just reminds me how alone I am. Maybe that's why I stayed with Lee for as long as I did—for fear of being alone if I left.

I haven't always feared being alone. When I was younger, it was easier to meet people—friends and boyfriends alike. But as I got older, I was only reminded how alone I'd be thanks to Lee alienating me from anyone I'd previously been friends with. So, I stayed because it was easier than starting again. But all that is behind me now, and I intend to be happy. With or without a boyfriend, a woman can be happy. I don't need a man to validate me.

Brogan swooned as I told her about the soul-searing kiss. She's a dreamer, that one. She believes in the foot-popping kind of kisses from films. She thinks that there's someone like that for everyone. All I know is, if that were true, then Lee definitely wasn't mine. His kisses didn't set butterflies swirling in my stomach. They didn't make my blood sing in my veins as it had with Nate.

Wanting so much to believe he was my destiny, Brogan talked about how I could waltz back into the tattoo studio and ask to see him. In her head, I'd lock gazes with him and he would smile a megawatt grin. He'd walk up to me, wrap me in his embrace and kiss me deeply, with a passion only felt in romance novels. His kiss would make my toes curl, my stomach somersault, and whatever other clichés she could think of.

In reality, I wasn't going to walk back in there and ask to see him. He wasn't going to look into my eyes and see straight to my soul. He wasn't going to kiss me until I melted into a puddle of something gelatinous at his feet. In reality, I was going to go about my life, as would Nate. We are not destined to be. Although, that kiss awoke something long dormant in me. Desire.

Riley walks into the bar and places a bunch of flyers on the bar top. He smacks his hand on them, making me jump.

"Ladies, there's something I need you to do for me."

"Yes, Riley, what is it we can do to help?" chirps Brogan from behind me.

"We're having ourselves a speed dating event in two weeks' time. These are the flyers. I need you two to make the customers aware."

"Can do, boss," Brogan says as she swipes a flyer from the top of the pile.

She reads the flyer aloud and it takes all I have not to cringe—externally anyway. Events like this have never been my cup of tea. I can't see the customers being interested either, but then I guess some people might do it for a laugh. That's the problem though. People will do it for a laugh instead of because they actually want to meet someone. The younger customers might do it as a way of hooking up with someone. I personally hate the thought of a "hook up" or "bunk up" or whatever the hell today's youth call it. I don't do one-night stands. Never have, never will.

Promoting this event will be tough. I just can't imagine the customers wanting to do it when my face displays my disdain for such nights. I guess I'll either rely on Brogan or I'll have to pull up my big girl panties and whip out my plastic smile.

"Sure thing, boss," I answer as he stares at me—almost like he's reading my mind. He was looking for my co-operation and I have no choice but to agree.

He leaves us to it, and I pull a face at Brogan.

"Suck it up, buttercup," she says before poking her tongue out at me.

"Nice, real nice."

I nudge her in the ribs as she passes to serve a customer and she just laughs at me.

So, this is what has become of my life. Promoting hook-up events. Yay for me!

***

I fall into bed after what felt like an extra-long shift. My comfy memory foam mattress greets me like an old friend. I'm in shorts and a tank as it's so bloody hot outside, with a fan at the end of my bed. Why do we not have air conditioning units in this sodding country? People in the States are so lucky. They get to remain cool while I get to moan like a bitch that my skin feels like it's going to melt right off my body.

Tossing and turning, I try to get comfortable, but no position feels right. I get up to take a cool shower in my en suite in the hopes of cooling off a little.

I close my eyes as the water pours down over me. The kiss plagues my thoughts and I wish there was a repeat performance on the cards.

I towel off, drop my used towel in the hamper and redress in my tank and shorts. It's going to be a long night if this heat persists.

Grabbing my laptop, I wait a moment for it to boot up and I grab my glasses, so I can work on a rough design idea I've had for Marcus Dudley.

Dudley & Sons was his father's baby really, but as he lost his father a couple of years ago, Marcus has had to take the mantle and wants something that reflects him as well as his father. They were diametrically opposed—or so he told me—which is why the rebrand is happening. His brother works for the company but doesn't want the pressure of helping run the business, so all I have to do is please one of the late Mr Dudley's sons. Thank goodness for that.

After working for an hour or so, I feel my eyelids becoming heavy, so I decide to switch everything off and get some much-needed sleep. If only that kiss doesn't replay in my dreams.

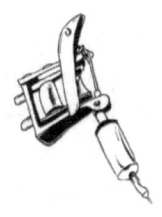

Chapter Four

Nate

After a restless night, I get into work and realise in horror that my reflection doesn't show the composed guy I usually am. I run my fingers through my hair and decide that the three-day-old scruff on my face will just have to do for now. I overslept this morning thanks to little sleep last night, so I was in too much of a rush to shave. Or to even look at my reflection by the looks of it.

Star comes in and greets me with a smile.

"Thought you could probably use this, boss," she says as she hands me a takeaway coffee cup.

"Thanks, Star. You're a lifesaver!"

"I saw you from across the street and thought you didn't quite look awake yet." She finishes her sentence a little sheepishly.

"You'd be correct in your assumption. Thanks Star."

I walk into my room and start to set up for the day. Feeling better with caffeine running through my system, I switch on my iPod in its dock. What to listen to this morning, that's the question.

A Fever You Can't Sweat Out is a favourite album, so I select it and set the volume so that it doesn't bother the customers too much. I just hope they don't mind a few expletives. As most of my customers are regulars, they know my taste in music by now though.

It's been a week since that toe-curling kiss with the blonde beauty. Just thinking of her conjures up an image of her eyes, the way she looked at me as we broke apart. The sparkling green orbs shone with lust before Steph had knocked on the door, making her look like a deer caught in the headlights instead.

Josh, my long serving best friend, has suggested we go to a speed dating event at The Siren Song, a pub just on the edge of town. I couldn't contain my enthusiasm as I eagerly agreed to go…said with sarcasm coating every word.

I really don't want to go, but he said he needs his wingman. Having been married to a bitch from hell for far too long, he wants to meet someone who doesn't just use him for his bank balance. I told him he won't find that at such a tacky event, but he's a persistent fucker—excuse the language. So, I found myself agreeing in a resigned voice. I don't even drink in that pub as a rule; I much prefer to get out of town on a night out. Our town is full of the same women—women I've met, women I've bedded or flat out refused to bed. Hence, I don't drink round here.

Thankfully, I still have another week to prepare myself for the worst night out in history.

Cranking up the tunes on my break, I sit in my room and close my eyes, as that's the only way I get to see Jenna.

***

After visiting with Gramps, I feel drained. I feel terrible for thinking that way, but he didn't who I was and so I'd ended up pretending to be my father, Daniel. I was only eight years old when he passed away, so I don't know what to do when Gramps mistakes me for him. I end up making it up as I go along. The last thing I want to do is remind the poor guy that his son died over two decades ago. There's no need to upset him. Maybe some people wouldn't agree with me pretending to be somebody I'm not. But, even though I hate doing it, I prefer that to the alternative—reminding him he lost his son and having him cry on my shoulder the way he did the one and only time I refused to put up the pretence that I was Daniel.

These days, if he calls me Daniel, I gently try to remind him I'm Nate, and it can go one of two ways; he remembers who I am, and we carry on our visit, or he tells me not to be daft because Nate is only little, and then I pretend to be the man I wish my father was around to be.

Turning up the volume when Kings of Leon come on my iPod, I belt out the lyrics as I drive home.

As I get home, I throw my keys in the bowl by the door and hang my jacket before taking my shoes off and walking through to the kitchen to grab a much-needed beer.

I decide to do something I've been meaning to do for a while. I boot up my trusty MacBook and look for graphic designers. I think the shop could do with a facelift. Or at least the branding. Especially if I aim to open up another site. Which I fully intend to do. I just don't know when.

Knowing it's too late to call anybody for this type of job, I decide to send an email to a couple of designers. I've taken a look at a couple of websites to see their portfolios and there are two strong contenders. At least there are if either of them has the time to help a guy out.

Hitting send on my second email, one to Morgan & Co Design, I log out of my email account and close down my Mac.

I decide to shower before bed. It's been a long, hot day, so I set the temperature to cooler than normal. Looking at myself in the mirror, I grab my shaving kit to get rid of the scruff on my chin.

***

After another long week, all I want is to lounge around at home with a beer in my hand, but Josh has sent me a text demanding my presence as his wingman. I reluctantly let him know I remember he requires my assistance to pull because, with a face like his, he was going to need all the help he could get, or so I told him. He reprimanded me for being an arsehole, so I told him I wouldn't go if he spoke to me like that. To which he apologised profusely, albeit insincerely. It was funny to see him beg.

That's how I find myself in ripped black jeans, and a black tank top with a red and black checked shirt over the top, driving to The Siren Song with Kaiser Chiefs' "Hole in My Soul" playing full belt.

Pulling into the carpark, I cut the engine and effectively put an end to a song that sums stuff up well—'Everything is Average Nowadays'.

Seeing Josh at a table outside the pub, I walk up and fist-bump him as he stands. He hands me a bottle of Corona and I tip my head in thanks.

"Do I really have to do this?" I ask in a bored voice.

"Yup!" He pops the "p" and nudges me as he walks past me into the pub.

Well, there goes my entire night of rewatching *Game of Thrones* ahead of the new season. God, what I'd give to be in the comfort of my lounge pants with a Corona or six. At least I have the bottle in my hand. And many more to come if this is the way tonight is going to go.

If I walk in and they are playing romantic, girly songs, god help me. I'm going to need a whole keg of beer to get me through the night. Thank goodness it's only a couple of hours. But I think I'll challenge myself to see how many I can drink. But—oh shit—I drove here. Damn. It's either grab a cab home and fetch the car tomorrow, or make sure Josh is in a state to drive us—even though I detest other people behind the wheel of my car. If he's looking for a woman to date, he can't exactly get shit-faced, can he?! Oh lord, I hope not. He might want to drown his sorrows, but knowing Josh is a—and I use a quote from one of his many exes—bloody handsome bastard, I don't see that happening. Unless all the women are his idea of ugly, anyway.

Pulling up my big boy pants, I walk into the pub with a plastic smile on my face.

I see the woman with the sign-up sheet on her clipboard and reluctantly tell her my name. She gives me a stupid fucking sticker, displaying it to everyone. I don't rip it off until I'm out of her eyeline. I gave her a fake name anyway.

Hearing whistling over the speakers, I'm comforted by a song I remember my parents listening to—'Wind of Change'. It's almost bittersweet, but erring on the side of sweet.

Looking around the room, there isn't a face that stands out of the crowd. Good job I'm not really here for myself.

The song ends and a woman clears her throat as she holds a microphone.

"Ladies and gentlemen, welcome to The Siren Song's first ever speed dating event. I'm Brogan."

I tune out as she goes over the rules of the night. I have my card in my pocket—a list of names where you indicate if you're interested in someone, and they do the same on their card. If you both indicate each other, then you're matched. Yeah, I think the rules are pretty simple.

Some sappy love song comes on after Brogan finishes reciting the rules. I'm pretty much trying to make myself invisible, but Josh comes over from the bar with another bottle for me. That perks me up a bit. Just not enough to really go through with this shit.

"Come on dude, fake it for me," he says as he sits next to me.

"That's not something you're going to say to anyone else tonight is it?" I ask with a wink.

"There'll be no faking anything, dude."

"No, because there's no going home with anyone tonight."

Josh's face falls, like someone just kicked his puppy, or his puppy peed on his favourite trainers. I swear I don't know what's more important, his French bulldog or his limited-edition collection of trainers.

"You have to drive me home, shithead. No women slobbering all over you in my car. So, no; no hooking up tonight. Them's the rules if you want me as your wingman."

"Screw that; fetch your car tomorrow."

"Nope. You dragged me here, so the least you can do is drive my drunk ass home!"

His face is crestfallen, but I just don't care. Sod that. He can do what he wants, whenever he wants, three hundred and sixty-five days a year. So, my way this once won't hurt him.

***

These women are the dictionary definition of boring. Dull as dishwater. They're either actually this bad in real life, or I am just not the one that makes them any less dreary. Yes, I've had them ask for my number. No, I haven't given it to anyone. Yes, they've ticked their little box on their checklist right in front of me. No, I haven't reciprocated.

I had two more Coronas in the break and Josh stared daggers at me the whole time. So I picked up another before Brogan could ring her little bell, indicating the second half of this mind-numbing night.

I've got to be having the most lacklustre night of my entire life. What the hell was I thinking when I agreed to come? I tried to be a good wingman during the break and tell women what a catch my best friend is. But I can't talk him up a storm when I'm sitting opposite these women, considering I'm meant to be telling them all about me.

Giving them a fake name makes me a jackass, but I don't want them knowing anything about me. I tell them all I'm a builder called Jack. Should they try and track me down after this event ends, they won't find me. Unless of course someone comes into town to get a tattoo, but I'll cross that bridge if I have to.

The last woman of the evening sits opposite me. Chocolate brown hair and sparkling green eyes. I see something flare in those eyes.

"So, Jack, is it?" she asks as she takes her seat.

"Umm…"

"Not, oh I don't know, maybe…Nate?"

Her tone is playful. She knows my real name.

I look down at the stupid list of names on the card I've not paid a shred of attention to. Oh shit!!

"Let me introduce myself as you clearly don't remember me. And no, before you ask, not another notch on your bedpost. Maybe this will clear things up…"

She pulls her hair from over her shoulder and I see my work bold as day in front of me.

I never thought I'd see her again. And she's a brunette, not bleach blonde like I remember. But there's no mistaking my ink on her skin.

Chapter Five

Jenna

I see recognition flash in his eyes. Then something like appreciation. I guess I can forgive him for not instantly recognising me, considering several things; one, I'm a brunette now; two, I'm dressed in my very best "little black dress" instead of jeans and a tank; and three, I've got my hair down and straightened rather than how it was when we met. So, yes, I'll forgive him—if he even wants me to.

"Jenna," he says as he leans forward, "I didn't think I'd see you again."

"You would have done eventually; I received an email from you."

He looks a little puzzled and doesn't say anything in response. He's surely not speechless? This handsome, enigmatic man without words.

"I'm sorry, I'm a little confused. An email?"

"Yeah, asking me to rebrand the studio."

Surely he hasn't forgotten. And I haven't got it wrong, considering he included the business name in the email. Blank Canvas. It's not like I'd forget that name in a hurry.

"Umm…"

He takes a swig from his bottle, still looking puzzled.

"You sent an email to Morgan & Co Design, didn't you?"

"Umm, yeah."

"That's me. Jenna Morgan."

"I didn't know. I'm sorry, I must look like a prized prat right now."

"No, just a puzzled one. So, you didn't know I ran the company?"

"I honestly had no idea. I looked you up in our appointment book and all I saw was a first name. No surname, no phone number…"

"You looked me up? Should I be worried that you're some psycho stalker who uses his appointment book as a list of people you'll track down and murder in their sleep?"

He laughs a deep, rich laugh. It sends a shiver through me and I have to clench my legs together to abate the feeling.

"I'm not a serial killer," he finally replies.

"Oh, so, you've killed once then?"

"What?"

"Well you said you aren't a 'serial' killer," I say, air-quoting the word, "but you didn't say you weren't a killer at all. So, by my calculations, that means…"

"Oh my god!"

He rubs his hand over the day-old stubble on his face.

"And that's all we have time for tonight, folks. Please hand in all your cards so we can sort out any matches," my best friend Brogan says as she rings a bell, ruining my evening completely.

"Jenna." My name sounds like both a prayer and a curse as it falls from his lips.

"Sorry, Nate, she rang the bell. If the lady says that's the end of the evening, well then, she's the one in charge, so…" I let my words trail off.

"Please," he whispers.

He's standing so close to me I can almost feel his heart beating.

"If you hand in your card, Brogan will let you know if you've been matched with anyone."

"That's a bit hard when I haven't checked any boxes. And … I gave her a fake name," he adds in a whisper.

"Well, if you want to see me again, you'll put a little tick in the box next to my name on your card. Then—well, then, you'll have to wait and see if I've done the same."

"Jenna, please."

I turn my head to look him in the eye.

"Just hand your card to Brogan," I reply quietly. "Oh, but be sure to put your *real* name on the card."

I turn and walk in my best friend's direction, handing her my card. It's not long before Nate follows and hands her his card too.

"Did you put your name on the card, *Jack*?"

I have to stifle a giggle as he looks at me.

"Oh, well, you'll just have to wait and see. Maybe I didn't even tick your box, so it won't matter. It was nice meeting you, Jenna."

He tips his beer bottle in my direction before placing it on the bar and walking off into the crowd.

"What was that? Was that what I think it was?" Brogan quizzes me.

"Depends what you *think* it was."

"Sexual tension."

"Jeez, get straight to the heart of the matter why don't you?"

"Babe, he's bloody gorgeous!"

"Hmm ... he's alright ... if you like that kind of thing."

"What kind of thing? The bad boy vibe? I'm totally digging it! If you don't want him, maybe I'll—"

She doesn't finish her sentence when I give her the blackest look I can muster.

"Have you at least ticked his box?"

She pulls my card out and sees the two little ticks I've put neatly in their boxes.

"Oooh. You've ticked two boxes— *two*, Jenna, you little minx."

"Well, being fair, if I'd known *he* was here, it would only be *one* box."

"But which one?"

I don't answer, and she gets all excited like a little puppy.

"Ugh."

I finish my drink in one big gulp before going behind the bar and pouring myself another.

Seeing Brogan rifle through the cards, I watch as she almost drops them in in her hurry to find one in particular. I know she's looking for Levi's card. He was the only other one I ticked. And I was being honest with her; if I'd known Nate was here, I would have only ticked one box, not both.

To be perfectly honest, I wasn't going to tick any at all. I didn't even want to come tonight, it was Brogan's persuasion that got me here. But I admit to it being Levi that made me tick his box. I didn't need any bribery from my best friend to do that.

Levi is ... well, he's hot. He's smart. He's a lawyer. He looks damn good in a suit. Even though I wouldn't have said the local pub running a speed dating event warranted a suit. But a suit he wore, and he wore it well. Tailored, expensive looking, like it was made especially for him.

You could tell, even through the suit, that he's buff; he must work out. Blonde hair, styled to perfection, cerulean blue eyes that you could fall into and take a leisurely swim. He really is the image of perfection. If you like that kind of thing.

The question is, do I like that sort of thing? I mean, I ticked his box. There's no denying he's handsome. But Nate … there's something undeniable about the chemistry with him. If I were to score it on a scale of one to ten, it would read off the charts. That kiss—it might only have been the one, and it might be over two weeks since it happened, but it's fresh in my memory every night when I close my eyes. It's like it only just happened.

Looking at him, Brogan's right—he's got a "bad boy" vibe. Tonight, he was smart casual in ripped black jeans, a black tank, and an open checked shirt worn over the top. He has tattoos, which I guess you would if you're in his line of work. His blue-green eyes are intense. If Levi's are the swimming pool to take a leisurely swim in, then Nate's are the ocean and you're waiting for a wave to swallow you whole.

***

Standing in my en suite, I look at myself in the mirror. I'm not the kind of woman to date two men, but my best friend's parting words of wisdom still ring in my ears regardless.

"You never know, they might just surprise you. Dating both of them doesn't mean committed relationships with both of them—that would *never* work—I just think you need to play the field a little. Look at what your husband did to you; he made you a nun."

It's true I haven't dated since Lee and I split. I guess—minus the habit—I may just have become a "nun" so to speak. Am I sexually frustrated? Heh, maybe! But am I going to date two men to "get out of my dry spell"? Umm…no. Well, maybe. God, I don't even know.

I could date them both. It doesn't mean I have to sleep with them both. Jeez, why am I even contemplating this? I should just pick one of them … or neither of them … but they both have attractive qualities.

Let's see, listing them in no particular order…

Nate.

Extremely good looking … maybe dangerously so,

Charismatic.

Charming.

Looks at you like you're the only person in the room.

Great kisser—theory tried and tested!

Causes a feeling akin to electricity to travel from my head to my toes with just a small touch.

"Bad boy" vibe. Is that a positive or a negative? I don't know yet.

Sexy.

Is in great shape.

Gorgeous eyes that stare straight into the depths of my soul.

Has tattoos—a thing I think I'm starting to like more and more.

And then there's Levi.

Good looking.

Charming.

Has a steady career. Why is that on my list of attractive qualities?

Seems genuine.

Has a great smile.

Wholesome kind of a guy, who has his head screwed on … I think. I hope.

Okay, so, there are more points favouring Nate there. But I'm sure if I got to know Levi more, I'd find things to add to the list. Brogan asked me who I found more attractive, and, based on the chemistry I feel between us, I was tempted to say Nate. But I haven't had a chance to test the chemistry between me and Levi yet. It could be amazing. And, in all honesty, as for who is more attractive, that can't be based on looks alone. It's about the man as a whole. Of course, when I told Brogan that, she thought I was crazy. She said that looks aren't everything, but they are *something*. They are what you first notice about someone, after all. She also said that Nate was "über-hot." But then she likes a bad boy with ink. One of the last things she asked me was if he owned a motorbike—to which, I said I don't have a clue—because that would make him all the more attractive. She has a thing about motorbikes. Who knew?!

I turn the shower up hot and strip, grabbing a fresh towel to hang on the rail. Stepping under the jets, I stay still and allow the hot water to beat down on me like a hail of bullets, massaging away some of the tension I feel knotted in my shoulders.

Once I'm feeling thoroughly refreshed from my shower, I wrap a towel around my hair and slip into my pyjamas. Maybe after a good night's sleep, I'll have an epiphany over what to do about Nate and Levi. Well, I say that like it's a foregone conclusion that they both actually want me. But Brogan did let slip that both men had ticked my box—and my box alone—on that stupid little card. So, that means that they'd both like to see me again at least once, doesn't it?

Feeling as though that epiphany isn't on the cards after all, I unwrap the towel from my hair and lie down to let sleep claim me—if it even can, in this heat. I'll have bed head in morning, but that's tomorrow's problem.

***

Two weeks have passed by, and Brogan has been riding my ass about arranging a date with Nate and Levi. Turns out—as she already let slip that night—that they both want a date, and she says you only live once, so I should at least date each of them once.

I'm just putting the finishing touches to my makeup when the doorbell rings. He's bang on time, a tick in the right column.

Opening the front door, I am greeted by a handsome smile, perfectly straight and perfectly white teeth.

I look him up and down and drink in the sight of him. He's dressed smart casual, in blue jeans and a light grey shirt, open at the collar. A charcoal grey suit jacket completes his ensemble. Some men can't carry off the jacket-jeans combo, but boy can this man rock it. His blonde hair is a messy sort of stylish—I'm not sure what that's all about, but he makes it work.

"Come in, I won't be a moment," I say as I walk back towards the living room to grab my handbag.

"You look gorgeous, by the way. Sorry, I should've said that sooner," he says as he follows me.

"Thank you. I'm lucky I've managed to get my hair to play ball tonight. It's been so hot recently that it just ends up looking really lacklustre."

I don't know why I just said that. I obviously need to be taught the art of making conversation. What I *should* have done is paid him a compliment in return, but it's a little too late now and I don't want to look even more of an idiot.

"I've had similar problems, hence why it's not as neat as usual," he says as he smiles at me.

I watch those cerulean blue orbs look me up and down and I swear I see them twinkle a little when he looks at my legs. Feeling a little shy all of a sudden, if I had to guess, I'd probably say I'm blushing.

We leave and get into his sleek red BMW i8. I would know, considering I kind of wish I owned one. It's a little out of my price range though. It wouldn't be if I allowed myself to fall back on the inheritance my grandmother left me, but I refuse to touch it. I want my parents to see that I can make something of myself without that money, or theirs.

"Closer To The Edge" blasts out as Levi starts the car. He turns it down to a more comfortable volume.

"Sorry, I like my music loud. I didn't think to turn it down before I got out."

"Thirty Seconds To Mars weren't made to be listened to quietly," I reassure him.

"My friends make fun of me for listening to them at all, but I've never been one to do what all the sheep do. I'm the black sheep, the one who does what he wants, his own way."

"I have pretty eclectic tastes in music. For instance, you might not think it, but I love country music. But on the other end of the scale, I like electro pop. For instance, Depeche Mode were the band of my youth."

"New Order, Nine Inch Nails, Alice in Chains, Elvis Costello ... any of those float your boat?" he asks as he looks at me and flashes a grin.

"Umm ... honestly, don't shoot me for this but ... well, only New Order. The others, not so much."

I shudder in my seat as I think of the musical tastes of my ex. Nine Inch Nails and Alice in Chains were his sort of thing, but not mine.

"You more of a Westlife and Boyzone girl?"

"What kind of girl do you have me pegged as?" I say in exasperation. "Actually, yes. I liked both. What can I say? Cheesy pop was my jam in the nineties."

"Your jam? Do people really say that anymore?"

"Oh my god, two minutes into this date and you've offended me twice." I make sure he hears the mock offence in my voice.

He laughs and shrugs his shoulders.

"Sorry."

"But you're not though, are you?"

"Well ..." he doesn't finish his sentence.

If this is how the rest of the date goes, then I think we'll get on well. He seems sort of carefree. I don't have any butterflies fluttering around in my stomach at the moment, but there's plenty of time. The night—as they say—is still young.

***

Levi walks me to my front door and I'm not sure whether to kiss him goodnight or not. Do I kiss him on the lips? The cheek? Just a simple hug instead? Or do I do nothing? Should I invite him in for coffee, or would he take that as code for sex? I mean, that is what they say, after all.

We've had a good night. He's made me smile with stories of his siblings and his parents who he's made out to be just as stuck-up as my own. Not that I'd say that to him. Well, at least not about his parents. But I did tell him my parents see me dating a businessman who travels the world, owns a yacht, is a member of the country club—all the cliché things that rich parents want for their children. Whereas I want to be with someone for love, they want me to be with someone for status.

My first marriage was pretty much out of spite as much as anything. Lee was a nobody, with nothing much to his name. Hearing that had made Levi laugh. It's not that I didn't love Lee, it's that I *thought* I did but it turned out I was wrong. Biggest mistake of my life. But at least I got out while I'm still young.

Turning the key in the lock, I open the door slightly, then turn on the doorstep.

"Thank you for a nice night. I had fun."

"Does that mean you'd be up for doing it again?" he says with a hopeful look in his eyes.

Does it? I don't really know. I mean, he's genuine, down-to-earth, friendly, funny … but there's something lacking. Maybe it's just because it's the first date. But isn't that when you're meant to feel the butterflies the most? Or is it supposed to be in anticipation of the second date? God, why does dating have to be so hard? Why isn't there an instruction manual?

"I'll take that as a no?"

His face falls flat, and I realise I hesitated too long in answering him.

"I'm sorry, I didn't mean no. I just … well … I'm not used to this dating thing and I just …" I begin to ramble.

"It's okay. I'm a little out of practice myself."

"I'd like to see you again, that's if I haven't offended you."

"I'd like that. And no, you haven't offended me. You were quiet for a moment there, so I thought you didn't want to do this again."

Leaning in to kiss me on the cheek, Levi's hand brushes down my arm and he takes hold of my hand lightly in his.

"Until next time then."

And with one last smile, he turns towards his car. He has a nice ass in those jeans. I had noticed that earlier and now I get the perfect opportunity to check it out again.

He gets in the car and waves before backing out of my drive.

Walking into the house, I smile to myself. Levi seems just the kind of guy my parents would adore. But do I? Will I? Can I? I'm going to need a little longer to figure it out.

"He took me for a meal at that new place on the waterfront, if you must know," I tell Brogan over loudspeaker as I change into my pyjamas.

"Ooh, Mr Moneybags. That place looks great. Was the food nice? Everyone I know is raving about it, but it's booked up months in advance."

"It was lovely, yes. But that wasn't the main criteria of the date, believe it or not."

I roll my eyes like she can actually see me before shaking my head at my own stupidity.

"Was he as handsome as you remembered? What did he wear? What kind of car does he drive?"

"Yes, clothes, and a BMW i8 in red."

"Oh, wow, spare no detail," her voice drips its usual sarcasm.

"Look, I'm going to bed now. You know you'll nag me for detail at work tomorrow, so there's no point in me having to go over it all twice."

"Spoilsport."

I can almost hear her poking her tongue out at me.

"See you in the morning, Brogue." "You *know* I hate it when you call me that."

"I do. Now goodnight."

I blow her a kiss and hang up. I know she'll rake over the minutiae of the date tomorrow and I'm too tired to go over it all tonight.

Lying in bed, I find that instead of thinking about the date I've just got home from, I'm daydreaming about my upcoming date with Nate. Just closing my eyes, I picture the colour of his eyes, the shape of his lips.

He hasn't told me where we're going or what we're doing, but he's told me to dress casually. That gives me no clue at all. I know he said to wear comfortable shoes, but that could just mean that I'm going to be on my feet all day.

I find myself drifting off to sleep with the twinkle in his eyes on my mind.

***

A sleek black Miata pulls up on my drive. The purr of her engine alerts me to his presence and I find myself suddenly nervous.

I take a look at myself in the mirror in my hall. My outfit consists of a band t-shirt, ripped skinny jeans and my favourite black pair of Converse. My hair is pulled back in a high ponytail, an attempt at keeping it off my neck in the heat. My makeup is minimal, natural, the way I prefer to look instead of caking it so thick on your face that you could write your name in it. I'm not vain—I don't use fake tan; I don't overdo my makeup in an attempt to look better than I naturally do. I only like to highlight my eyes and lips slightly, but still in nude shades, which I find suit me best.

With a final spritz of my favourite perfume, I pick up my bag and grab my housekeys from the bowl on the dresser in the hall.

I open the door and am greeted by an enormous bouquet. I'd recognise the logo anywhere, considering I designed it for Venus in Rhapsody.

"Good morning," I say as I move to one side, so he can bring the flowers in.

"Good morning, Jenna."

He brushes past me as he places the bouquet on the dresser, and I feel a little spark like static electricity only more appealing.

"These are in water, so don't worry about finding a vase before we go out."

I already knew they were in water, considering I know the bag used to cover up the bag of water at the bottom of the bouquet.

They brighten my hall, with their shades of blue, pink, purple and white. I admit they look stunning.

"Thank you, they're beautiful."

We walk out of the door, and I turn to lock it behind us.

The gorgeous car I peeked through the blinds at is absolutely gorgeous. It isn't the i8, but it's no less of a sleek, stylish car.

Nate holds the car door open for me and closes it once I am seated.

"What kind of music do you listen to?" he asks as he takes his seat next to me.

"Oh, all sorts."

"You like Joy Division?" he asks, nodding at my t-shirt.

"To be honest, I prefer them as New Order, but this is the album cover for one of their most iconic—or maybe just better-known—albums."

"Okay, well, do you like The Cure?"

"Yes."

I almost clap my hands with glee that this guy has taste.

Turning on his iPod, he selects an album and then backs out of my drive. "Friday I'm in Love" blasts from the speakers and I find myself singing along.

Having no idea where we're going stresses me out a little, I normally like to know things in advance, but I find it easy enough to go along with whatever he has planned. Partly because it might give me an insight as to what makes him tick.

It takes a while to get to our destination, and Nate apologises for the time taken. I don't mind though because it gave us chance to chat about things like our musical tastes—and, although we differ on some bands, I must agree the boy has good taste. He asks me what I do for a living and I tell him about working at The Siren Song and my graphic design business. He is impressed to learn that Marcus Dudley has been my most recent client, even when I tell him it seemed Marcus was a bit anal retentive. Nate just laughs and says he went to school with Marcus and he's always been that way. I don't normally say things like that about my clients, but he asked my honest opinion of the guy and I gave it.

Nate also asks how the design for Blank Canvas is coming along and says he's glad it was me he contacted because he wanted to see me again but didn't know how to find me, and if he hadn't attended the speed dating thing, he would still have been able to see me when I went to take a look around the store for his concept. So, he still would have bumped into me at some point and he would have then known how to contact me in the future.

I think it's sweet that he tried to find me, even though he had no luck. Although, as luck would have it, he really had, just without knowing it.

He also tells me how he only attended the speed dating thing because of his best friend Josh, and I tell him I only went at Brogan's insistence. Seems we both have irritating best friends. Something else we have in common.

Pulling up outside a theme park, I laugh at his choice of destination. I'm also glad I only had a piece of toast for breakfast. Not that I get sick on rides, but I'm glad I don't have to chance it.

Coming around to open my door, Nate takes my hand to help me out and doesn't let go as he closes the door and locks the car. I like the feel of my palm in his. It sends crackles of electricity up and down my arm and makes my heart soar. It just feels so right.

After he refuses to allow me to pay my entry fee, I tell him lunch is on me. To which he politely declines and says a lady never pays on a date. Maybe a touch old-fashioned, but I dig that about him.

Getting a really good look at him, I admire his profile. He looks good enough to eat in a pair of ripped jeans and beaten Converse—seems we had the same idea of casual. When he turns to face me, I notice his t-shirt has the Stereophonics on it. The boy really does have taste. I would marry Kelly Jones if I could. A man that can sing and play guitar ticks all the right boxes for me.

We queue for our first ride of the day: Rita—nicknamed "Queen of Speed".

"Did you know this ride was once temporarily renamed Camilla – Queen of Speed?" I ask as we stand in line.

"Why would they call it that?" he replies with a look of utter confusion on his face.

"It was to celebrate the marriage of Prince Charles and Camilla Parker-Bowles. And no, I'm not a royalist, I just happen to love this place, though I haven't been since they built Wicker Man."

"A girl who loves her rollercoasters … maybe you are the dictionary definition of perfect after all."

"You mean I wasn't before?" I feign being offended but he just laughs.

"No, it's that I literally know nothing about you, yet I thought you were pretty perfect when we met."

He kisses the tip of my nose and I giggle like a teenage girl.

"Well a man isn't a man unless he can handle the biggest of coasters. So, I'll refrain from judging you until I know if you're a wuss."

"Challenge accepted."

His megawatt grin tells me he's as much of an adrenaline junkie as me.

Once we've come off Rita, we head for Th13teen. Nate says we should work our way from the back of the park to the front so that we'll be at the exit for closing time.

"So, you love this place, huh? What's your favourite ride?"

"Umm"—god I have to think for a second before I answer—"I guess to date it would be either Thirteen or possibly Oblivion. I love the anticipation of the sheer drop. It makes my stomach turn—the sign of a truly good ride. What about you?"

"Out of the newer rides, maybe Galactica. The originals though, I'd have to say Oblivion or Nemesis."

"Galactica used to be Air, right? But now instead of flying over the theme park and Staffordshire, you're flying through space with VR headsets."

"My girl knows her stuff."

A shiver runs down my spine when he calls me his girl. It might irk other women to be called that so soon, but it isn't an unpleasant feeling as something warm coils through my stomach at his words.

"What can I say?" I shrug nonchalantly, "I told you, I like big rides and I love this place. Though honestly, I haven't been on that one since the change. I've only really known it as Air."

"Then let's make our way in that direction next. We can ride Blade on the way. What do you say?"

"Let's do it."

***

After hours spent queueing and riding—even with our fast-track tickets there are still queues—we finally sit down for something to eat. If we hadn't been having so much fun, I might have noticed my stomach rumbling before.

We look over our photos of us on the rides—that Nate insisted *he* purchase, not me—as we wait for our food to arrive. I'm pulling some funny faces on several of them, but you're not meant to be picture perfect on a rollercoaster. I'd go so far as to say it's impossible.

Chatting as we eat, I tell him about my stuck-up parents and their need for control over everything. He doesn't say much about his own family, and the look on his face says it's a touchy subject, so I steer the conversation in the direction of Josh and Brogan.

"He's a douchebag, but he's been my best friend for more years than I care to admit," he says before biting into his burger.

"She's a bitch, but she's my best bitch. I met her while working at the pub."

"Tell me more about your work. Graphic design and bar work don't exactly go hand in hand."

"Well, graphic design was more of a hobby that Lee didn't like me working on, so it could only be done while he wasn't at home and I couldn't fit many clients into that time. I make book covers for authors, teaser pictures to go with them, logos and branding; hence why I diversified into logos and branding for bigger companies when it became a viable business after my decree absolute came through. I'm just now building it into what I want it to be. It can be quite a solitary job though, except for going to meet the clients. So, bar work was to get me out of the house and, as it's a customer facing job, I meet all kinds of people."

"That's good. What do you do in your spare time?"

"Well, actually, I don't have much of that considering I have three jobs."

"Three?"

His puzzled expression reminds me I never told him about my main job.

"Yeah, I umm … well I own a business in town."

"Tell me more," he urges when I go quiet.

"It's called Venus in Rhapsody."

It takes a second, but I see in his eyes the moment the penny drops.

"Shit! I bought you flowers from your own shop?"

A look of horror flickers across his handsome features.

"Well, in your defence, you weren't to know."

"I saw your friend this morning and she commented on the flowers, saying she hoped they were for a special someone and that someone had better be you and nobody else. I assumed she owned the place."

"She works for me. She needed more work than just the odd shift at the bar and I needed someone bubbly, friendly, and good at interacting with customers. She's the perfect fit."

"I feel like such an ass."

"Language," I say as I playfully smack his arm.

Tomato ketchup from the burger he's holding drips down his fingers and I have to laugh.

"Seriously, I feel like such an idiot. I wish Brogan had given me some warning."

"Don't worry. I love flowers. Whether they're for a customer or for myself, I love the colours, the different scents, the way they can brighten up somebody's day. You aren't an idiot. You did something thoughtful and I can't fault you for that."

He wipes away the ketchup as I talk.

"I won't make that mistake again—that is if you even want a second date."

I look at him and his gaze locks onto mine. I'm momentarily silenced as I swim in the depths of those blue orbs.

"You don't?" he asks, breaking the connection.

"What makes you say that?"

"Well, you didn't answer."

"I didn't hear it as a question, more a statement."

"Oh, okay. Well, Jenna, would you do me the honour of considering a second date with me?"

"I'll take it into consideration."

I wink at him and he smiles so wide that it could split his face.

"Can I take that as a yes?"

"Yes."

***

After a couple of hours driving, we finally pull up outside my house. As seems to be his style, Nate comes around and opens my door for me. Taking my hand, he helps me out of the car and doesn't let go as he shuts the door and walks me to my doorstep.

"Thank you for a wonderful day and for reminding me what fun stomach-churning rollercoasters are," I say as I take my keys from my bag.

"Thank *you*, Jenna. I had a great day," he says, smiling at me. "It reminded me how to have fun," he adds in a somewhat sombre tone.

"Would you like to come in for a coffee? It's been a long journey and I know I could take a caffeine hit right now."

"That would be lovely."

I lead him into the kitchen and tell him to take a seat at the island.

My kitchen is one of my favourite rooms in my whole house. It reminds me so much of my grandmother. She left the house to me, as well as the money held in a trust fund until I reached twenty-one. I only dipped into the money once and that was to build an extension on the house so that I had room to grow here and didn't have to someday leave for something bigger.

My grandmother was an amazing woman, and I miss her dearly. But this place has always been my home. My mother and father were away a lot over the years, building a business empire, I guess some might say.

They weren't always home for long periods and, to save disrupting my schooling, I pretty much lived with my grandmother, Annie.

Home has always been this feeling that my heart and soul belong right here. I know that you can tear a house down, but you can never erase your memories of being there. However, I don't want to tear down these four walls. I want to be here until I die, just like Annie was. To some, home is a feeling deep down in your bones, and this place is it for me.

"How do you take it?"

"In an I.V. drip if possible," he responds, making me laugh. "If not, just white, one sugar please."

"Sorry, I'm all out of I.V. drips. I can boil the kettle and pour it straight down your throat with some coffee granules and sugar if you like."

"Ugh!"

He shivers, and I giggle as I turn on the coffee machine. It's an old style one, but it's the best damn coffee you ever tasted.

"Relax, I'm kidding. None of that instant coffee shit for me."

"Thank goodness for that. I almost got up to leave you to your instant muck alone."

After making a decent cup of coffee, I sit opposite him at the island and hand him his mug.

Looking at him, I realise I don't want this date to end. Nate is handsome and incredibly funny, and we seem to have this inexplicable connection. It's like my soul matches his, calls out to it like a siren singing her song.

"You're so beautiful," he says, startling me and making me spill a little coffee.

"Thank you. You're not so bad to look at yourself."

I move to grab some kitchen roll to wipe up the coffee and as I turn around to mop up the spill, I feel a hard wall of muscle blocking my way. He braces his hands on either side of me, trapping me against the worktop.

"Not so bad, hey? Is that all you've got for me?"

He dips his head to kiss the side of my neck and a shiver makes its way from my head to my toes. This man is intoxicating. What is he doing to me? Apart from turning my insides to jelly with one tiny kiss, that is.

"Well, that depends," I manage to say before he kisses the hollow of my throat, taking my breath with him.

"Hmm…depends on what?"

I can't move, breathe or talk and I'm pretty sure he took all cognitive thoughts with that kiss.

"On if you keep kissing me," I manage to form those six words, and it feels like somewhat of an achievement.

"I think I can do that. But tell me this, does it make me better looking if I keep kissing you?"

"No."

"No?"

His hands skim my waist and I don't know what to do with myself. A hand slips under my t-shirt and goosebumps break out across my skin.

"You couldn't be better looking," I admit, surprised that I can form a coherent sentence.

"Is that right?" he questions before nipping my earlobe with his teeth, then kissing it to soothe the sting.

"Mm-hmm," I mutter as his hand grazes the underside of my bra.

"Good to know."

Suddenly his lips crash down over mine and it takes me a moment to respond. My brain doesn't seem to register what's going on.

Having his hands on me is an amazing feeling. Only the lightest caress—like a feather trailing over my skin—but for some reason, I feel almost hypersensitive to his touch.

My lips respond hungrily to his kisses. His fervour is hypnotic … tantalising … and prompts me to respond even more passionately.

His thumb brushes over the material of my bra and my nipple reacts to his touch. He slides his other hand underneath my shirt and brushes his thumb over my other nipple before greedily cupping my breasts in his hands.

What's going on here? I didn't think tonight would end this way. I'd decided to date both Nate and Levi for at least a few dates each, before deciding who I feel more for. Or at least that's what I thought I'd decided. But the chemistry with Nate is electric and undeniable. It's like trying to deny that the sky is blue, or the grass is green.

Nate's lips leave mine and I instantly miss his touch, but he soothes the ache by kissing a path along my jawline, down my throat. His moans are addictive. I'd give anything to hear that sound all the time.

"We can't do this," Nate says breathlessly as he pulls away.

I feel my face pull down in a frown as I let his words sink in.

"You don't ... want me?" I ask hesitantly.

"No, you misunderstand me Jenna. I want you, like, *really* want you. But we shouldn't do this now. We don't want to rush things and then end up with regrets."

"You think we'd regret sleeping together?"

"No, I'd never regret sleeping with you. Even if it was just once. You are intoxicating, and I want more, *so* much more. But I want to build something with you, Jenna. I don't know the right words to say so that I don't upset you. I do want you, I want you so much. I just don't want you to regret us sleeping together so soon and then second guess things."

"You haven't upset me. I mean, okay, part of me feels a little sad at the loss of your lips on mine. Part of me wants to take it further. But you're right. We don't really know each other and I'm not a one night kind of a girl. If we sleep together, I want it to be the start of something, not just an easy hook-up."

"So, you get what I'm saying? I haven't pissed you off or hurt your feelings?" he asks quietly. "I don't want to cause offence or make you think you're not an intensely desirable woman. I just think we should wait. Let me take you out again. Let's see where this goes."

"You haven't hurt my feelings. In fact, if anything, you're right. I don't think I'd wake up and regret it in the morning, but I can't guarantee that. So, you're right, we should see where things go first."

His lips claim mine in a sweet kiss. My arms wrap around his waist and I nuzzle my head into the crook of his neck as we break the kiss. He's warm and comfortable and smells damn good. It feels all kinds of right to be in his arms. But, if I'm honest, if we had slept together tonight, it would have been wrong. Not wrong, exactly. But it would be unfair. He doesn't know I've been on a date with Levi or that, until tonight, I had considered seeing Levi again. Maybe I would have ended up with regrets, just not the ones he thinks I'd have. Perhaps I'd regret sleeping with him on the first date, or perhaps I'd regret sleeping with him when it isn't just him in my life.

I know what I need to do, and I need to do it soon. I need to choose between him and Levi. It isn't fair to string them both along. That's not the kind of woman I am. I think I let Brogan talk me into it. But, if I'm being honest, it wasn't all her fault. I could have easily said no, but I didn't. I expected it to just be a bit of fun. It was me who let it get this complicated, so now, I need to uncomplicate it. My one regret would be to have hurt Nate in any way. He's a good guy—or so it seems—and he doesn't deserve to be hurt in the process of me figuring out what I want.

"I should go, otherwise I might not be able to keep my word about this not going further," he whispers in my ear.

Goosebumps skitter across my skin and the hairs at the nape of my neck stand on end. His warm breath caresses my skin gently, and it takes all I have to step back out of his hold.

"That would probably be wise."

Slanting his mouth over mine, he hungrily kisses me, bruising my lips in a punishing kiss. That toe-popping kiss of the movies is so overrated. This right here is so much better than anything in any film or romance novel. It's the real deal.

My heart feels like it wants to break free of its constraints, and my resolve starts to falter as his tongue duels with mine for dominance over the kiss. His taste is something I desire much like a plant needs water or a person needs oxygen. Intoxicating was his choice of word, but it doesn't describe me—it's him to a T.

I feel my nipples pebble and I have to clench my legs together because of the feeling pooling in my abdomen like molten lava as it begins to bubble.

His one hand is tangled in my hair, while the other hand sits on my hip. I know that he wants to move it higher—I can tell by the twitching in his hand, the fact that he can't keep it still.

My arms loop around his neck and I play with the hair at the nape of his neck as he kisses me passionately. I want so much to touch him, not just exploring the planes of his sculpted torso, but I want to explore the hardness he presses against me as he pulls me flush to his body. I want desperately to feel the silken touch of his deft hands on my skin. Why does my heart want him so much when my head knows it's too soon? Why can't my head and heart be on the same page for once?

"Nate," I whisper on a ragged breath.

A phone ringing breaks the silence around us. It isn't my ringtone, so I pull back from him, allowing him to put his hand in his pocket to retrieve the object making so much noise.

He looks at the screen and then looks at me.

"Sorry," he mouths as he moves away to take the call.

I turn to put the coffee machine back on. Anything to make use of my hands, hands that want to do so much more than stand here making coffee.

A few moments later, Nate returns.

"Sorry about that."

"There's no need to apologise. Do you have to go, or would you like another coffee?"

I want so much for him to stay for another coffee. Another kiss. Another touch of his skin against mine.

"I don't have to go, but I think maybe I should."

Trying hard to hide my disappointment, I turn and smile at him. It mustn't quite reach my eyes though as he reaches out a hand and cups my face in his palm.

"I'll be back soon, Jenna. That's a promise. Well, as long as you'll allow me to come back, that is."

"Hmm … I might need to think that one over for a while," I say playfully.

"Don't take too long."

He leans in and presses a chaste kiss on my lips. One last lingering touch.

"Don't leave me hanging," he says as he takes my hand in his.

Neither of us speak as I walk him to the front door. He opens it, allowing the cool night air to surround us. It's too soon. I don't want to let him go. Alas, I must. It's the right thing to do.

"Goodnight, Jenna."

"Goodnight, Nate."

"Until we meet again," he says and then lifts my hand to kiss the back of it.

He walks to his car and I just stand here, rooted to the spot, even after he's backed out of the drive and is out of my sight.

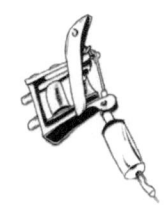

Chapter Six

Nate

"I know you said he was okay, but I came to see if I could see him, even for five minutes, just to put my mind at rest."

The staff nurse in charge looks at me sympathetically.

"It's after visiting hours, Mr Peterson. I really shouldn't buzz you in, but ..."

The sound of the buzzer is loud in the still air of the reception of Haven Lodge.

"Thank you. I won't be long. I promise."

I smile at the nurse before taking off down the long corridor.

Standing in front of the door, I take a deep breath and ease it open quietly. Peering around to his bed, I see Gramps with his eyes closed.

Walking to the end of his bed as quietly as I can, I take in the sight of him. He's sleeping peacefully, and I don't want to disturb him. I just needed to see him with my own two eyes. I don't see any sign of anything wrong, but then the nurse had told me that he'd only taken a bit of a tumble and would be okay. She said the bruises would probably start to show up a little over the next few hours, but that, for now, he seemed in good spirits. Typical of the old man. He's tough as nails. Externally, anyway.

"I know you're staring at me, boy. Did your grandmother and I never teach you it's rude to stare?" he says as he turns his head to look at me.

"How did you know it was me?"

"Because the nurse's heels click-clack on the floor and you sound like a herd of elephants as you stomp around."

"I do not!" I feign indignance.

"Yes, you do, boy. Now what do you want? I was sleeping until you stomped your way in here after visiting hours."

"Good to see you too, old man."

"Oi! Less of the old. I'm still in my prime."

"You might think you are, but I know better," I reply as I pull up a chair next to his bed.

"You're here because that nurse told tales out of school, aren't you?"

"If you mean Linda, and by 'telling tales out of school' you actually mean she rang me to inform me you'd taken a spill earlier this evening, then yes."

"Goddamnit," he curses under his breath, "I told her not to bother you."

"Gramps, I'm your next of kin. She has a duty to inform me. Don't blame Linda for doing her job."

"Pour me a brandy, son?" he asks as he shifts to sit up in bed.

"Not a chance, old man."

"For medicinal purposes," he replies with a twinkle in his eye.

"Not happening on my watch. Plus, you know you're not allowed alcohol, so where would I even get brandy from?"

"In there," he says as he points his wrinkled finger in the direction of a small cupboard.

I get up and open the cupboard. Sure enough, there's a small bottle of brandy in there. It's only three quarters full, so he's already had a nip of it at some point.

Standing to my full height, I look over at my grandfather and frown.

"When did you open this bottle, Gramps?"

My tone is stern and leaves no room for him to brook argument.

"I had a nip earlier when Jackson brought it in for me."

"Jesus, Gramps. Is this the reason you fell?"

He looks at me and I can tell he's considering his answer, weighing his options carefully. It's obvious that today is one of his more lucid days.

"Answer me, Gordon Peterson. And whatever comes out of your mouth had better be the truth."

"Okay, okay," he says in exasperation. "It wasn't the reason I fell. Well, not the whole reason. That damn coffee table was the reason I tumbled. Bloody thing was in the way."

"That table has been here for as long as you have, and it hasn't moved, so I call bullshit."

"It's true. I turned around and bumped into it."

"Because of the brandy?"

"Boy, I've been drinking longer than you've been alive. I can hold my bloody alcohol."

"Nobody is suggesting you couldn't—when you were younger. But that was then, and this is now. You're on medication that you shouldn't drink with. And, while we're at it, where the hell did you get this from?"

"I told you, it was Jackson."

"Jackson? Fine, I'll go wake him and ask why he's bringing you contraband shall I? He can't leave the home either, Gramps, so someone has to have got it for him."

"Possibly his granddaughter, Abigail. Or maybe his grandson, Robert. I don't know."

He shrugs, and I know he's lying. He knows exactly who smuggled it into the home and gave it to Jackson. I know he doesn't want to get them in trouble, but boy I could murder someone right now. Gramps is the only family I have left, and he isn't getting any younger. He won't be around forever. But I want him to be around for as long as possible.

It might not be a big deal to a lot of people. It's not like everyone is at Haven Lodge for the same reason. Jackson's family have snuck him a bottle in and most likely not for the first time. And, if I'm being realistic, this won't be the first time Gramps has snuck a drink.

However, big deal or not to other people, it's a big deal to me. He can bet all the money he has that I'll be informing Linda.

Before he can protest, I twist the cap off and pour the contents down the sink.

"That's better," I say as I put the bottle in my pocket and sit back down next to him.

"What the hell did you do that for, boy? It's the only fun I get around here. You're such a spoilsport."

"I don't give a shit if I spoil all your fun, Gramps," I say through gritted teeth. "You're not going to be getting hold of any more alcohol. Ever!"

"That isn't your decision, Nathaniel."

"Oh, you bet your ass it's my decision."

"Have you no respect for your elders?"

No respect? Seriously? I can't sit here a moment longer. I'm itching to punch something. Preferably Jackson's grandson, but that won't get me very far.

"It's late, Gramps. I'm going home. I'll call tomorrow."

I get up and put the chair back where I found it.

"You're just going to leave?"

"Either that or we end up in an argument, and I really don't want that. So, I'm leaving before I say something that I regret, something I can't take back."

I walk out and want to slam the door, just to show how pissed I really am, but realising that's childish, I shut the door quietly behind me.

I walk to Linda's office and knock on the door. I'm greeted with a smile that quickly turns sour when I show her the empty bottle.

"It won't happen again, Nathaniel. I'll make sure of it," Linda says as I get up to leave.

I didn't want to get Jackson or his family into trouble, but I had to tell her where the bottle came from.

"Thank you, Linda. I'll see you in a couple of days. I'm going to cool off before I come back and see him. I know there's a chance he'll forget what happened, but I won't. I just need to get my head straight before I come back."

We say goodbye and I head back outside into the cold night air. I unlock the car and open my door. Sitting with my head against the steering wheel, I consider how rude I was to Gramps. I didn't want to fall out with him, and I guess I could have handled it differently. Maybe not been as hacked off that he'd had a nip of brandy. I mean, it doesn't sound like something to be annoyed at on the surface, it's just that he's already fragile. I don't need something like this making him worse.

Taking a few deep breaths, I start the car and pull out of the parking lot.

***

Finally, I cut the engine and head into the house. I can't help but feel exhausted. Physically and mentally. An amazing date that took every ounce of strength not to end with me taking Jenna to bed, followed by an emotionally exhausting time with my gramps. Bittersweet. That's what today has been.

I wish I had somebody to talk to about it. I think about texting Jenna, but then decide not to. She doesn't need to be burdened with my crap. She barely knows me. We've only been on one date after all. An incredible date, yes, and she seems like the kind of person who you can talk to about anything, but … well, I guess sharing my innermost fears about Gramps dying isn't something I'm willing to do. Not yet. Maybe one day when we know each other better.

I head to the fridge and grab a beer to sit and decompress but think better of it and grab a cold bottle of water instead.

***

It's been two days since my argument with Gramps, but I still haven't been back to see him. I've called Linda for updates, and she said he hasn't had any other problems. She also told me she'd had a quiet word with Jackson and his family. Jackson had then called me, having got my number from Gramps's address book. He was contrite and said he hadn't been thinking. He also hadn't meant to leave the bottle with Gramps, it wasn't meant for him, other than a small tipple. Crafty so-and-so had taken the bottle while his friend wasn't looking, and Jackson had been looking everywhere for it. I apologised for tipping the bottle down the sink and told him I'd replace it, but he refused to let me, on account of what had happened and him blaming himself.

I haven't seen Jenna again, but we've been texting, and I've been trying to think what we can do for our next date. I don't think I thought Alton Towers through fully, considering I don't know how to top that for a date.

I didn't know she was such an adrenaline junkie, so Alton Towers actually turned out to be way more fun than I had expected it to be. She wanted to go on the biggest rides and said that the sign of a good ride is if you get off feeling sick—the sicker you feel, the better the ride. A girl after my own heart.

The good thing is, we had a lot of fun on our date and the chemistry was off the charts. The bad thing is, I left her house with a serious case of blue balls. But, having said that, I have major respect for a woman who won't "put out" on a first date. So, that's another good thing. If I ever had a checklist, then Jenna would be ticking all the right boxes.

I've been working a lot of hours recently; the business is doing so well that we're booked up months in advance. So, I've decided to hire another tattooist. I've got interviews lined up for this afternoon, but all I can think of is Jenna. I keep picturing her beautiful smile or the way her eyes twinkle with mirth as she laughs at me. I really need to get my head back in the game though, so I head for a shower.

Turning my iPod on in the bedroom, I grab a towel and head for my en suite. Kaiser Chiefs blast through my sound system as I stand under the jets as the water beats against my skin. I can't help singing along to "Love's Not A Competition, But I'm Winning". The older songs are the best.

After showering, I dry myself off and grab some fresh clothes. Black jeans and a white vest, with a black shirt, sleeves rolled up to the elbow. At least this way, I look semi-smart, ready for interviews. I just don't go in for the suited and booted look, considering I'm a tattoo artist, not some corporate mogul.

I grab my phone and car keys and slip my feet into my Iron Man "Vans". Comfortable and stylish, although more casual than smart.

I hop into my car, roll the windows down, slip my sunglasses on and turn the music up. New Order's "Blue Monday" plays, and I can't help but smile as I think of Jenna. She was wearing a Joy Division top, even though she prefers them as New Order. She's a walking contradiction alright, considering it was their debut album and nowhere near the time they became New Order.

As I arrive at work, I see Steph has opened up and Star is sitting at the reception desk, her bright smile in place. She really has the sunniest disposition.

"Morning, Star."

"Morning, boss. Steph's in her room and the coffee machine is on."

"Great stuff, thanks Star. What time is the first interviewee due?"

"Umm…" She chews the end of her pencil as she looks over the appointment book. "Ten a.m."

I look at my watch and see I have forty-five minutes to spare.

"I'll be in my room; would you come get me when they arrive?"

"Sure thing, boss."

Walking down the short corridor, I see Steph in her room. I walk into the small kitchenette and make two cups of coffee.

"Here you go, Steph."

"Oh, thanks, boss. Didn't get time to grab myself one on the way in. The wife allowed me to oversleep. We didn't get much sleep, if you know what I mean."

She winks at me and I let out a laugh.

"I can't possibly imagine what you mean," I reply in jest.

"Only cos you're not getting any," comes her witty retort.

I like that my staff are as sarcastic as I am.

"You're getting enough for both of us."

"True!"

"I thought people's sex lives went downhill after marriage?"

"Nope. Not a chance. Well, not with Luna anyway. If anything, she's gotten hornier."

"Oh my god, this is so not a first thing in the morning conversation."

"Like I say boss, only cos you're not getting any. If you were getting laid…"

"I wouldn't be telling you how horny she was."

"Only because you're mean."

Steph pokes her tongue out at me, and I chuckle as I retreat from her room.

"Catch you later, Steph. Interviews for your replacement will be starting soon."

"You wouldn't replace me. You'd rather lose a limb."

"You'll be missing a limb if you don't stop rubbing your sex life in my face."

"Oh, I think Luna may well kill you if you cut off any part of me."

"And now I need to scrub my mind with bleach. Will you please shut up?"

She lets out a proper belly laugh that I can still hear as I enter my room. Steph and Luna's sex life isn't something I want to be picturing. It would be like picturing my sisters having sex—if I had sisters.

Steph helped me big time when it came to setting this place up, and she had a hand in making it as popular as it is today. Not that I'd tell her that. I'd make her ego bigger than it already is and trust me, she doesn't need it. She's already sassy enough as it is. Goodness knows how Luna puts up with the blue-haired nightmare that is Stephanie Casey.

***

After interviewing six candidates, I could use a caffeine boost. I think I've found the right person for the job, but I'm going to have her come in for a sort of trial so that I can see how the rest of the staff like her and how well she fits in. I can't just say she's got the job without feeling out how she's going to fit in with our setup.

I make myself a coffee and decide to check my emails. Seeing one from Jenna has my face splitting in a wide grin, à la Cheshire Cat.

Opening it, I nearly spit my coffee out when I see the amazing job she's done of the rebranding. I forward the email to Steph to get her opinion. Although I'm the boss and the owner, I'd never give this place a look that the staff didn't agree on. We're like family here, and so I like to have their say in anything that affects the company as a whole.

A knock on my door startles me, and I turn to see the blue-haired nightmare chuckling at my expense.

"Sorry, boss, I didn't mean to make you jump."

"Yeah, yeah. Whatever. Come on in."

She makes herself comfortable in the leather chair I use for clients.

"So, your non-girlfriend did an incredible job of the design, huh?"

"Jenna really incorporated the whole vibe of this place."

"She really did. She's got talent. So, are you going to get new signs made and everything?"

"I am. And it's great that I can carry this brand off if I want to open another parlour."

"A chain of Blank Canvasses. I can just see it now."

I can just picture it too. It's something I've been working towards for a long time.

"You approve of the design then?"

"I sure do. I asked Star what she thought, and she agrees it looks amazing."

"Then I say we get to rebranding."

"Are we going to go all out and have a grand reopening?"

I hadn't thought of that, but it sounds like a plan.

"Can I count on you to help organise it? Maybe we could do a discount for the first customers."

"That could be good. Would we include piercings in that?"

"Of course. We could open on a day that we'd normally be closed, like a Sunday. We could advertise on social media that we're doing a discount for anyone who books in with us on that day. What do you think?"

"I think that sounds like a brilliant plan. I have to say, I like Jenna's plans for the new social media campaign too."

"She really thought of everything. She's gone above and beyond what I expected."

"You know you get a twinkle in your eye when you talk about her don't you, Nate?"

"I do?"

"Yup."

She gets up to leave and winks at me.

"It's a good job I'm married, otherwise I'd make a play for her myself, give you a run for your money."

"Then I'm glad you're married."

Steph laughs as she walks out of my room. I might seriously have had some competition for Jenna if Steph made a play for her. Although I don't think Jenna is that way inclined, I still think Steph would have given chase and tried to make it harder for me.

My phone rings, and I smile as I see her name on the screen.

"You didn't like it did you?" she greets without even a hello.

Her tone sounds worried. I look at my laptop, only to see that I hadn't hit send on my reply to her. Shit! No wonder she sounds worried"No, Jenna, I love it. It's incredible."

"Oh, thank goodness. I was a little anxious awaiting your response."

"I'm so sorry. I had typed out a reply but hadn't hit send and I've only just realised."

"That's okay. I was just worried it wasn't what you'd pictured. I was worried I'd screwed up."

"I asked Steph what she thought, and she asked Star. They both thought it was amazing too."

"What a relief."

Her relief is actually evident in her tone and I kick myself for not double-checking I'd sent her my reply.

"Would you like to get a drink tonight to celebrate a job well done?"

"I'd love that, but I'm afraid I can't. I have other plans. How about this weekend though? I'm pretty busy this week what with juggling three jobs."

"Sure. I'm free on Saturday. I was actually hoping to talk to you about the social media rebrand. I kind of want to do a grand unveiling, and Steph suggested a grand reopening of the store when we have new signs made up."

"Sounds like a good idea. I can send you all the high definition images now you've agreed the proofs. That way, you can do what you like on your own timescale."

"Great, thanks."

For some reason, I'm stuck on what to say to her. I don't want to just talk about work, but I don't want to mix business and pleasure either.

"Well, I'd better get going, I have a shift at the pub tonight."

"Okay, well I'm sorry you had to call, but I'm glad I got to talk to you."

"It's good to hear your voice too."

She sounds like she wants to say more. Either that or my imagination is playing tricks on me.

"I'll text you about Saturday then?"

It comes out more of a question than a statement.

"Yeah, sure. I'm at work until the pub closes tonight, but I can answer the odd text."

"Speak soon then. And Jenna … thanks."

"You're welcome. I was only doing my job, but I'm glad you liked it."

When I hang up, I sit and wonder why the hell I felt so weird talking to her. I think it was because of the whole business-pleasure thing. I wanted so much to talk to her about anything other than work-related stuff.

Shaking my head, I stand and tidy the desktop my laptop sits on, making sure everything is orderly for when I come in tomorrow.

Having only worked a half day today, I leave work early after saying goodbye to Steph and Star.

I decide to drive home and fetch my bike, feeling like taking a ride out through the open countryside. My red 959 Panigale Ducati is one of the sexiest motorbikes I've ever seen in my life—or at least within my price range.

On my way out of town, I stop in at The Siren Song for a quick drink—or at least that's what I'm telling myself. It has absolutely nothing to do with the fact that I know Jenna is working today.

I park my bike, walk into the pub and immediately feel my lips lift in a smile. She looks beautiful. Her long hair is tied back off her gorgeous face, showing off her cheekbones and those stunning eyes. Her eyes light up at the sight of me—or at least that's why I hope they're shining like the world's most precious gem. Good lord. What's happening to me? I'm beginning to think like some mushy-gushy romantic. Not an image people around here have of me. No, I'm the bad boy with tattoos and a motorbike. There's no conceivable way those two things could go together, not in the small minds of people around here.

"Hey, you," she greets as I take up residence on a stool at the bar.

"Hi."

"What's your poison?"

"Just a Pepsi, please."

"That goes with your hard man image," she says as she throws a wink my way.

"Well, if anyone asks, I'll say it's a Jack and Coke."

With a laugh, she pours my Pepsi.

"So, what brings you here on this gorgeous day? Aren't you supposed to be at work?"

"Half day. I had interviews for a new tattooist and decided to take my bike out in the open country air this afternoon."

"Ah, a bike? That goes with the image I have of you."

"You have images of me?"

There's a hopeful tone to my voice.

"Slip of the tongue, I meant that *other people* have of you."

"Damn. There was me getting my hopes up."

"What kind of bike is it?"

I don't miss the blush of her cheeks as she quickly changes topic.

"A red one."

"Oh, wow. That's the best kind."

Sarcasm is laced in her tone as she deadpans me.

"Sorry, it's a Ducati."

"I have to say, I do like motorbikes. I know next to nothing about them, but I know what I like when I see them."

"You should come see mine; I have her parked out front."

"Her?"

"Yes, it's a her. She even has a name. Bet that lines up with the image *other people* have of me, huh?"

"Depends what her name is."

"Molla la Donna. She's named after a rockabilly pinup model from Finland."

"Any particular reason why you named her that?"

"Other than the fact she's gorgeous?! She's got red hair. Red hair, red bike … umm … yeah, makes me sound shallow naming it after a hot pinup girl, doesn't it?"

"I don't know, I guess it depends *how* hot she is."

"The girl or the bike?"

"The girl, silly."

I have to quickly Google a picture of Molla as Jenna serves another customer. When she comes back to me, she takes the phone from my hand.

"She's smoking! I would name a bike after her any day."

"I just happened to see a photo of her with a bike the once and thought she was gorgeous. I'm tempted to say you'd look sexier on the back of my bike than she would though. But if I said that, you'd probably tell your boss I was sexually harassing you, right?"

She laughs and smacks me in the chest with the back of her hand.

"Don't be a dick. I would *not* do that. And no, *she* would definitely look sexier on the back of your bike."

"Care to test that theory? You could pull a sickie and come out on my bike with me."

"And just how would I pull a sickie when my boss has seen me here and I don't look in the slightest bit sick?"

"You could say it was … umm … women's problems."

She laughs at me and swats me in the chest again.

"Take me to see this bike of yours; I'm due a short break."

She comes out from behind the bar, and the first thing I see is legs that go on for miles.

"My eyes are up here," she jokes.

"Sorry," I reply as I flick my gaze up to hers.

Her eyes twinkle with mirth as she smiles that gorgeous smile at me. She really is gorgeous. Long, shapely legs. Curves in all the right places. Yes, I've noticed her ample cleavage, but her face is her best feature—physically anyway. Her eyes really are stunning. Her soft, kissable lips and the way they feel when they're moulded to mine … she's the image of perfection.

But it isn't just a physical attraction I feel for this woman. There's something soul deep that connects me to her. She's kind, genuine, down-to-earth, funny, compassionate; but they are only a few of her attributes. She's also intelligent. So, some would say she's the total package—brains and beauty. She's a man's holy grail of everything he wants in a woman. But she isn't here to be objectified. By me or anyone else.

I walk to the door and hold it open for her. Jenna walks ahead of me but stops short when she sees my bike.

"You weren't kidding; she's hot!" she says as she walks over and runs her hands over the handlebars.

"Take a seat."

"What? No way."

"It's on the kickstand; you won't fall. Plus, do you really think I'd let anything happen to you?"

"I—" she starts but doesn't manage to say anything else.

I hold out my hand to her and help her as she swings her leg over the seat. Once she's sitting, I release her hand and walk to the front of my bike.

I know some women think a man on a motorbike is hot, but the image I see before me blows me away. A woman riding my bike—no, this woman riding my bike—is a fantasy come true.

I take my phone out of my pocket, tap the icon for the camera and take a candid shot while she isn't looking.

"Hey, beautiful," I call.

She looks up at me and I snap another photo. A gentle breeze stirs her dark hair over her shoulders and across her breasts. I'm seriously thinking my bike needs renaming Jenna at this point.

Jenna strikes a pose and pouts at me, making my cock stir in my jeans. I take a photo, wanting to capture this moment so that I can relive it later. Another pose and another picture taken—this girl will be the death of me, and I'm not talking figuratively.

Walking around the bike, I sidle up to her and run my fingers over the handlebars. My fingers trail down over the petrol tank and softly graze her thigh. Her sharp intake of breath has my senses on high alert.

"Scoot back," I say, my voice coming out in a husky whisper.

Jenna does as she's told, and I carefully swing my leg over and position myself in front of her.

"Wrap your arms around me."

I feel her warm body snuggle against me and her arms wrap around my waist. I love the way she feels against me. It feels right, like she was made for me.

I start the engine and feel it rumble beneath me. Jenna holds me tighter and I take my phone out to capture this moment in time. I take a selfie of us both and her smile lights up the whole screen.

"If I had another helmet, I'd take you for a ride."

My heart squeezes in my chest as she lets her lips trail across the skin of my neck. She places a simple kiss just underneath my ear and I swear I feel like I've died and gone to heaven. One simple touch from this woman, and my blood sings in my veins.

"I'd like that. Maybe we can do this again sometime."

Her words make me smile like a cat who got the cream.

Cutting the engine, I revel in her touch a moment longer before dismounting and helping Jenna to do the same.

"I'd better get back before they start to miss me."

We walk back inside, and I can't help but admire her sweet little ass. It's shaped like a delectable peach, enticing me to take a bite. My cock stirs to life again, and I have to think of anything other than how exquisitely beautiful this woman is to make it stop in its tracks. The last thing I need is to sit here uncomfortably with a raging hard-on in front of the patrons of the pub.

Finishing my Pepsi, I thank Jenna for the drink and leave a tip in the jar on the bar top.

I don't want to say goodbye, but I feel the wide-open roads calling me and Molla to go for a ride. I need to shake off all thoughts of this brunette beauty, temporarily at least.

"Don't forget you owe me that drink," Jenna says as her lips curve up in a sweet little smile.

"An IOU will have to do, considering you're working, but I'll hold you to it."

"I'll make sure you do."

I slip my sunglasses down and flash her a grin before slipping quietly out of the room.

***

The vast expanse of road in front of me makes me feel something like nothing else I've ever felt. It calls to me, and it sounds like freedom. The confines of normal everyday life are stripped away as I ride further out from town.

I park up on the side of the road, take off my helmet and soak in the rays of sunshine beating down on me. Slipping my sunglasses on, I walk over to the little bridge I see in the distance. The vibrant green grass beneath my feet is wet with dew from the rain we had just before the sun came back out. The sights and smells around me make me take in deep breaths of fresh, crisp air. I'm wet from the light rain, but I don't care.

Standing on the bridge, I look down into the water. It's so clear here, unpolluted by the pollutants of the town just a few miles away. I walk down to the water, cup my hands together and submerge them. The water is cool and feels good as it runs through my fingers.

Sitting at the edge of the stream, I look across the expanse of green fields and see where the blue sky converges with it on the horizon. Such a glorious day was made to be shared with someone special. I dry my hands on my jeans and pull my phone out.

Looking at the photos I snapped of her earlier, I feel a pang in my chest. We could have something so good. If only I could bring myself to be honest and share the whole of me with her. But some things are better left unsaid.

Feeling a tightening in my chest, I scroll to the number for Haven Lodge, stored in my contacts. I hit call and put the phone to my ear.

"He's had an okay day, but he asked about you. He asked why you haven't been to visit, so I told him you were busy with work and would come as soon as you were able."

Linda's words cut through me, like a hot knife through butter. I'm an idiot. I've let my anger at Gramps blind me to the fact he needs me.

"I'll be there in about twenty minutes. I'm sorry you've had to cover for me, Linda."

Guilt laces my words and tastes bitter on my tongue.

"Don't beat yourself up, Nate. Gordon's in good hands, and you know we'll take good care of him."

"But you're lying to him for me, and you shouldn't have to."

"Nathaniel." Her soft tone squeezes my heart like a vice. "Stop. You are not to blame. You only needed some time to yourself. And you took that time away for both your sakes. If you hadn't, you would have been mad at him, and he wouldn't necessarily remember why. Don't you think that would feel worse?"

"You're so good to me, Linda."

"I like you, Nate. You're a good guy, with a good heart. You're fiercely protective of your gramps, and that is commendable."

"He's my world—what's left of it. That's the only reason I was so mad at him. I know it might seem silly to anyone else, but drink is the devil when you're a man in his position."

"I know. Don't worry; Jackson has promised it will never happen again, and we are being more stringent in his interactions with other patients too. We're keeping a careful eye on him."

"Thank you, Linda. I just worry about losing him. He's all I have left. I can't see him buried too."

"Nate, I can't make any promises for a man in your grandfather's position. But Parkinson's and dementia aren't a death sentence. He could have several more good years in him. Just cherish the time you have with him. Take each moment and absorb all the goodness whilst letting all the bad fall to the side. Make happy memories with him. And know that wherever he is physically, he's always in your heart."

My throat is clogged with emotion and I can't trust myself to speak, so I let the silence linger.

"Are you still coming over to see him?"

"I'm on my way," I manage to say around the lump in my throat.

"See you shortly."

I end the call and look down at my reflection in the water. A droplet splashes on the surface, and it takes me a moment to realise my face is wet. I can taste the salt on my lips where my tears have fallen unbidden.

Admitting, even just to myself, that my gramps hasn't got infinite time left upsets me more than I care to admit, but if you scratch beneath the surface, I'm a scared kid. So afraid of losing my only living relative that I throw my toys out of my pram when he has a nip of brandy.

I make my way back to my bike and pull my helmet on. Starting the engine, I feel her purr underneath me, and it calms my frazzled nerves a little.

Making my way in the direction of Haven Lodge, I practice my plastic smile. They say to fake it until you make it, so I'll fake it until it feels more real.

Chapter Seven

Jenna

After Nate left the pub, Brogan came in to start her shift. She'd closed Venus in Rhapsody for the day and walked in with a smile on her face.

Her playful banter has me in hysterics and our boss is looking at us like we were two silly teenagers.

I tell her about Nate, and she has a face-splitting smile as she listens to me prattling on about how it felt to hold him as I sat on the back of his bike. She laughs when I tell her he'd named his bike but says she didn't blame him because Molla la Donna is hot. I guess it's just me who's never heard of her until today.

"You're smitten. Admit it."

"I can't. You know I'm supposed to be going out on another date with Levi."

"Do you have to? I mean, you're obviously into Nate, so there's no need to dip your toes in the water any longer. You should call it off with Levi and just see where it goes with Nate."

"I don't like breaking a promise."

"But what will you do if Nate finds out about Levi and vice versa? They'll both get hurt, and so will you when they say they can't see you again."

The girl has a point, but I don't want to admit it. If I'm honest, Nate makes me feel ... I can't even sum it up. It's like riding a rollercoaster blindfolded—you have no clue where it's going or where it's going to end, but you still have a feeling in your gut. It's anticipation of things to come. It's riding the high and enjoying the thrill of the butterflies in your stomach as you climb higher and higher. But what if it all ends in disaster?

Whereas with Levi, things feel … safe. You feel on terra firma. On our date, there were no butterflies in my stomach, no anticipation, just … just what, exactly? He doesn't make my pulse race. There were no kisses hot enough to make me spontaneously combust like there were with Nate. Levi felt like the safe choice—even though that doesn't always mean the *right* choice. The kind of person my parents wouldn't hit the roof if I dated. They'd welcome him with open arms. A lawyer; a career-driven, solid man for me to marry and depend on. Not that I necessarily *want* to marry again. After all, my experience of marriage taught me it isn't all it's cracked up to be.

"Hello, earth to Jenna," Brogan says, waving a bar towel at me.

"Sorry, I was miles away."

"On the back of a sexy red motorbike with a handsome bad boy?"

"Oh, shut up!"

I swat her away and get back to work.

The door opens, and I see a familiar figure walk in. Have his ears been burning?

"Evening," he says as he takes a seat at the bar.

"Good evening. Good day?"

"Well, a lawyer's work is never done. Even when we're not on the clock, we still take our work home with us. So, I'm pretty tired actually."

Sounds like a dull and tiresome job. Not that I tell him that.

"Well, we all need some downtime. What's your poison?"

"Poison?"

He looks at me as if I've spoken a foreign language.

"What can I get you to drink?"

"Oh, sorry. I'll take a Jack and Coke, please."

"It's bottled Coke, is that okay? We have Pepsi on draft, if you'd prefer."

"Bottled is fine, thanks. So, what have you been up to?"

"Working hard. Well, I would be if Brogan would stop cracking jokes and making our boss scowl at us like we've been caught doing something naughty."

I pour his drink and hand it to him. He takes a large gulp before thanking me and handing me his money. Looks like someone has had a hard day. Or maybe he's like this every day. After all, I don't actually know much about him.

Come to think of it, I know more about Nate than I do about Levi.

Conversation after that is stilted with Levi and, dare I say it, boring. He leaves after a short while and Brogan has gone decidedly quiet, which isn't like her. She's always got something to say.

"He seemed ... nice," she finally says as we're cleaning down the bar after closing time.

"Yeah, he's nice."

"At least you wouldn't need sleeping tablets."

"What?"

"To send you to sleep at night. You'd just listen to him for five minutes and you'd be out like a light."

I look at her, aghast, and she cracks up laughing. I can't help but join in because she's totally right. However, I'm still loath to break my word to him about our second date. Maybe today was just a crap day at work. Perhaps he's just taking work home with him like he said lawyers are prone to doing. He certainly didn't seem as boring on our date. He'd got good taste in music and made me laugh—although that could have been a one-off, or he was trying hard to win me over—he'd been a total gentleman. But, in hindsight, maybe I didn't want a gentleman. Perhaps I'd wanted him to kiss me until I melted into a puddle at his feet. But no, he'd stayed firmly on his side of some invisible line he seemed to have drawn.

"Are you going to let him down gently?" Brogan asks, interrupting my train of thought.

"No."

"No?"

"No. I'm going to keep my word and go out on another date."

"You're what?"

Now it's her turn to look horrified. She looks well and truly mortified, actually.

"I don't understand. He's enough to drive a woman to drink just to put up with his drivel."

"Brogan, that's not nice. Maybe today was just a bad day. We're all entitled to a second chance."

"Yeah, but ... well, think about what I said earlier. It's not like you can date them both. You like Nate. You click with Nate. You laugh with him and you swoon over him like some lovesick teenager."

"You're right, I do. But what if it's all sunshine and roses at first, and then it all ends in disaster?"

"Honey, that's called dating. That's the risk of dating *anyone*, not just Nate. It could end in disaster with Levi."

"It's less likely to happen with him. He seems … dependable and solid."

"And boring. He seems like an eighty-year-old man in a younger man's body. Yes, it's a hot body, I'll give him that. But honestly, he seems as dull as dirty dishwater. And I'm not saying that to be cruel. I'm just trying to say that you'd have more fun with Nate."

"And more chance of getting my heart broken."

"What did I just say? That's the risk of dating anyone. Look at you and Lee. That ended in disaster. And Levi seems a lot like him from what you've told me of your ex-husband. He's solid and safe, but he's boring and risk-free. Well, as risk-free as a relationship can be anyway. But it all ended in divorce for you and your first Mr Boring. Do you want to make the same mistake twice just because you're scared?"

"I don't know." I take a deep breath and it comes out as a long sigh. "I know that no relationship is guaranteed to work, but Nate just seems dangerous for my heart."

There. My fear spoken out loud. Nate could wield the power to shatter my heart irreparably.

"Well, let me just say this; being risk-free isn't a guarantee and nor is it fun. Being a bit of a risk can be exciting. In the right context anyway."

"I know that I'm doomed to make the same mistakes over and over if I date the safe kind of guy like the jerk-off I married. I mean, look at my marriage; I thought he loved me, thought he'd take good care of my heart, but he cheated on me with some little slut in our marital bed. I mean, the bed isn't the big issue there, but it did desecrate the sanctity of our marriage, the fact he'd bring her home and fuck her in *my* bed. Did he do it because it added an element of danger, excitement? Or did he just not care about taking someone else to our bed and screwing her there where he stood to get caught? You say a little risk is exciting. Well, Lee took that risk and it blew up in both our faces."

Brogan sits on the bar stool opposite me as I lean on the bar top. She takes my hand in hers and looks me in the eye.

"Lee was a damn fool. He was blind to the woman in front of him. He took you for granted, and he hurt you in a spectacular fashion. But, and this is a big but, not all men are wired the way he is. I'm not saying that Levi is a bad guy, I'm sure he's lovely and would be perfectly suited to a Miss Boring. But, babe, you are not her. I know it's a decision you need to make, so I can only offer advice. Look at Nate without thinking bad boy. Look at him and see him for who he is. Remember the date and how much thought he put into it. He wanted to whisk you away for a day of fun. Did Levi do that?"

"No, our date was far safer. Feet planted firmly on terra firma all the time. But is that what's important? It's not the dating; it's the relationship on the whole. Maybe Nate can offer me fun and excitement, maybe he gives me butterflies in my stomach and sets my heart racing. And perhaps Levi doesn't offer me any of that. However, Nate might only be trying so hard to win me over. Maybe once he has me, he'll stop trying."

"Your worst fear isn't Nate stopping trying. Your worst fear is you falling hard for him, only to be hurt in a few years' time, and it all coming to an end. You're scared to give him your heart, only to find that he doesn't treat it with the care it deserves."

She's got me there. Everything she's said makes sense, and I don't want to be Miss Boring. I have already been her for so long. Lee held me down, never let me grow into the woman I could be. I had the potential to really flourish and he nipped that in the bud. Since the ink dried on the decree absolute, I've chosen to allow myself to grow, to learn, to become who I was always meant to be. The ashes of my divorce allowed me to rise like a phoenix from the flames. When a phoenix dies, it turns to ash and then is reborn, a baby phoenix, waiting to grow and rise. That's what I am right now. A baby bird wanting to spread her wings and fly. I want to soar above it all, the way I feel I was always meant to.

"You're right." My tone sounds defeated. "My fear is that I give him my heart, entrust it to his care, and then he rips it out of my chest, jumps up and down on it like a trampoline, sticks it through a shredder and then forces it back into my chest, upside down and back to front, bruised and barely beating."

"Wow, don't hold back on the description, will you? I had pictures in my mind of complete evisceration."

"That's what I'm scared of. Complete and utter evisceration."

"I have one thing left to say. A question really. How do you know that's what a future with Nate holds? You don't. He could be the other half of you. The yin to your yang. He could even be scared of you doing the same thing to him."

"I guess."

Sighing in resignation, I pick up the bar towel and look at my best friend.

"Life is a game of waiting and seeing. I wish we had the foresight to know what was coming."

"I do too. But the main difference between you and me is that I live in the moment. I don't spend my time worrying about what might happen in years to come. I feel like I'll miss out on all the moments in between if I act that way."

"How did you get so wise?"

She smiles a broad smile at me.

"I'm an old soul. Always have been."

***

After confessing my innermost fears to Brogan, I feel like a weight has been lifted off my shoulders. I feel like some of the burden has been removed, like Brogan made it disappear somehow.

I stand under the jets of my shower and turn the temperature up a little. The water works on the knots in my shoulders, and I close my eyes, allowing it to relax my sore muscles.

When I'm dried and dressed in my pyjamas, I pad downstairs to the kitchen and pour myself a glass of filtered water from the jug in the fridge.

I sit at the kitchen island and look around the room. Everything in here reminds me of my grandmother, Annie. I haven't redecorated since she died. She actually had pretty good taste and, of course, it makes me feel all kinds of nostalgic.

My old bedroom here was one of my favourite rooms. I had Polly Pockets galore, some of which are still in the attic today. Then there were my Barbie dolls, of course. Plus, my Quints, which were five little baby dolls with their tiny cots for them to sleep in. I had a Sally Secrets doll that had things like stickers that came out of her tummy, and a stamp and ink pad in the backs of her trainers. I also had tons of My Little Ponies, and the original Little Mermaid doll with Prince Eric, Flounder and Sebastian. I loved Ariel. You could slip off her mermaid tail and discover her human legs before putting her into her pink princess dress. I think she's still in the attic too.

My grandmother spoiled me as a kid. Her house was the only place I could play with dolls and stuff. My parents didn't think playing with dolls was something that I should do. They didn't see how my imagination ran wild, and I'm glad they didn't. They hated anything that they considered wasteful. Time spent playing with my Barbies was time wasted.

Instead, they'd pay for riding lessons, and I had a private tutor who taught me how to play the piano. They thought my childhood should be constructive. And, whilst I enjoyed riding horses, I hated playing the piano. I was proficient enough at it to appease my parents, but I never had fun learning to play.

I didn't see anything they wanted me to do as being things I would still do when I grew up, and it turns out I was right.

I don't feel the first tears fall, but they fall nonetheless. I taste the salt as I go to take a sip of my water, and that's when I realise my face is wet.

Annie was without doubt the best part of my life. Not just because she allowed me to play, allowed me the time to really be a child, and encouraged my creativity instead of stifling it. No, she was the light of my life because she showered me with unconditional love. She inspired me to be whatever I wanted to be, to do whatever I wanted to do. She was like the lighthouse in the storm. She called me home and guided me well. Her boundless love for me was reciprocated every inch of the way. I utterly adored her, and it broke my heart when she passed away.

I didn't come out of my room for days. My parents couldn't get me to eat. Or should I say, their maid couldn't. My mother was upset about her mother passing away, but at the time, it felt like I took it the hardest. The staff my parents employed all tried their hardest to console me, and they actually seemed to care more than my mother and father.

My father hasn't always been an emotionless void. It's mostly when he's around my mother. With me, he's different. With me, he cares. He doesn't show it much around my mother and her friends, but underneath his hard, polished exterior, he's a big old teddy bear.

I finish my water, wash the glass and leave it on the draining board as I head up to my room.

I've taken over my grandmother's old room now. I can feel her surrounding me, loving me from wherever she may be now.

Lying under the covers, I think of the past and the present, worrying what will come of the future. Is Brogan right? Should I take a chance on Nate? The last thing I want to do is get hurt, but isn't that the inherent risk of any relationship?

If I was to date Levi, would I be destined for a repeat of my marriage? Worse still, would I end up like my parents? They might really love each other, or they might just be staying together because they're too scared of starting over at their age. But I'm not too old to start over. I need a fresh start. I know it began when I started with my graphic design business and working at the pub, but where will it lead?

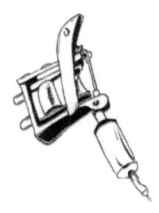

Chapter Eight

Nate

Gramps didn't remember our argument when I went to visit the first time after it happened. I was glad of that to be honest; I didn't want to have to relive it. But I did feel guilty for not visiting him for a couple of days after it happened.

He was glad to see me and, luckily, it was one of his more lucid days. But having spoken to Linda about an upcoming doctor's visit, I'm a little worried about the progression of his Parkinson's. It's been something he's had for a while now and the symptoms haven't been too bad. It didn't interfere too much with his daily life. But now it's affecting his speech, and his movement is slower than it used to be. Signs it could be getting worse.

Many people live with Parkinson's, and it's said you can live ten to twenty years after diagnosis. It's different with each individual, and I can see it's starting to show more obviously now. Coupled with his dementia, you'd be forgiven for thinking he's a feeble man, a shadow of his former self. And, in a way, he is. On his less lucid days. However, on the more lucid days he's still a funny, gentle, caring man. He might be slower than normal in getting around, but he's getting older, so that's to be expected anyway.

But Linda seems to think there's a little more to it than that. I don't want her to be right. I want my gramps to be around for many more years to come. He's the most important thing in my life. He's always been my guide. My moral compass. A man I looked up to and aspired to be. How am I meant to cope without him still in my life, even on the days he mistakes me for my father?

I asked Linda if I can take Gramps out for the day, but she spoke to the doctor and said we shouldn't risk it. His dementia might make him wander off and not recognise people or places that he's known all his life. He might get scared, and it isn't worth risking it just to take him out of the confines of Haven Lodge. She knows I would keep my eye on him like a hawk, but it's just not safe enough.

Instead, Linda suggested a picnic out in the communal garden. I could pack a hamper and we could sit out there in the sunshine. It's not what I wanted, but I'll take anything I can get.

This morning, I'm working on a back piece that I've been working on for a while. The client has a steampunk obsession, and she wants her whole back to look as though it's open and you can see cogs and gears inside her.

Sasha is pretty in a quirky kind of way. Her hair is dyed a shocking orange, but she rocks it. She's young enough and seems confident enough to pull off something so bold.

"Hey, Nate," she greets as she opens my door and smiles at me.

"Hi, Sasha, how are you?"

"Excited. I can't wait for this piece to be finished."

"I can't wait either; it's been so much fun to work on. I haven't done many steampunk tattoos, to be honest. Seeing this one taking shape is awesome."

"You wouldn't know you haven't done many of these before. It's a masterpiece."

"Thank you, that's very kind of you. Why don't you come and get yourself situated on the bed while I set up the needle?"

She strips her top off without any shyness. She's brazen as she takes her bra off and lies down on her front. Maybe I'm wrong, but I swear I saw her smirk as she exposed her bare breasts to me.

To be honest, she may be young, bold, attractive and sweet, but I can't help but wish it was Jenna lying before me. Sasha is someone I may have taken an interest in before Jenna came barrelling into my life, but not now. There's nobody else I'd rather see naked than her.

My cock starts to twitch as I picture Jenna naked, so I stop my train of thought before Sasha mistakes it for interest in her. She's flirted with me each time she's been in, but she hasn't made any moves, so maybe she's just naturally flirty and not shy about showing her body off. She has a good figure, so I don't blame her, but I prefer women who aren't so brazen. Did I prefer my women that way before Jenna? I don't think I did. I think it's her and her inhibitions that are so attractive to me. It's all her.

Do I see her as a challenge? Yes, but not as a notch on my bedpost. I like seeing her walls come crashing down when my lips meet hers. I like that I push her buttons and make her let her inhibitions go.

"Earth to Nate, are we getting this show on the road?" Sasha calls.

I have to shake my head to clear away all thoughts of my favourite stunning brunette.

"Sorry, yes, I was just thinking."

I get to work and make small talk with Sasha as I get to finishing up the masterpiece she said her tattoo is.

"I love the feeling of a tattoo needle on my skin."

"Me too, there's nothing quite like it," I respond as I work on the piston at the bottom of her spine.

"There really isn't. But then there's something to be said for the feel of flesh on flesh."

"Hmm," I murmur noncommittally.

"What, you don't agree? Are you a monk or something?" she teases.

"No, definitely not a monk."

"You're not married because you don't wear a ring."

"How can you tell? I'm wearing gloves."

"I've studied your hands without the gloves on. And the latex would stretch differently over metal."

She's studied my hands? What an odd thing to do. And to admit to.

"No, I'm not married."

"Gay then?"

I consider saying yes, but don't see the point in lying.

"No, I'm not gay either."

"Just not interested then?"

"In what? Sex?"

"Me."

I have to stop what I'm doing before I make a mistake that will ruin her tattoo.

"Sasha, I … Look, I'll be honest here. You're very attractive. Young, bold, vivacious. In another life, yes, I probably would have been interested."

"But you're not?"

"No. I'm sorry."

I carry on where I left off and silence descends. It's an uncomfortable silence, so I turn around to flick on my iPod.

"Sorry, I shouldn't have said anything. My mother always says I speak before I think."

"It's okay. The truth is, I have just started dating somebody."

"What's she like?"

I'm not sure I want to discuss Jenna, but my best friend Josh has been tied up with a woman he met that I really don't have anyone to turn to except Gramps.

"She's gorgeous. Funny. Kind. Sexy."

"What's she like in bed?"

I cough and splutter at her direct question.

"We haven't got that far yet."

"Oh. Sorry. Like I say, I speak before I think sometimes. I didn't mean to pry. Sorry."

We settle into another uncomfortable silence, but this time I'm glad for the music that distracts me.

"We're nearly done here," I say a few minutes later.

"I can't wait to see it. Is it going to be okay to uncover it in a couple of hours?"

"Once it's wrapped, it should stay that way for a while. Why?"

"I have work and they won't want to see a big thing covering the base of my spine."

"Oh? What do you do for a living?"

"I'm an exotic dancer."

"Oh! Umm … can you at least leave it for a couple of hours?"

No wonder she's not bothered about taking her clothes off in front of a near stranger like me. She does it for a living.

"Yeah, I have work at lunch time though."

I wonder how there'd be any trade during the day for someone in her line of work, but I don't voice my thoughts.

Finishing up the last bit of shading on her tattoo, I let her know she can check it out in the mirror before I wrap it.

She sashays over to the full-length mirror without her top on, so she can inspect my work.

"Wow, Nate, it's amazing. Look at my heart and the way it looks like the cogs are tearing through my skin. I'm stunned."

"I'm glad you're pleased with the end result. I know you've been itching to get it finished and, now it is."

"I'm more than pleased. I'm ecstatic."

Her enthusiasm as she eyes her tattoo is a boost for me. It's always good to know that people are pleased with their art.

After I've wrapped the bottom of her tattoo, she pulls her clothes back on and winks at me.

"If things don't work out with whatsherface, you know where I am."

"Her name is Jenna," I snap, making her jump.

"Whatever."

She walks out and slams the door shut behind her.

I clean up my work station with a little more force than intended, knocking a bottle of ink over as I go.

"Heard that door slam from a mile away," Steph says as she enters the room. "Unhappy customer?"

"Not with her tattoo, no."

"Ooh, so she made a move and you rejected her?"

"That's about the size of it. If you don't mind, Steph, I'd rather forget it."

My words come out more forceful than I intended.

"Sorry, boss, I just came to see what all the fuss was about."

"I'm sorry, Steph. I shouldn't snap your head off."

I close my eyes and take a couple of calming breaths. When I open them, Steph is nowhere to be seen. I guess I should go and apologise.

Handing Steph a coffee, I try for a smile, and she gives me a sympathetic one in return.

"I had no right to snap. Sasha, the last customer, she made advances and I rebuffed them."

"The girl with the orange hair and a face like thunder?"

"That's the one."

"Saw her stomping down the corridor. She looked pissed."

"Yeah, well, some women can't handle rejection."

"You'd normally be in there like a shot. This Jenna must really have an effect on you."

"She does."

I smile my first genuine smile as I think of her. I pull out my phone and I scroll to the selfie of us on my bike. Turning my phone round, I show Steph. She smiles and takes it from me.

"Wow. She looks smitten. And so do you, actually."

"I don't know about that. She is beautiful though. And funny, kind, sweet ..."

"But you're not smitten, no?"

"Don't start," I warn.

Steph just laughs and scrolls through my phone. Her eyes lighting up as she sees the other photos of Jenna.

"Someone's got it bad, huh, boss?"

She smirks at me and I just feign nonchalance.

***

I hear my phone ring, so I dry my hands and grab it from the pocket of my jeans which are lying on my bed. Seeing Jenna's beautiful face lighting up my screen makes me smile.

"Hey," I answer.

"Hi, Nate."

Even just the sound of my name on her lips sounds divine.

"What can I do for you?"

"Well actually, it was what I can do for you."

Colour me intrigued.

"And what would that be?"

"I was thinking of your grand reopening. I had some ideas. I mean, you don't have to use any of them, I was just thinking and, well, I don't know, I thought you might be open to ideas."

Her rambling is kind of cute. Any other time we've spoken, she's seemed in control, but now she's flustered.

"Hit me with them. I'm open to suggestions."

We talk work for a while before making small talk about her day. I tell her about my encounter with Sasha, and she laughs. She actually has the audacity to laugh at me. But it isn't long before I'm joining in.

I want to ask her on another date, but I haven't even had time to think about what to do. I don't think I can top the theme park date now I know she's an adrenaline junkie. There's a new restaurant opening in town next week, Bella's. I hope she likes Italian food. I know the owner and am sure I can score us a table on opening night.

"Are you busy on the fourth?" I ask before I can chicken out.

"Umm ... let me just look at my diary," she says, and I hear rustling on the other end of the line. "Nope. I'm free as a bird."

"Would you like to go out?"

"Ooh, that's a tough question. Another night in your company?"

"Well yes, unless you wanted to go out with someone else?" I tease.

Her laughter is loud. And is a sound I could listen to over and over again.

"I'd love to go out. Where are you thinking of taking me?"

"That's a surprise."

"Oh, come on, just a little hint."

"No. All I'll say is this; the dress code is anything but casual."

"Okay."

"I'll text you the time I'll pick you up because I'm not one hundred per cent sure yet."

"I'll be waiting."

We say our goodbyes and I can't stop the wide smile that splits my face from ear to ear.

I pack up and head home for the evening. I don't have any more appointments until the day after tomorrow. Tomorrow is picnic day with Gramps at Haven Lodge, so I've booked the day off. It meant I had to move some appointments around, but luckily we've had some cancellations, so I didn't need to postpone my customers for long.

I don't really like juggling my appointments and feeling like I'm letting people down. But my gramps comes first.

Slipping my helmet on, I straddle my bike and turn the engine over. Instead of going straight home, I decide on a whim to go and see if Jenna is working at the pub. I forgot to ask her earlier if she's working tonight, but if she isn't, I'll just have the one drink and head home.

***

I'm sitting at the bar ogling her pert ass as she bends over to restock the mixers. If I'm not careful, I'll start drooling next. She really does have a tremendous ass though, so you can't blame a guy for looking when it's right there in front of him.

"Hey, mister, my eyes are up here."

My gaze snaps to hers and I see hers dance with mirth.

"Hey, I'm a red-blooded male and you were bent over. Find me a guy that wouldn't do the same."

"At least you're not denying it."

"No point. You caught me red-handed. Plus, I don't care if you catch me staring. You're gorgeous and so is your ass."

Her smile is wide and genuine. I think she took it as a compliment. I sure meant it as one, but some women might take offence.

"Well, just so you know, I could feel your eyes burning holes in my ass while I was busy stacking those bottles."

"Like I say, I'm not bothered."

I shrug and throw her a wink.

"Brogan warned me about men like you," she says in a jovial tone.

"Men like me? Would you care to share what that means? What exactly am I like?"

"Well," she whispers conspiratorially, "you're an alpha male. You might as well beat your chest with your hands."

"Oh, I do, regularly."

"Thought as much."

"And what else am I? Handsome? Muscular? Irresistible?"

"All of those, plus a great kisser. But that's not what I meant when I said men like you."

"So, enlighten me then."

"You're flirtatious, driven, like to get what you want, don't take no for an answer."

"That about sums me up."

"You're confident. You ooze charisma. You're also a typical bad boy."

"That's what the rumour mill would have you believe. The bad boy bit, I mean."

Another customer distracts her attention from me, and I smile as I watch her. She's utterly gorgeous. Inside and out.

Her hair is pulled back in a messy bun this evening, but she makes it look stylish. She's wearing light makeup, and for that I'm glad. I like the natural look rather than when women cake their faces in products to cover up.

She's wearing light blue jeans that hug her ass, a pair of worn Converse, and a tank top that says "Fresh Sarcasm Served Daily".

"Another Pepsi?" she asks as she returns to stand in front of me.

"Please."

She pours my drink and I hand her the cash, telling her to get herself a drink too.

"What time do you get off?"

"Ten. Why?"

"I just wondered if you fancied that ride on the back of my bike?"

"Do you have a second helmet?"

"Not with me, but I'll go home and grab it and pick you up at ten. *If* you want me to."

She doesn't say anything for a moment, and I can tell she's actually thinking it through instead of jumping at the chance.

I'm not used to that. If I'm honest, I could ask a woman and she'd agree before the whole question had left my lips. I'm not trying to be big-headed; it's just the way things are. But I don't necessarily want them to be.

"I'd like that, but what would we do when we got on the bike?"

"I can take you home, or we can take a little detour, so I can show you something first."

"Sounds intriguing. Are you sure I'm safe with you late at night? You're not, like, an axe murderer or something?"

"That's a risk you'll have to take."

"I'll just remember to borrow Riley's baseball bat then."

Her eyes sparkle as she laughs at me.

"Is it called Lucille?"

"Yes, actually. And the barbed wire is said to really fuck you up."

"Miss Morgan, did you just swear at me?"

She shrugs, and I just laugh. I'm glad she got my reference to *The Walking Dead*, even if I did stop watching it last season.

"I'll see you and Lucille at ten then," I say as I stand and gulp back the last of my drink.

"I'll look forward to it."

Leaving the bar is a tough task. My feet feel like lead. I don't want to leave her; I want to sit at the bar and keep chatting to her for the rest of the evening, but I know I can't.

I get on my bike and head for home.

***

Pulling on my leather jacket, I smile to myself as I think about Jenna. She's intriguing, utterly beguiling and such a beautiful woman—just as much on the inside as she is on the outside. She fascinates me and holds my attention in a way no other woman has for a very long time.

There was once a time when I thought I was in love with the most amazing woman on the planet, but it turned out that all that glitters isn't gold. She hurt me more than I ever thought possible when she slept with my—now ex—best friend, Marshall. Not content with just sleeping with my friend, she did it in my house, my bed. I was unfortunate enough to catch them in the act. I walked in just as he was fucking her over the end of the bed. Just thinking about it makes my heart squeeze in my chest.

Moaning, panting, and shouts of "Yes!" catch my attention as I enter the house. I follow the sounds upstairs. My best friend Marshall and I share a house, and I'm assuming it's him and some random that he's hooked-up with.

I decide to go to my room to grab my iPod and headphones. I'll grab my sketchbook to sketch a design for a new tattoo for my girlfriend Nikki. Anything to distract my mind from the noises that animal is making. And it really does sound like two wild animals mating.

Opening my bedroom door, I'm greeted by a bare ass and a sculpted back. I'd know that backpiece tattoo anywhere, considering I designed it. He doesn't turn his head upon hearing me enter, too distracted by the woman he's currently pleasuring, in my room of all places.

Looking at her, I gasp in shock. That fiery red hair, her creamy smooth skin, accentuated by a tattoo on the nape of her neck ... Marshall holds her hair in his hand as he pulls it back ... I'd know that body anywhere, anytime, blindfolded. Nikki Anders, my one true love. Or so I'd thought.

Moans of pleasure escape her as Marshall fucks her, her legs spread as she bends over the end of our bed. He slaps her ass and she lets out a sound of sheer exhilaration, while I stand rooted to the spot. I'm unable to form a coherent thought, never mind words.

Anger burns through my veins as the betrayal stings my heart. I can feel my blood beginning to boil, and my temper only heightens as Marshall shouts at her to come for him.

Finally able to move, I launch myself at him. The first punch connects with his jaw and I watch his head rock back. He looks at me, shock evident on his face. But there's no sign of remorse. Nothing to suggest he's sorry for sleeping with my girlfriend.

The second punch connects with his eye socket, and Nikki screams as I pummel him to the ground. Rage floods every molecule of my being.

Spinning around, I look at Nikki, the love of my life, the one woman I saw a future with, and see the horror on her face. She wears a duvet round her as if to cover the body I've worshipped a thousand times. If I had to guess, I'd say my expression is one of pure disgust. I am a millisecond away from snatching that duvet and smothering my sorry excuse for a best friend with it. Maybe wrap his body in it when I'm done with him.

But even as angry as I am, I know that no good would come of beating him senseless. I've already given him enough of a beating for him to be broken and bruised for a good while to come.

Walking out of the room, I release a breath I didn't realise I was holding. I barrel down the stairs and out of the house, jump on my bike and ride as far away as I can, before pulling up at the small creek and sitting with my head in my hands. I sob my heart out, letting the grief pour out of me.

My best friend and my girlfriend. How long has it been going on? Was today just a one-off, or is it something more? Is it serious between them? Is it love or lust? Do they really not care about the consequences of their actions? Too many questions and not enough answers.

Shaking my head to rid me of unwanted memories, I pull my helmet on and straddle my bike. I pull off my driveway and head towards what I hope is my future.

Chapter Nine

Jenna

I hear a motorbike pull up outside the pub and a sudden feeling of nerves makes me feel giddy. I feel like a teenager waiting for her crush to arrive. But I'm a grown-ass adult who's waiting for her crush instead. Crush. What a weird word. But I have no other way of describing it. My heart races when I hear his name mentioned in conversation, not to mention when I see his name on my phone from an incoming text. I get butterflies in my stomach at the sight of him. By the time he gets to touch me, my whole body is tingling. The hairs at the nape of my neck stand on end, goosebumps break out across my arms ... I am an incoherent jumble of nerves and anticipation. And that's how I feel right now.

Brogan winks at me as I look across the bar to where she's standing, wiping down a booth. The bar towel I'm holding drops to the floor along with my jaw when Nate walks in looking like a modern-day James Dean. He's got that swagger going on, and boy is he rocking the hell out of it.

My stomach does this kind of triple somersault that any gymnast would be proud of pulling off to perfection. My mouth feels dry, and I wonder for a second if I've swallowed a load of sawdust.

"Hi."

Good god, even his voice oozes sex appeal.

"Hi."

My reply comes out as a sort of sigh like some swooning teenager, but I can't find it in me to be embarrassed.

"Are you ready to go?"

"Sure, give me a second to grab my bag."

I walk into the back room of the pub to retrieve my jacket and bag.

Looking in the mirror, I check my appearance isn't too dishevelled after a long-ass shift on my feet. I apply a bit of extra lip gloss, slip it back into my bag and head back to the bar.

"Break her heart and I'll break every bone in your body," Brogan says with a tone of menace to her usually friendly voice.

"I swear I won't. Scouts honour."

"Were you ever a scout?"

"Umm … okay, you got me there. But you have my word, Brogan, I won't hurt her."

I clear my throat to announce my arrival and see the sheepish look on Nate's face. I'm guessing he's intimidated by my bestie. I have to say, she can be a real Rottweiler when it comes to defending her friends.

"Don't worry, her bark is worse than her bite."

Brogan chuckles and whips my ass with a bar towel.

"Get out of here before I show you my bite."

I poke my tongue out at her as I take the arm Nate is holding out to me.

"You better have a second helmet."

"Oh, my goodness, will you get off his case? Of course he has a second helmet."

Nate holds the door open for me, and I offer a small smile of gratitude. He might look the part of bad boy with his leather jacket and motorbike, plus the tattoos I've seen on his arms, but he's a big softie really.

"Have fun. Don't do anything I wouldn't do," Brogan calls after us.

"That doesn't leave much then does it?" I call back.

Nate sniggers. He tries to disguise it as a cough but fails spectacularly.

Handing me his second helmet, he pulls his own on and I follow suit.

"Hold on tight and, whatever you do, whichever way I lean, you lean, or we risk falling off."

"This isn't the first time I've been pillion on a bike, Nate."

"Good, then you know what to expect."

I sit behind him and snuggle in nice and close, wrapping my arms around his middle. The engine rumbles to life and we pull out into the traffic. I have no idea where we're going, or if Nate even has an actual plan. All I know is that, when he asked earlier, I couldn't bring myself to say no to a ride out with him.

***

As we pull to a stop, my heart settles back in its rightful place. I wasn't lying when I said it wasn't my first time on a bike, but it was my first time with him and that made my heart race like a horse in the Grand National. It was exhilarating being on the open road, snuggled into the warmth of his broad back.

I take off my helmet and shake out my hair. In my mind, I look as gorgeous as when women do it in films, but in reality, I probably look a fright with my hair everywhere. Giggling at that thought, I pass Nate the helmet and receive a funny look in return.

"Something funny?" he quips.

"Not really. Just me being stupid. Ignore me."

"That's easier said than done."

"What is?"

"Ignoring you. How could anybody ever do that? You're stunning."

My pulse spikes as his compliment probably makes me blush.

"You're a smooth talker, Mr Peterson."

"Nope, I just speak the truth. With me, what you see is what you get, and I say exactly what comes to mind. Yeah, sure, that gets people into trouble sometimes, but I know when *not* to say something. I don't go around upsetting people on purpose. But if you ask me a question, I won't lie."

"What's your full name?"

"What?"

"Well you said you won't lie when asked a question. So, I'm going to ask you some questions."

"Nathaniel Peterson."

"No middle names?"

"Nope."

"How old are you?"

"Thirty-six."

"Favourite colour?"

"Green."

"Did you always want to be a tattoo artist?"

He leads me to the edge of a small creek, where I sit on the grass and slip my shoes off, then dip my feet in the water. It's cool and refreshing. It's nice to sit here under the moon and stars. The darkness isn't all-consuming; it's lit by a million stars that provide us with enough light to see each other and our surroundings.

"Not always. I wanted to be a fireman when I was about five. A policeman when I was about ten. It wasn't until I studied art at high school that I thought about practical ways of earning money from my art. I didn't want to be some struggling artist."

"Do you want to get married and have children?"

He pauses for a moment before answering and I see his Adam's apple bob as he swallows.

"Yes, to both."

"Why did you hesitate?"

"Because I lost my parents when I was young, and it was my grandparents that brought me up. I guess I just thought that I'd never have kids in case something happened to me. I didn't want them to grow up without a dad. But then, I realised that I can't go through life thinking "what if". So, yeah, I want kids … one day."

"I'm sorry, Nate. I didn't know."

I could kick myself for upsetting him.

"It's okay. It is what it is. I can't go back and change it. I would if I could. But you can't keep living in the past. You've got to live for the future. You've got to really live, not just exist. I came to the conclusion that life is a series of fleeting moments. Some are happy, some are sad. You have to take each moment as it comes and play the cards you've been dealt. Take the happy moments and really squeeze them of every drop of pure bliss. Store them in your heart and mind so that when the sad moments pass through, you have something to get you through them."

"That's so true. I've always believed you have to play the hand you've been dealt. There's no changing it. So, you do what you can to make the best of what you have."

I didn't expect the conversation to take such a dramatic turn. I wanted to keep it light and playful.

"That's why I set up Blank Canvas. I wanted something that was mine, somewhere to be my happy place. I'm always content when I'm being creative. There's something about tattooing people that just brings me happiness. It's like a sense of accomplishment when they tell you how much they love your art."

"You are pretty amazing."

"Thanks, you're not bad yourself."

His salacious grin makes butterflies unfurl in my stomach.

"You know what I meant. Your artwork. You're extremely talented."

"Thank you. I'm glad you approve."

"Oh, I approve. But trust me, when my mother finally sees this phoenix, she's going to have kittens."

"What's she like, your mum?"

"Kind of stuck-up. Prissy. Irritating to the nth degree. She wants me to date a doctor or a lawyer, or someone with lots of money and a good, solid background. She thinks I need someone from—and I quote—good breeding. Whatever the hell that's supposed to mean. I totally piss her off when I say that I want to marry for love, not money or status."

"What about your dad?"

"He's softer than my mum. He's a big old teddy bear. Don't get me wrong, he's still a little bit stuck-up like my mum, but that's only when it comes to business and stuff. When it comes to family, he's a total sweetheart. My mum thinks he babies me because he's loving and tender, the exact opposite of her cold, icy heart of stone."

"What does he think when it comes to you dating?"

"He has to be seen to agree with my mum, because otherwise she'll give him an ear-bashing. But when it's been just the two of us, he's made it clear that he wants me to be happy. He knows my first marriage failed. He knows that just because Lee had a good job didn't mean our life was perfect. Our relationship had its problems and ultimately ended in divorce."

"What did your mum make of your divorce?"

I take a deep, calming breath before answering.

"She—how can I put this? She blamed me. Said I hadn't put in enough effort. She told me that you only get out of a relationship what you put into it, therefore, it was clear that I hadn't worked hard enough. But she was wrong. So bloody wrong. It was Lee that didn't give a damn about the sanctity of marriage. He was the one caught cheating in our marital bed."

Tears prick my eyes and I'm glad I have the cover of darkness to disguise them.

"I'm so sorry he did that to you, Jenna. You didn't deserve that. No woman does, but especially not you," he says as he lifts his hand and places it against my cheek. "You're so beautiful, inside and out. You're enchanting. Any man would be a fool not to want you and only you."

My stomach does that weird little flip-flop again. He just called me enchanting. Me. Plain old Jenna.

"I'm not sorry he did it," I confess. "It showed me his true colours. It was the catalyst for me leaving. Okay, so I didn't see myself being a divorcée at my age, but I'd rather that than be married to a cheating rat."

"Everything happens for a reason, even if we don't find out the reason until quite some time later. Things have to happen in order to get us to where we need to be. I wouldn't be who I am or where I am in my life without every little thing that has happened. Be it big or small, happy or sad, these things shape us in ways we don't necessarily see at the time."

His hand leaves my cheek and instead comes to rest on the back of my hand. It's an odd sensation—most likely because Lee didn't like to hold my hand—but I like it when Nate's skin comes into contact with mine and sets my pulse racing.

My heart squeezes in my chest. He's so right. I guess I was too caught up in what happened to actually sit back and appreciate that it set me on the path to becoming a better version of myself. I wasn't really me when I was married to Lee. I was a shell of my former self and it wasn't until I left him that I made my way back to being me.

"What's your favourite colour?"

His question takes me by surprise, but I'm grateful for the change of direction.

"Purple."

"Any middle names?"

"Yes."

"I'm waiting."

"What?"

"Well I asked if you had any middle names and you just said yes, you didn't tell me what they were."

"You didn't ask what they were, just if I had any. I only have one. Louise."

"Jenna Louise Morgan."

He acts like he's testing my name out on his tongue. A smile graces his lips and he looks so handsome.

"What star sign are you?"

"I'm a Leo. What about you?"

"Ahh, a reason for your feistiness! I'm a Libra."

"I think I'd be feisty regardless of my star sign."

He laughs and it's such a wonderful sound.

"Where do you see yourself in five years' time?" he asks as he strokes the back of my hand.

It's such an electric feeling. It's just a simple touch, but it feels like so much more. Like he's trying to communicate something via his touch. But I don't know what.

"Well, I'd like to slow down workwise. No, not slow down, I would just like to stop juggling three different jobs. I want to be successful enough with my two businesses that I don't need to do the bar work. Not that I don't like it, because I do. But you can only burn the candle at both ends for so long. I don't do the bar work because I need the money. The truth is, I really don't. I just do it for human interaction because graphic design can be isolating. And the flow of customers isn't the same in a florist as it is a pub."

Nate stands and takes my hand, helping pull me to my feet. I grab my shoes in my free hand and we begin to walk along the side of the creek. The moonlight reflects in the water, making it shimmer iridescently.

"What about you? Where do you see yourself in the future?"

"Honestly, I don't know. I would like to expand Blank Canvas, like a chain of studios. Hence why I had you rebrand the way you did, so that it wasn't solely for one premises. Other than that, well, I guess I'd like to be settled down with someone. I guess I'm figuring that part out along the way."

We stop short of a little bridge over the water.

"You might want to put your shoes back on now."

I bend to slip my shoes back on and almost topple over. Thankfully, a strong arm saves me and wraps around my waist. He doesn't let go when I stand, and I feel comforted by his touch. He leads us across the small bridge and stops as we get to the centre.

"See that star up there," he says softly as he points his arm in front of us. "That one right there. I want you to close your eyes and make a wish."

I do as he says. Scrunching my eyes tightly closed, I make a simple wish. A wish to be loved for just being me. A man shouldn't want to change me, to mould me to be who he wants. He should want me for me, no hidden agenda.

Opening my eyes, I see Nate's face. His eyes are closed; he's making a wish. I find myself really wishing I could read his mind, to see what he's asking for.

***

Nate pulls up in my driveway and I reluctantly get off his bike. I instantly feel the loss. It's not just the rumble of the engine beneath me that I miss, it's the warmth of the body I was clinging to.

He climbs off his bike and walks me to my front door. I want to invite him in, but I'm not sure where it would lead, or even where I would *want* it to lead. I feel safe with Nate. He makes me happy. There's a real chemistry between us, a connection like a combustible energy. I haven't felt this way in a long time, and the more time I spend with him, the more convinced I become that I've *never* felt this way before.

Lee never made me feel like this, not even in the early days of our relationship. Searching my memory, trying to grasp onto something that felt even remotely close, I come up empty.

"Would you like to come in for a coffee?"

"It's late; don't you have to be up early in the morning?"

"Brogan's opening the shop, so I don't have to be in until ten. But I'm the boss; I can make my own hours."

I flash him a grin and he mirrors it with a beaming one of his own.

Opening the door before I can change my mind, I walk inside and hear Nate following closely behind. I walk into the kitchen and turn the coffee machine on. I grab two cups from the cupboard above, set them down on the worktop and stand there, waiting for the machine to do its job.

As soon as the two coffees are made, I turn to Nate and hand him his steaming cup. His fingers brush mine and it sends a tingle through my arm. The harsh light of the kitchen should highlight his flaws but, after searching, I realise he has none. Not a scar or a blemish. His skin is smooth and tanned. He looks good dressed in jeans and a leather jacket. I'm sure he'd look good in anything … or nothing. I really should get my mind out of the gutter, but that's hard when he looks so magnificent. It's as though somebody decided to make Michelangelo's *David* come to life and put him in my life. Only he's much better looking.

"Cat got your tongue?"

His question startles me, and I realise I've been silently staring at him.

"Sorry, I just—"

"You don't have to be sorry for being caught looking at me," he butts in.

"Who says that's what I was doing?" I quip.

"Well unless you're blind … you were looking in my direction. There was nothing else there; you couldn't see beyond me. So, in conclusion, you *must* have been looking at me."

"Okay, I surrender."

I hold up my free hand in surrender and he laughs.

Nate places his coffee on the kitchen island and walks around to my side. He looks like a hunter stalking his prey, and that's exactly what I am. Prey. And I don't mind one little bit.

He gathers me in his arms, places my coffee down and backs me up against the worktop. His lips meet mine and it's as though I'm oxygen and he's fire. He seeks entry to my mouth with hot, demanding kisses. I'm only too willing to surrender. I'd give anything to freeze time and just be here in this moment. Hungry kisses and roaming hands. I could gladly accept this as my fate for an eternity.

Large hands skim my waist underneath the hem of my top while his tongue duels with mine for dominance over the kiss. He's passionate and pours every ounce of himself into this moment right here with me.

My heart beats a staccato rhythm in my chest. It feels like it wants to break free. It's like it has a mind of its own and it wants to jump into Nate's hands for him to cherish it.

I can feel his heart beating under my palm as I slide my hands up over his chest. Our breaths are heavy, intermingled with each other's.

Coherent thought leaves my mind, and the only thing I can think of is Nate. His passion, his energy, his sculpted body … how I wish there was less clothing separating us from each other.

His mouth leaves mine, and I feel bereft until I feel hot lips kissing a trail along my jawline. He nips at my earlobe and then kisses it to soothe the sting. Moments later, he's kissing down to the hollow of my throat, with one hand wrapped up in my hair, gently pulling my head back to expose my neck to him.

Soft moans leave me as my chest heaves. Every part of me feels heavy with lust. It's like he's poured petrol over every fibre of my being and then struck a match. The fire burns through my veins and has a direct line further south of my waist. His hands cup my breasts over the soft material of my bra. A gasp bursts from me as he deftly pulls my nipple taut between his thumb and forefinger.

Groans of appreciation rumble through his broad chest as his hands reach around my back to undo my bra. Large hands cup my breasts and a tingle travels straight to my core. It's a dizzying sensation as he leans towards me, capturing my lips. Far from being a soft tender kiss, I'm almost sure it will leave a bruise. But I'm also sure I don't give a damn.

He moves one hand and the loss is instant. My body craves his touch. His free hand plays at the waist of my jeans and my chest rises and falls rapidly as his fingers slip between the denim and my skin.

My fingernails dig into his shoulders as I hang on to him, feeling like my legs will give way beneath me at any moment.

Momentarily moving his other hand, he tugs at the button of my jeans before sliding the zip down. My back arches as his thumb finds my clit. I bite into my bottom lip to keep from moaning in ecstasy. I don't really want the neighbours banging on the door, telling me to keep the noise down. My one neighbour is a grumpy cow and would probably interrupt me mid-orgasm.

Nate slips a finger inside me and his hooded gaze meets mine as he watches for my reaction. I slip my arms around his neck and lean in to kiss him. He offers no resistance as I take what I need. I bite his bottom lip as he slips another finger inside and hooks them both to hit the right spot. I kiss his lip to soothe the sting as I slip one hand down to the waistband of his jeans.

Sliding my hand down between his jeans and his soft skin, I realise he's gone commando. I shiver at the thought and slide my hand further down to stroke his growing erection. Nate's moans are lost as I kiss him harder, hungrier than just a moment ago.

Until we got here, I wasn't sure this was what I wanted tonight. I didn't know if it was too soon. But now it just feels right.

Not a word is spoken between us, but they say actions speak louder than words anyway.

Nate's fingers slide in and out of me in a punishing rhythm as I stroke my hand up and down his cock. He moans as I increase the pressure of my grip, upping the rhythm of my own movements to match his.

"Jenna, stop ..." he whispers.

My heart drops as I think he's regretting letting things get so carried away.

"No, baby, no," he says as his eyes gaze deeply into min., "I just don't want this to be over too soon. I want to make love to you so badly, and if I come now, it might be a while before we get going again."

"Oh," I sigh in relief.

His mouth slants over mine in a deeply passionate kiss. His fingers move deeply inside me, pushing me ever closer to the edge. The warmth coils within me and I have to brace myself with my hands on the worktop behind me.

Nate's lips leave mine, and his free hand exposes the skin of my stomach to him as he lifts my top.

Trailing soft kisses across my abdomen, he ventures upwards and captures my nipple between his lips. This time, I can't hold back the moan that bubbles up from somewhere deep within me. I sound like a wild animal, but there's no room to be embarrassed when Nate's playing my body like he's done it all his life.

All too soon, his lips leave my skin again. He gazes up at me as he slowly gets down on his knees. His deft fingers hit the spot over and over, but I clench my walls around them, trying to stave off the impending sensation. I don't want it to end. If what he said about life being a series of fleeting moments is right, then I want to stay in this moment right here for as long as humanly possible.

Before I have a chance to comprehend what's about to happen, Nate spreads my legs a little further apart and his tongue darts out to circle my clit. I fight to keep my eyes open to watch him masterfully seduce me, but they close against my wishes.

My head falls back and my chest heaves as a passion I have never felt before washes over me.

Before too long, I realise I can't hold back any longer. I ride against his fingers as he pushes them harder in and out of me, pushing me further than anyone has ever bothered before.

My orgasm rips through me like a tidal wave. I moan ecstatically into the night as his movements slow. Riding out the little aftershocks, I'm panting like some wanton woman as he licks me languidly.

I fight to open my eyes and I look down at Nate in time to see him lick my essence from his fingers. Another moan bubbles up from me as I look at one of the most erotic things I've ever seen.

Sex with Lee had been missionary and boring for so long. I didn't know ecstasy like this existed. It's like my own personal high. Who needs drugs or some artificial high when they have Nate Peterson? I certainly don't.

I feel as though I should be embarrassed at being half naked in my kitchen, but I can't bring myself to care. Nate certainly seems to like it, so I don't let it faze me.

***

I rub my tired eyes with the heels of my hands. My eyelids are still heavy with sleep and I really don't want to wake up, but the sunlight is streaming in through my open curtains, bathing my room in a bright glow.

Looking over at the pillow next to me, I feel a pang in my chest as the memories of last night return. I've been on my own for so long that it feels weird seeing a naked body in bed next to me. But I quickly realise that it isn't a bad weird—it's just unusual.

My eyes take in the sight before me. Sculpted muscles, intricate tattoos, that V that I've never known the name of, but it drives me wild nevertheless ...

"My eyes are up here," a sleepy voice says, startling me.

I look up and see his eyes dancing with mirth.

"You told me I shouldn't be embarrassed to get caught staring."

"That's very true."

I lean down and place a soft kiss on his lips. His reaction is instant and fiery. He doesn't wait for an invitation, but instead slips his tongue inside to dance with mine.

A hand reaches up to cup the back of my neck, bringing me closer to him. Any closer and I'd be straddling him ... but maybe that's what he wants.

Breaking the kiss, I look to my bedside table for the time on my alarm clock. It's already nine thirty and I'm due in work at ten. I might have to forego my morning shower and just put my hair up in a messy bun for the day.

"Hey, Nix, come back here and kiss me like you mean it."

"Nix?"

"Yeah. Your tattoo. Phoenix. But that's not as cute a nickname."

"You are not calling me that. I don't even let anyone shorten my first name to Jen."

"You don't?"

"Nope. Don't like being called Jen. Haven't since my grandmother passed away."

My throat clogs with emotion. I swallow it back down as much as I can.

"Oh. I'm sorry. Was it something she called you?"

"Sort of. I was her little Jen-Jen as a kid. Then as I got older I was just Jen."

He looks at me with compassion in his blue-green eyes.

"Then Nix it is."

"Oh no it isn't," I reply as I throw my pillow at his chest.

"What time do you have to be in work, Nix?"

"Ten o'clock, and *stop* calling me that."

I get out of bed and can't help but notice when Nate's eyes roam over my naked body. I've never claimed to be a supermodel—I couldn't hack the diet of rabbit food, for a start. I'm much happier being slender with curves in the right place. Thankfully, for a woman of my age, I have pretty perky breasts, and Nate certainly enjoyed lavishing them with attention last night.

"Can you call in sick?"

There's no mistaking the lust in his voice. And there's no mistaking the neediness I suddenly feel.

"I hear my boss is a real bitch."

"Oh, I kind of heard that too."

"Oi."

I look around for something to throw at him but come up empty.

"Actually, I heard she's a sexy woman with the most amazing body known to man."

"Oh, now you're just trying to butter me up. That won't work, jerk."

I poke my tongue out at him and walk to my closet. I start pulling things out in a hurry but am stopped in my tracks when two warm, strong arms wrap around me. His erection presses against my ass and I can't help the sigh that escapes me.

"How about you text Brogan and say something has come up—no pun intended—and you're going to be a little late."

"I guess with a text she won't be able to tell I'm lying."

I sigh in defeat and turn around to grab my phone from the bedside table. I'm blocked by a wall of muscle that doesn't budge, so I stand on tiptoes and ghost a kiss over his soft, full lips.

"If you don't get out of the way, I can't text Brogan. So you're not doing yourself any favours."

"Okay, Nix. I'll move. But only if you promise me we can finish what you started with that kiss."

Playfully backhanding his chest for his insistence on the nickname I'm pretending not to like, I walk past and grab my phone.

>Hi Brogan, I'm really sorry but something has come up and I'm not going to make it in 'til at least midday. Will you be okay 'til then or do you want me to find cover?

I receive a reply almost straight away telling me not to worry, so I turn around and crook my finger at Nate.

"What did you say to her?" he asks as he walks towards me in all his naked glory.

He really could have been sculpted in marble. In fact, they ought to erect a statue of him instead of *David*.

"Just that I wouldn't be there until around midday. Now come here and let me make good on that promise."

I watch as he walks over to the bed, his gaze hooded with lust and a salacious grin playing on his lips. God, those lips. They were made for sin, just as much as every other wicked inch of his body.

Chapter Ten

Nate

I couldn't believe it when my little Nix let me spend the night worshipping her divine body last night. There isn't a millimetre of it that I haven't touched, kissed, licked. I only have to close my eyes and I'm back there in her bed, making love to her as the sun streamed in this morning. If we hadn't both had to turn up at work at some point today, I'd still be in bed with her … or perhaps the shower.

It took all the willpower I possessed to get on my bike and ride away.

Work was long and tedious. I usually enjoy creating art the way I do. It's usually something that brings me joy. I feel like the person can tell if I put my heart into it or not. But nobody has complained about awful tattoos, they've given me nothing but compliments, so maybe I'm wrong.

It isn't that I don't love my job. It's more that I spent the entire day wishing I was back in bed with Nix. My body might have been physically at Blank Canvas, but I was with Nix in spirit.

I can smell her on me and it's addictive. The scent of her strawberry shampoo, the scent of her skin … I close my eyes, and visions of her play out behind my eyelids. Her creamy, soft skin. The curves of her body. That great ass. Those perfect, perky breasts and succulent nipples. My cock begins to twitch just picturing her.

"Nate."

Steph's voice startles me back to reality.

"Sorry, Steph, I was miles away. What can I do for you?"

"Miles away with a certain sexy brunette, by any chance?"

"I don't know what you mean," I reply with a smirk.

She knows she's hit the nail on the head; I can tell by her smile. Damn the blue-haired know-it-all.

"Denial isn't just a river in Egypt, you know?!"

We both crack up at her lame-ass joke.

"She's really something, Steph, you know?!"

"Finally, he admits it. So, come on, spill."

"This man doesn't kiss and tell."

"Really? Where's the real Nate and what have you done with him?"

Okay, so I used to be the type to kiss and tell—or should I say brag.

"This is different, Steph. *She's* different. She brings out a softer side in me—as you can tell just by the fact I'm admitting that."

"Wow, you're a total goner."

"What?"

Her shit-eating grin speaks volumes. She knows what I won't admit, even to myself.

"Your private life is your business, boss. I'm just pulling your leg. But if you really like her, then I'm happy for you. Maybe she'll be good for you. Better than that bitch of an ex."

"Ugh."

Shudders run through me as I remember the bitch I wanted to marry and have a life with. Nikki. I can't even stand to think of her name. She was a heartless bitch that screwed my ex-best friend.

"Your next appointment is here," Star says from the doorway, where she stands behind Steph.

"Thanks, Star, let them through."

"I'll let you get back to it, boss," Steph says as she turns on her heel.

"Wait. What was it you wanted?"

"Oh, I was just wondering if I could book a day off next week. It's my anniversary."

"No worries, just put it in the diary, Blue."

"Thanks, boss."

She gives me a mock salute as she walks out the door.

I'm busying myself with setting up the tattoo gun when I hear a voice that makes my stomach turn inside out. Good job I didn't have breakfast, else I'd be cleaning it up right now.

"Hey, Nate," she says in that saccharine sweet voice.

I look up and see her in the flesh. Standing in my room like butter wouldn't melt. I haven't seen her for years, and I would have preferred to keep it that way.

"Nikki," I greet, in a voice devoid of any emotion.

"It's good to see you, babe. How have you been?"

"I'm not your babe. I haven't been for a long time, Nikki. What do you want?"

I haven't got time for her shit. Not now, not ever.

"I'm here for a tattoo."

"What?"

I blanch at the idea of having to touch her skin, even in a platonic way. Even if it means losing business, I'd rather she takes her money and shove it up her—I won't finish that thought.

"I'm your next appointment. Don't act like you didn't know. I booked it weeks ago."

"I don't look at the diary, Nikki. That's Star's department. I had no idea you were coming. I would have cancelled the appointment or put you with someone else."

"Now there's no need to be like that, babe. A lot of time has passed since we last saw each other. Time heals all wounds."

"No, Nikki, it does not. There are some things I'll never forgive or forget. Watching my ex-best friend fucking you over my bed is one of those things."

"Oh, babe, it was just sex. You weren't exactly short of female attention, as I'm sure you aren't now. Still the same old Nate."

"I'm not the one who cheated, Nikki. You think because women flirted with me that it gave you a right to fuck my best friend? And what the fuck was he thinking when he was doing it? Actually, screw that, I don't want to know."

"Oh, cry me a river, Nate. Just get over it already. It doesn't do any good to harbour ill will."

"That's it,, Nikki, get the *fuck* out. Star will happily refund your deposit. And while you're at it, never, *ever* come back here."

"Calm down, babe. You'll burst a blood vessel."

"What did I just say about calling me babe? GET OUT!"

I can feel my blood boiling. I don't get angry often, but fuck if she doesn't bring out the worst in me.

"What's the commotion, boss?" Steph's voice comes from behind Nikki.

Nikki spins around upon hearing her. Steph's face registers shock, as if our talking of the devil brought her to our doorstep.

"What the hell?"

"Nice to see you too, Stephie."

Steph's face morphs from shock to rage.

"What the fuck? Don't try and play like we like each other. And my name is Steph."

"No need to get angry, Stephie. I'm just here for a tattoo, nothing more."

I stand and walk to Nikki's side. Grabbing her elbow, I try to steer her out of the room past Steph. But Nikki digs her heels in, and Steph looks like she won't let her through. This is so not the best time to be airing shit. It's my place of work, for Christ's sake.

Trust Nikki to come along and burst my happy bubble. Not a slow puncture either, just complete annihilation. She always did go for the jugular.

"Nikki, I asked you to leave. In fact, I made it pretty goddamn clear you're not welcome here. I suggest you get the hell out and forget this place exists."

"I want my tattoo," she replies indignantly.

"Get the fuck out of here," Steph says as she moves forward towards Nikki.

She shrugs my hand off her elbow and puts her hands on her hips.

"I came here to get a tattoo and I'm not leaving until it's done."

"Then I'll call the police. They can escort you out."

"And what would you tell them, Stephie? That a lady wants a tattoo that she booked in for weeks ago and the tattooist refuses to do it? Wow, they'll take that shit seriously."

I see a derisive smile grace her ugly face. This isn't going to end well.

"I'd tell them that some little psycho bitch won't leave the premises. You've had fair warning to leave of your own accord, Nikki."

"What the hell is this circus?" Hélène asks from somewhere behind Steph.

"A storm in a teacup, Hélène, nothing to worry about," Steph answers before I can even open my mouth.

"It sounds like a bit more than that. We can hear you from my room. What's going on?"

"Sorry, Hélène. It's really nothing to worry about."

I really don't want to give our newest employee the impression that this place is nothing more than a circus. She's a good fit with us and a fantastic tattoo artist, so I don't want to lose her.

"I heard mention of police, so it can't be nothing," she replies tersely.

"I'm here for a tattoo, but your boss is refusing," Nikki says.

"That's his right. He can refuse clients if he has grounds to," Hélène says.

"But I haven't done anything wrong."

"Not today, you haven't," I butt in.

God give me strength; I really want to strangle her.

"I haven't done anything."

"Not today, Satan," Steph chimes in.

"Look, I think you should just leave. I don't know you or your problems, nor do I want to, but you're causing a scene and making yourself look silly," Hélène points out.

At least Hélène talks sense. I can feel my temper rising, simmering under the surface.

"I've had enough now, Nikki. You've caused a commotion like always. You've drawn attention to yourself like the attention-seeking whore you are. That's it. End of. Get out!"

Taking her by the elbow once more, I manage to steer her past Steph and Hélène. She digs her heels in, but my upper body strength outmatches hers.

Steph stands back out of the way with a look of thunder on her face. I know she'd like to slap the stupid look right off Nikki's face, but violence solves nothing.

Forcing her out into the reception area, I see other clients waiting. God, what will they think of this floor show? I don't have time to care; I need this bitch out of my place of work.

"I know you like it rough, Nate, but this is a new low even for you," Nikki says as I tug her to the door.

"No, Nikki. You're wrong. I don't have to explain myself to you, so I'll save my breath. Just get out."

I hold the shop door wide open with my free hand and gesture for her to leave.

"I didn't expect such hostility, Nate. Honestly, I would have thought you'd have gotten over the past a long time. But I guess you're better at holding grudges than I thought."

"Nikki, you have to be stupid to think I would ever forgive and forget. You haven't been part of my life for a long time and you never will be again. Give my love to Marshall."

"Oh, I will."

She smirks and then flicks her hair over her shoulder like some stupid teenager. That's when I catch a glint from something sparkly. Looking closer at her hand, I see a stupidly large rock on her ring finger.

"Yes, that's right, Marshall and I are engaged," she says as she catches my eye.

"Never have two people been more right for each other," I answer derisively.

"You're quite right. We're a better fit than you and I were."

She smirks, and I want to slam the door in her face, but I can see clients trying not to look at us as they sit in the waiting room.

"Cheats deserve each other."

I step back and let the door close.

"Sorry about that, folks," I say as I pass.

Walking back to my room, I see Hélène has gone. Steph, however, remains standing by my door.

"Well, that was a trip," she says as she follows me in and closes the door.

"Wasn't it just?"

I scrub my hands down over my face and feel the stubble on my chin. I want to rip chunks out of my hair or punch a hole in something, but that would only be a temporary relief.

"Want to get out of here for a while?"

"What?"

I look up at her and she offers me a small smile.

"I don't have any customers until two this afternoon, so I'm off for an extended lunch. Care to join me as you have an hour free unexpectedly?"

"Probably a wiser choice than sitting here stewing. What are you doing for lunch?"

"Popping to the Siren for a Bacardi and coke."

"I could use a large whiskey after that ordeal, but I'll join you for a soft drink considering I'm on my bike today."

"I'll just grab my bag and meet you out in reception."

Off she swishes with a flick of her blue mane.

***

After a soft drink and shooting the breeze with Steph, I feel much better. It's a shame Nix isn't working at the Siren today; I was hoping to catch a glimpse of her. Instead I decide to send her a quick text.

>Hey gorgeous. How are you?

I see three dots, meaning she's typing back already. I stare at my screen and will a message to come through as quickly as technology can handle.

>> Hey! I'm good. Busy though, got a wedding to make the bouquets and posies for. How are you?

>Shit day at work to be honest. Went to the Siren for a drink, hoped to see you. Forgot you weren't on shift.

>>Damn! Would have been nice to see you. I've had so many pricks today it's unbelievable…from the roses, that is, so get your mind out of the gutter ;)

>Aww, do you need somebody to kiss your boo-boos better? ;)

>>That would be…pleasant.

>Oh, trust me, it would be a hell of a lot more than pleasant!

I try to get my mind back on work but fail when I hear my phone chime again.

>>Are you free this evening?

Dammit. I'm seeing Gramps this evening, but I still haven't told her about him. He knows about her. You can't get much past Gordon Peterson … on a lucid day, anyway. He's sharp as a tack.

>Sorry, I'm busy this evening. I couldn't get away until around nine.

I feel like shit for wanting to see her and Gramps, but not being able to be in two places at once. I don't know whether it's too soon to mention him to her. I mean, I know stuff about her family, and she knows next to nothing about mine. I guess you could say I'm a private person. But this—whatever "this" is between us—is going well. She's a great person—funny, sexy, down-to-earth, genuine … I really like her and can see it going somewhere between us. Gramps isn't exactly a secret, I mean, he's my only family. I love the man to bits. And I want him to see me happy. He'd be over the moon to see me settle down. Are we settling down? It's hardly that … yet. But it could be. Maybe. Hopefully. Ugh, I want to bang my head against the wall.

My phone chimes with another text.

>>I haven't got to work tomorrow, if I get all these posies finished tonight. And by the time I'm finished here, even with Brogan's help, I couldn't see myself being ready before eight-thirty anyway.

Before I can overthink things, I shoot her a message back.

>Would you like to meet someone who means a lot to me?

Those three dots make me antsy again.

>>Colour me intrigued

>I'll reveal all later but suffice to say except for you and my best friend Josh, this is the one person who means the most to me in the world. Should I pick you up from home around nine?

>>Can't wait. Must get back to these damn roses. Tell me, what kind of bride wants a bunch of pricks in her bouquet? ;)

>She's probably already had a bunch of pricks before the one she's marrying.

That didn't come out quite right, but I sent it anyway.

>>OMG I can't believe you just said that. Brogan peed herself when I read it out.

>You're reading my texts to Brogan?

>>No, just that one because it was funny. Don't worry, what we say stays between us.

>Okay. I'll believe you. See you at nine, Nix.

>>Stop calling me that!

> Miss you, Nix. See you later xx

I laugh at her false hatred of her new nickname. She pretends to be offended by it, but I can always tell by the look on her face that she doesn't actually mind it as much as she makes out.

>>I need a stupid nickname for you. Hmm… I'll see what Brogan and I can come up with.

She didn't call me out for saying I miss her, so she mustn't mind.

"What's got a shit-eating grin on your mug, boss?"

"Shut it, Smurf."

"Jenna."

"So intuitive. Yes, it's Nix. I've been texting her. She knows how to make me smile."

"Nix?"

"On account of the phoenix tattoo she got. She gets irked by the name, so I use it as often as I can."

"You're a dick."

Steph laughs at me and hands me a mug. I inhale the rich aroma of the steaming hot coffee.

"Thanks, Smurf. You off for the day?"

"Yep. You?"

"Not yet. My last client should be here any minute. Told him I'd stay open for him. You know I can't say no to Josh."

"Oh, jeez, I'm glad I'm done for the day."

I can't say I blame her. Josh always teases that he's the guy to turn her straight. Even when he's not single, he still teases her.

"You know he's harmless."

"Yeah, but still a big flirt. I'm heading out; I just thought you could use a coffee. See you tomorrow."

"Nope. Day off."

"Oh, okay. You back Wednesday?"

"Yep. Not until about eleven though. Don't have appointments earlier than that."

"Okay. I'll see you then."

"See you then. Oh, and by the way, Smurf, thanks for earlier."

"No problem, boss. And stop calling me Smurf."

"Catch you later"—I pause as she walks back to the door—"Smurf."

She flips me off over her shoulder and disappears.

***

Josh's tattoo took a little longer than planned, so I quickly washed up in the shop restroom. I could use a shave, but that'll have to wait. I have just enough time to pop home to collect my second helmet and then over to Nix's by nine.

It turns out Josh is actually really digging this chick he met the night of the speed dating event, but he's keeping tight-lipped about who she is. I'm his best friend and he won't even tell me.

His tattoo turned out to be better than we both imagined. It's of a woman's face inside a lion's mouth, done in black and white. It's a piece he's been booked in for since forever, but he knew I had a pretty full waiting list, so he's been patient. I mean, he did get it done at mate's rates, so he can't really complain.

I jump on my bike and head for home. The house is dark as I arrive, but the outside light comes on as I pull up. I love this house so much. I've lived here since Gramps went into Haven Lodge. It was his and my grandma Lillian's house for many years before she died, and then he lived here alone while I lived with Marshall. After what that bastard did to me, I moved in with Gramps for a while, then it was decided he would move into Haven Lodge because I couldn't keep my eye on him twenty-four seven.

I still feel bad about that decision to this day. But he knew he was going to get worse, and we talked at length about our—or should I say his—options. He was happy enough going to Haven Lodge. He knew he'd be well cared for and, because of the security cameras, nurses, carers, and everything they have in place, we knew it was the best place for him to be.

Letting myself in, I grab the spare helmet and look at my watch. Eight forty-five. Just enough time to get to Nix's place. Sending her a quick text to say I'm on my way, I slip my phone back in my pocket and lock the house up again.

Arriving just before nine, I knock lightly on the door. The light is on in the living room, so I know she's home.

The door opens, and I look up at the woman before me. Dressed in faded blue jeans, an oversized jumper, and a pair of worn-in Converse, she looks amazing. It doesn't matter whether she's dressed casual, smart, or a combination of both, my heart still squeezes in my chest every time I see her.

She grabs her jacket and turns to lock the door behind her. I pass her the helmet and expect her to put it on. Instead she stands on tiptoes and ghosts a kiss over my lips. I cup the back of her neck and bring her in for a deeper kiss.

Nix awakens something deep within me. Something I didn't know existed, but something only she has ever been capable of evoking.

Breaking apart, our breaths are heavy as we stand smiling at each other.

"So, are you telling me where we're going or who I'm about to meet?"

"Nope."

I pull my helmet on and straddle the bike, waiting for her to follow suit. She snuggles in behind me, and I take a moment to revel in her touch before starting the engine.

Pulling out of her drive, I head in the direction of Haven Lodge. The place where my heart currently resides.

Chapter Eleven

Jenna

We pull up outside what looks like a nursing home, and I wonder why he would be bringing me here. He hasn't said a word about who we're seeing, so I just dismount the bike and hand him my helmet.

He gets off the bike and takes my hand. It feels as though it was made purely to fit mine.

We walk up to the door, and he presses the buzzer and gives his name to the woman that answers.

Holding the door open, he gestures for me to go in before him, then shuts the door and slips his hand around mine once more.

"Good evening, Nate," the woman behind the little desk says.

"Good evening, Linda. How's he been today?"

"He's on good form today. Could you please sign your guest in?"

He picks up a pen on the counter, and I notice his left hand is his dominant hand. How did I not notice this before?

"Good evening, it's nice to meet you. Any friend of Nate's is a friend of ours," Linda says.

I still have no idea who she is, or the "he" that they both referred to, but I greet her with a smile and a shake of the hand. She seems nice.

Looking around, I see some art on the walls interspersed between some doors. The doors are a way apart, so I'm guessing the rooms behind them are a good size. I'm not stupid, I know a nursing home is for the elderly, so I have some inkling that the gentleman we're about to meet is elderly, but it can't be Nate's father because he told me that, tragically, his mother and father both died some years ago.

He doesn't talk about family, so I'm guessing this is some old family friend that I'm about to be introduced to. I don't have time to wonder though, because Nate pulls my hand forward, so I fall into step beside him.

Nervous butterflies flutter around in my stomach. Nate and I haven't defined whatever it is we have going on yet. But if he wants me to meet someone he says he cares deeply about, then I have a feeling he sees us as starting something. I'm hoping this is only the beginning of something beautiful.

Yes, I swore off men after the ordeal with Lee. But meeting Nate was akin to being shot in the heart by cupid. Cheesy? Yes. But true, nonetheless. I didn't see him coming. I didn't foresee love or even lust being in my immediate future. Fate seems to have other plans for me though. And, although I may have sworn off men, I can't deny that I'm glad I met him. He makes me feel … well, I'm not sure how to define it. I feel alive, like I've been a statue, standing tall and still for so long, and finally someone has come along and breathed life back into me.

Nate knocks gently on a door and a voice beckons him in.

Walking in behind him, I see a handsome-looking gentleman sitting watching the television. He turns it off as we enter and looks at Nate with a huge grin on his face. Behind him, I see framed pictures on the walls. Some medals are framed too, and I wonder whether they're his and how he earned them. Was he in the army?

"Nathaniel, how good to see you boy. And you've brought a friend."

He smiles at me, and I offer him a smile of my own.

"Don't stand on ceremony, get over here and give an old man a hug, Nathaniel."

Nate does as he's told, and I see his face light up as he turns to me to introduce me.

"Gramps, this is Jenna," he says, before pausing to take a deep breath. "Jenna, this is my grandfather, Gordon."

"Oh, pish-posh, call me Gramps, young lady. And that's an order," he responds with a wink.

"Hi," I reply, extending my hand.

He brushes my hand aside and stands to embrace me in a big hug instead. I return his embrace and get a whiff of Old Spice. Traditional, I like it. "Take a seat, you two."

Nate pulls two chairs out at the small table in the little kitchenette

Les

of Gordon's room. He waits until I'm seated before sitting beside me.

"So, my boy, it's always good to see you, but I'm guessing you have a reason for bringing a young lady to meet me."

"Umm …"

"You've set me up on a date? In that case, young lady, don't call me Gramps, that wouldn't sound right on a date."

Gordon chortles and Nate grins like a loon.

"So, boy, don't keep an old man waiting, it's not polite."

"Well, umm … Jenna is my … umm …"

His humming and hawing brings a smile to my face.

"Friend," he says, at the same time as I blurt out, "Girlfriend."

"Well, which one is it? Friend or girlfriend?" Gordon asks, a shit-eating grin on his face.

I look at him in that moment and see the same smile Nate wears. It would be obvious that they're related, even if he hadn't told me; it's impossible not to see the familial link.

"Well, we just started dating, actually, Gramps. So, we haven't really defined it."

"Boy, you aren't getting any younger. Thirty-six years of age and still not married or given me great-grandbabies. Make your mind up which one you are. Are you her friend or her boyfriend?"

Jeez, I'm glad I'm not on the receiving end of his smart tongue. I can't help but laugh as Nate looks to me for help.

I squeeze his hand under the table and his eyes soften.

"She's my girlfriend, Gramps."

"'Bout time boy. You were about to die of indecision there."

Gordon chortles, and I can't help but laugh. I burst into a full-on belly laugh at the look on Nate's adorable face.

"Aw, boy, you're adorable when you're in love."

"Gramps, don't go getting ahead of yourself," Nate warns affectionately.

"I'm allowed to do what I like, thank you, young man. Don't forget who is the elder one here. You're not too old to be put over my knee and spanked on your bare ass."

"I'm not sure that's correct, Gramps. As you said, I'm thirty-six."

"As I said, not too old. Now shut up before I show you how right I am."

"Aw, Nate, Gramps is going to give you a hiding if you don't just quit while you're ahead," I butt in.

"Goddammit, now I have both of you on my case. Maybe bringing a woman I like to meet this miserly old git wasn't the right thing to do after all."

"You're cruising for a bruising, boy. Shut your damn mouth. Oops, sorry Jenna. Forgive my potty mouth."

"Your grandson isn't as polite as you, and I've heard him say worse, so you're forgiven."

"Hey, you're meant to be on my side," Nate says, casting a look my way.

"Why am I?"

"Because girlfriends always side with their boyfriends."

"Not when they're wrong."

I poke my tongue out at him, and Gramps laughs long and loud. Nate gives me a playful nudge in the ribs for my cheek but joins us laughing.

"You've got yourself a keeper there, boy. Put a ring on it. Isn't that what Beyoncé says?"

"Like you know who Beyoncé is, old man."

"How could I not know Queen B?" he asks with an—almost—serious face.

"Okay, prove it. Sing me some lyrics to any one of her songs."

"Care to lay odds boy?"

"How rich are you feeling, old timer?"

"Umm …"

Gramps proceeds to empty out the contents of his pockets onto the dining table. There's some pocket fluff, a handkerchief, a dice—goodness knows why—and some change.

"Okay, care to make a different kind of wager, boy?"

"Depends what you're thinking, Gramps."

"If I win, I get a kiss off this girl o' yours."

"Firstly, that isn't mine to promise you, and secondly, what do I get if I win?"

"All this change here, but not my dice. I need that for my game with Jackson later."

"Aw, I promise you a kiss if you win, Gramps," I reply before Nate can get a word in.

"You're on then, old timer. Sing us some Queen B."

Gramps proceeds to belt out the chorus of "Single Ladies". He's got a great voice, although it's not the perfect song for him. But a bet is a bet. So, I stand up and lean to give him a kiss on the cheek, but he turns just before the kiss lands and, instead, it lands squarely on his lips. Cheeky so-and-so.

"Hang on, that could be a fluke. The chorus is the most well-known part," Nate chimes in.

"A win is a win, Nathaniel," I chide.

"Oh, come on, that's so not fair!"

"Shut up, Nathaniel. A bet is a bet and a win is a win. I won; therefore, I got the prize."

"Okay, old man, you got me this time. I don't know how you pulled that off though. I think you were listening to the radio before we came in."

"If I was, I wouldn't have been listening to Beyoncé. Well, not by choice, at least."

"I thought you said she was—and I quote—Queen B."

"I did. But that's only because the nurse was saying so about half an hour before you got here. I tried teaching her a song only an old timer like me would remember and she tried teaching me a bit of Beyoncé. That was the real bet here, sunshine. And I won. I get hot chocolate *with marshmallows* before bed now. I even have witnesses."

He gestures to the two of us as he talks, and Nate's face morphs into a full-on Hollywood smile.

"You, Gramps, are a genius."

Somebody knocks at the door and Gramps calls them in.

"Here you go, Gordon. As promised, if a little early," the nurse says as she places a mug down in front of him. "Sorry it's early. It's just that my shift finished at nine thirty and I heard you singing as I passed the door, so I went back to the kitchen rather than getting Linda to bring it later."

"Thanks, Gayle. I'll be sure to enjoy this. Chocolate sprinkles as well. I must have been good."

"Well, Gordon, we could hear you in Flo's room next door. She asked me what the—let's just say *heck*—you were singing. I was bent over laughing as she tried to figure out what the lyrics were on about. Let's just say she was wondering why you kept repeating *oh oh oh*."

"OMG Gramps, I can't even …"

Nate bursts into laughter and I can't help but join him.

"Can't say I had fun trying to explain it to her," Gayle says as she turns to leave, "but thanks for the laugh, and never let it be said that I welsh on a bet. See you tomorrow for breakfast."

"Thanks, Gayle. See you in the morning, beautiful."

"Oh, you flatterer. Night night."

Gayle waves as she closes the door softly behind her.

***

"Your gramps is a hoot."

"Yeah, he's a riot. He's a pain in my ass, but he's funny and smart."

We walk back to his bike and grab our helmets.

"He's smart as a whip. I can see where you get your sarcasm from. And your good looks too."

"Don't let him hear you say that; he'll get a big head."

"You have the same Hollywood smile. All perfect, pearly white teeth."

"He's still got all his own teeth too, good for a man of his age."

"You have the same eyes too."

"I have my father's eyes, or so I've been told," he replies wistfully.

I still don't know Nate all that well, and he hasn't confided in me about how his parents died. All I know is that he misses them deeply.

"Then he had beautiful eyes too."

No more is said as we climb on his gorgeous red Ducati. I must say, it's one hell of a sexy beast. Molla, that's what he said she's called.

We ride back to my place, and Nate walks me to the door. He leans in and ghosts a kiss over my lips.

"Thank you for coming tonight. I can't tell you how much it means to me."

"No thanks necessary, Nate. It was a nice night. Like I said, your gramps is a comedian. Those dirty jokes he was telling, oh boy!"

"He's incorrigible. And you, you egged him on."

"All part of the fun. You want to come in for coffee?"

"Sure."

His eyes twinkle and his grin suggests he'd be up for the kind of "coffee" people normally invite people in for this late at night.

I open the door, and Nate follows me as I head down the hall to the kitchen. He pulls up a bar stool at the island in the centre of the kitchen. Resting his chin in his hands, he smiles widely at me as I put the coffee machine on and turn to grab two mugs from the cupboard.

Feeling his eyes burning holes in me, I turn slowly back towards him and watch as his gaze roams my curves. The look in his eyes says all he needs to say without words. He likes what he sees.

Thinking back to our conversation with Gordon, I realise that we announced whatever's going on with us as an actual relationship. A smile graces my lips as I set about making two mugs of steaming coffee. Nate's my boyfriend. He didn't complain or correct me when I'd said I was his girlfriend.

I'm of an age now where people don't really say things like "Will you go out with me?" anymore. That was the kind of thing we did in our teenage years, sure. But I'm in my thirties now and it can be quite difficult to put labels on things. You'd think relationships would get easier to define when you're older, but that's not necessarily the case. You might be grown up, but it's the same shit, just a different day.

"What's going on in that pretty head of yours?"

His question startles me, and I almost spill the coffee I place in front of him.

"I don't know. Nothing really, just thinking about things."

"What kind of things?"

"Relationships."

My mouth opens before my brain registers. I didn't really want to have "that" conversation.

"Oh? And what about them specifically?"

His grin is wide and smug.

"Just that we haven't defined this and then—"

"Gramps put us on the spot," he butts in.

"Yeah."

I shake my head and pull up a bar stool opposite him. He takes my hand over the top of the island and traces circles on the back of it with his thumb.

"You can take it back. Gramps doesn't need to know. I won't tell him."

"No, you misunderstand me. I don't want to take it back, that's the thing."

"You don't?"

The shit-eating grin nearly splits his face in half, and his eyes light up. They really are the most mesmerising colour. A blue-green—nobody calls the colour of their eyes turquoise, but his are—that reminds me of the beauty of the ocean. The vastness within them reminds me that the ocean is deep and alluring. You go to dip your toes in the edge of the water, but it calls to you, and you can't resist taking a swim. But you have to be careful. You have to know you're a strong swimmer, else you might get pulled under by the current. Nate's eyes tell me the same thing. I could get swept away by the tide. But I don't find myself caring. I'm willing to be brave and take the risk … if he is.

"No, I don't. The thoughts rattling around in my brain were actually about how much easier it is to define things as a teenager. The passing notes in class, the hushed whispers in the corridor. The best friend going up to the other person's best friend and saying something to try and urge them to get together. Saying 'will you go out with me'. That sort of thing."

"Oh, to be young again. You're right, it was easier then. Life doesn't get easier as you get older. Well, some things do, and for some people relationships are easy, while others battle against the tide, not wanting to be sucked under by a rip current."

"Very true. It gets harder to define things and put a label on them. Nobody really asks anyone out anymore. Some people don't even date. They have the kind of relationship where they just fall into each other's routines."

"I guess I'm old-fashioned then, because I like to go out on dates. The fun of going new places, trying new things … I guess Gramps raised me with a few ideas on how to treat a woman well."

"So where would your ideal date be then? Set the scene for me."

"Umm …"

He caresses my hand as he ponders my question. Little shivers run through me at just that little touch. I close my eyes and remember those hands touching me more intimately.

"I guess, if it was something adventurous, we'd try something neither of us have tried before, like a tandem bungee jump, or even base jumping if the other person was up for it."

"Well, that's me out then. I'm all for adventure, but base jumping looks terrifying."

"It is a little scary looking, but that's part of the thrill, I think. Anyway, if it was a romantic date, let's see, I'd say … a guessing date, I suppose you could call it. It would be something I'd have planned out weeks in advance. I'd make up little clues and lead her on a treasure hunt. The prize at the end is me. Like, I'd set up something to do together, like a picnic, or a trip to the theatre. Then I'd send the woman out on a hunt to find me. She'd get clues in sealed envelopes that take her all over the place until, finally, she gets to me."

"Wow, that sounds like fun."

I actually quite like the sound of that. Half the fun is in the clues, running around town and trying to figure stuff out. The other half of the fun would be reuniting with him at the end of it. Sounds romantic and fun. Something I wouldn't have pegged Nate as being the kind to do, but now that he's said it, I can picture him waiting at the end, wearing a suit and taking me to the theatre. Or dressed casual with a picnic hamper and blanket in his hands.

"What about you? What's your ideal date?"

"Hmm … I don't really know. Something fun that I haven't done before. But there's a limit to my adventurous side. No base jumping, no skydiving, nothing I could potentially break a limb doing. If you want romantic, he'd know my favourite show to see at the theatre, he'd be dressed in a sharp suit and I'd be in a cocktail dress. Only, we'd pretend like we don't know each other. The guy would 'bump into me' in the bar before the show and then he'd ask me to accompany him. I don't know, something like that."

Nate's eyes twinkle as he listens to me, like he's had an idea. Now more than ever, I really want to know what he's thinking.

***

We talk until the early hours of the morning, getting to know each other better. Silly things like favourite colour, taste in music, what we studied at school, where we went to school. It's good to know more about him. I feel more and more at ease with him, like I've known him in another lifetime. Like our souls call to each other. Maybe that sounds a bit weird if you say it out loud, but in my heart, I feel like I'm taking a risk on Nate, giving him my heart and hoping he won't break it.

I'm not at the "I'm in love with him" stage, yet, but it's definitely more than mere lust. That being said, I'm definitely lusting after him. It's two a.m., I should be tired. But looks like the one he's giving me stoke the flames of desire within me. The way he's looking at me right now, like he's undressing me with his eyes, makes me want to jump him right here, right now on the kitchen island.

My pulse races as he traces lazy circles on the back of my hand, like he's been doing on and off for the last few hours. But this time, instead of being a calming touch, grounding me, it feels more intimate. Goosebumps break out on my arms, and the hairs at the nape of my neck stand on end. I try to stifle the feeling by placing my free hand on my neck, but it doesn't abate.

Nate stands, rounds the island and comes to a standstill behind me. His hands trace gentle movements up and down my arms. It sends shivers down my spine and stokes a warmth in my abdomen.

Gently, he moves my hair to fall over one shoulder. My oversized jumper exposes the skin on my shoulder to his soft kisses. Each touch is as delicate as a butterfly's wings. They ghost across my skin as he moves to the side of my neck. His warm breath has me breathing heavily.

A soft moan leaves my lips before I can stop it. He murmurs an appreciative response.

I try to stand, to turn in his embrace, but he pushes me down gently, communicating the need for me to stay right where I am.

He nips my earlobe, then kisses away the little sting. Tracing his way along my jaw, he puts his hand under my chin, tilting it up to meet his kisses.

Bending to place his hands on my thighs, he turns me around on the stool. I look up at his hooded gaze, lust darkening his irises. My heart beats a staccato rhythm in my chest and it echoes in my ears.

Tracing feather-light kisses down one side of my neck, he bends down further and places a kiss at the hollow of my throat. My heart lodges itself firmly in my throat. It's torturous that he's going so slowly, yet it's so much more tantalising than a quick lay. He doesn't want to just fuck me for the sake of it. His heart is one hundred percent in this. I'm not saying it's love, but he doesn't seem to be using me just because he can. Why introduce me to his grandfather if he doesn't see this going somewhere? So, I'm hoping he's in this for all the right reasons. I know I am. Yes, I was undecided at first, because of my issues with men in general, and because I was attracted to Levi, but I've let Levi down gently, because when I am in something, that's it for me. I'm all in. No backing out.

I move my hands to his hips and pull him closer to me, between my parted thighs. We couldn't be any closer in this position. He sighs contentedly as he kisses down my exposed shoulder, pushing my jumper further down my arm.

Raising my arms above my head, I look into Nate's ocean gaze and he pulls my jumper up over my head. I'm left semi-exposed in just my lacy bra. His pupils dilate as he takes in the sight before him.

"Would you stand?" he asks quietly.

I stand without replying. He reaches to undo the button and zip of my jeans, before pushing them down my thighs.

Strong hands grip my waist and he lifts me to sit on the island. The cold would bother me if it wasn't for the warmth Nate is providing.

He pulls my jeans further down my legs before realising I still have my shoes on. He makes quick work of removing them and discarding my jeans along with them.

Sitting here in just my panties and bra, I should feel exposed, even shy, and if it was anybody else, I would feel like that. But not with Nate. With him, I feel safe, adored, hungry for what I know is coming.

He looks at me like I'm a veritable feast and he's a starving man looking for his next meal.

Slowly, he removes his own t-shirt and stands before me. His body is something to be admired, but he doesn't give me any time to do so. He leans over me and places a kiss in the valley between my breasts. Just one soft, silky kiss. It makes me shudder in delight.

Strong arms brace on the countertop on either side of me, trapping me between them.

"Beautiful."

His breath causes goosebumps to break out across my skin. That warmth in my abdomen blooms again. I close my eyes, revelling in the delicious feeling.

Before I know what's happening, I feel his strong arms lift me and cradle me against his bare chest. He walks to the stairs and carries me as if I weigh no more than a feather.

Placing me on the bed, he treats me with a reverence, the likes of which I've never been shown before.

I lie on my back and Nate walks to the end of my bed. I lift my head and watch as he strips out of his jeans and boxers. His erection is impressive, and I lick my lips at the mouth-watering sight before me.

"Delectable," I whisper as he braces himself over the top of me.

"You certainly are," he whispers, before claiming my lips in a soft and tender kiss.

I circle my arms around his neck and pull him closer in an effort to deepen the kiss. A groan reverberates from his chest as he kisses me more fervently. Our chests are heaving, and my body is craving his touch. I want him to take his time with me, kissing every inch of me like he did the other night. Then, there was no part of me left untouched. He worshipped me over again in the middle of the night when we both woke for no apparent reason, after which, I fell into the deepest sleep I've had in months. He took me to the edge and jumped off with me. The exhilaration made my body tingle and awoke a part of me I hadn't paid attention to for a long time.

Sex with Lee had been just that—sex. But Nate treasures me, worships me like I'm something truly special to him.

Nate kisses down my throat, along the swell of my breasts, then cups them in his hands before reaching around me to undo my bra.

I pull the straps down my shoulders and toss the material to one side. He looks at me with fire in his eyes as he cups my naked breasts and leans down to take one of my nipples into his hot mouth.

I revel in the sensation of his tongue before he gently nips it, pulling it taut. He moves to pay the same attention to the other nipple, and it shoots a feeling of desire straight to my core.

Moving further down, he kisses my abdomen before tracing the edge of my panties with his tongue. I shiver, and my hands grasp at the sheet below me. My back arches off the bed, and a moan of pure bliss leaves my mouth as he uses a finger to pull the material away from my body, letting his tongue roam closer to where I need him.

There's an ache in me. A yearning for the touch of this wonderful man. He brings me so much joy, and not just in a sexual way.

Dipping the material further, he kisses across my bare skin, but it isn't enough, I can tell he's barely restraining himself.

"I'm yours," I whisper.

The next sound I hear is material tearing as he pulls my panties away from my body. I won't lie, that is possibly the most erotic thing he's done up to now.

My body feels heavy with lust, want, need … I can't quite describe it, but it feels incredible.

He languidly licks a trail across my sensitive skin. I feel like I might spontaneously combust. Feeling him run a finger from my navel to my clit, I moan in delight. I feel like a wanton woman, the heady feeling of satisfaction making me climb higher and higher.

As he slips a finger inside me, I moan long and loud into the still air.

Everything feels electrically charged, as though lightning might strike at any moment. He slips a second finger in and I hear him growl like a wild animal as I squeeze my walls around his fingers.

Curling his fingers inside me, he hits the spot a few times before slipping them both out of me again. He sucks and nips at my skin as he slides them back in with a bit more force. My eyes fall closed, and I feel every molecule inside me as they come to life. He's breathing a life into me like I've never known.

"You feel so damn good, Nix. So wet and ready for me. Primed and ready for the orgasm of your life."

My blood sings in my veins, every fibre of my being hyperaware of the sensations he's invoking within me. I can't hold out much longer.

"Jesus, Nix, the scent of you … the taste … hmm."

As he hums against my skin a delicious tingle works its way up my spine.

"I can't … Nate, I …"

My eyelids close and I fall over the edge of the abyss, lost in the deep dark chasm.

Without giving me a chance to fully recover, Nate crawls over my body and aligns himself with me.

"Stay there, Nix," I hear from somewhere in the dark.

I feel Nate push inside me, stretching me to accommodate the size of him. He slowly inches his way inside until I'm fully wrapped around him. He lifts my legs so that they are around his waist, and it takes all my effort to concentrate on holding them there.

As Nate pushes in, slowly withdraws most of the way, and then sinks back into me, my hands grasp for something to hold on to. I grip onto him, my nails sinking into his flesh as he builds a steady rhythm. My hips meet him thrust for thrust and I cry out as he pushes me closer and closer to the edge once more. I haven't had chance to properly come down from the first high, so this feeling building inside me has me dangerously close to coming undone.

"Oh god, Nix, you feel fucking amazing."

Moving my legs up, he hooks them over his shoulders, and fuck if he doesn't feel deeper inside me than a moment ago. He thrusts harder than before, making my back arch off the bed. He leans back and slaps my ass as he lifts me higher to get a better angle.

"Holy shit, Nix, I'm … so … close …"

He pants heavily, and I can't deny it's a turn on.

"I'm yours, Nate. You own me."

I'm balancing on a knife edge here, just waiting for him to join me. It doesn't take him long and we both fall apart at the same time.

I feel sated, yet I want to devour him whole, to own him the way he does me. I'm beginning to think that love isn't *too* far off being the right word. He's worked his way underneath my skin, all the way to the core of me—this is more than just lust.

We lie side by side, looking at each other. Gazing into his eyes, I see his emotions reflected in them. I can't guarantee he feels as much for me as I'm beginning to for him, but I don't care. I'm scared of opening myself up to him, laying my heart on the line for him, and I think he's afraid of making himself vulnerable to me.

If and when he's finally able to offer me his heart, I will cherish it, nurture it and take care of it for as long as I can.

Can I guarantee him forever? No. Nobody with any sense could. It's impossible to see all the eventualities. But I can promise him that I will always try. I will always put the effort required into this relationship. Some people say, "if it's real, you don't need to try", but that doesn't hold water with me. My theory is that it's when you give up trying that you lose everything.

"I'm scared, Nix," he says, so quietly I would have missed it if the room wasn't so silent.

"Of what?"

"You."

"Me?"

I don't know whether I should feel hurt by that or not. Why should I scare him?

"Yes, you. I told you before that I loved and lost, big time. She did to me what Lee did to you. So, I built walls as high as they could go. I was seeing someone on and off as more of a fuck buddy than anything, because I didn't want strings. But then you walked into my life, and it was like I wanted all the strings. I want everything that you can offer me,"

He takes my hand in his and brings it up to his chest. I feel his heart beating against his ribcage. It feels like it wants to break free.

"I don't want to scare you," he continues. "I'm not saying we should elope and get married or anything like that. But I want you to know that I'm in this. You said before that I own you, but that isn't right. *You own me.* Mind, body, heart and soul."

I blink back the tears that spring to my eyes. My brain refuses to comply with my mouth to form a coherent sentence. We haven't even been dating long, but I know in my heart that I feel the same as he does. His words echo my earlier internal thoughts, but I can't speak. My mouth is dry, feeling like I've swallowed a bunch of cotton wool balls or something.

"I—"

I swallow and try again to form a sentence.

"Nate ... you ... I—"

"It's okay, Nix. We're not ready for those three little words. They're said too often, and often don't mean enough. When we say them—and yes I said *when*—I want it to mean the world and more."

"Oh, Nate."

The first tear falls unbidden, soon joined by a flood of its brothers and sisters. My heart feels full to bursting. I want him to know that I don't think I've ever been happier. In fact, I *know* I've never been happier. Nobody has ever left such an impact on my heart and soul.

Every girl dreams of meeting her Prince Charming, but, sadly, not all of them find him. I knew Lee wasn't my prince. He was a good guy—in the beginning and the middle of our marriage—but he wasn't my happily ever after, riding off into the sunset on a white charger. He broke my heart, or so I thought at the time. But actually, I came to realise that he'd done me a favour. He'd set me free.

They say "if you love somebody, set them free. If they come back to you, then you know it was meant to be".

Lee didn't set me free in the hopes we'd reunite, so it's not exactly the same. But he let me go, and it showed we weren't meant to be.

I've been holding back from feeling anything for anyone because I needed a little more time. But right here, right now, I know that Nate could make me so happy. My past nearly drowned me, but he came along and offered me something I never thought I'd experience. I'm just scared to voice those feelings ... yet.

His hand comes up to brush away my tears, and I curl myself up into him. I wrap my arm around his waist and my head into his chest. More tears fall, but for once, they aren't the sad kind.

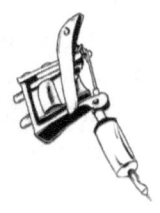

Chapter Twelve

A month later

Nate

Things have been going really well with Nix for the last month, and I don't think I could be any happier. We still haven't said those three little words, because I don't want to push her before she's ready. Both of us have been hurt by ex-partners that cheated. Both of us know what it is to say those three words. The words themselves may only be small, but the meaning of them is profoundly more than words can sum up.

We've visited Gramps, and the two of them seem to have this bond. I can't really explain it, but they get on like a house on fire and are as thick as thieves. Ever since Gramps won the bet over Beyoncé, they've just solidified their friendship. It's beautiful to see.

He always said he wanted to see me happy before he passed away. All I could focus on was knowing he was going to die; I just didn't know when. So, I couldn't make him a promise I didn't know how to keep. But it seems fate had big things in store for me, things I never foresaw happening to me.

I was hurt by Nikki and Marshall; I didn't see love being in my future. But ever since I met Nix, I've actually wondered what—if anything—I felt for Nikki. I think about the feelings I have for Nix, the emotions she brings out in me, and I realise I never felt this way with Nikki, nor with any other woman.

So, if this love, then I never really loved Nikki. I felt something for her, sure. But love? No. I can now say, unequivocally, no.

Today is my day off, and Nix has arranged for cover at work. She has no clue where I'm taking her, but I know she's going to love it. There's absolutely no doubt in my mind, this date will be different from anything either of us have ever done and I want it to be the best date yet.

Nix said that she and her ex-husband never really dated, they just ended up in a relationship and then her mother made sure that they got married. Her mother interferes a lot—I should know, I've seen it first-hand.

My god, that dinner we had with her family a couple of weeks ago, that was my idea of being in hell.

"You're thirty-five years old, Jenna, you should be a wife and a mother by now. Instead, you're fooling around with someone who can't offer you the life you deserve. This foolish folly needs an end putting to it now," she said from her place by the kitchen sink as Nix stood looking out of the window.

"Mother, you need to accept that things don't work to a schedule. Nothing in life can be planned and executed to perfection, much to your chagrin, I know. Yes, I'm thirty-five. Yes, I'm divorced. No, I don't have children. And all that sticks in your craw. I know all that. I know it and I don't care. You can accept Nate as part of my life or not. But it's not up to you. This isn't some crush I have. It's more than that."

"That's why you need to end it now. You know, Lee has cleaned up his act and he wants you back. He's desperately sorry and wishes you'd give him a second chance."

"And just how do you know that? Have you been in contact with my dick of an ex-husband behind my back?"

Just the tone of Nix's voice would have been enough to set me on edge if I was her mother. But she wasn't intimidated; she wasn't even slightly flustered.

I'm standing by the kitchen doorway, peeking round every so often, but trying my hardest to stay hidden. I shouldn't eavesdrop, but I'd gone to take some crockery into the kitchen and was caught by their argument. I should walk away, but curiosity has got the better of me.

"Please don't use such language in my home, Jenna, you should know better. As for speaking to Lee, yes, we've been in contact. He knew he couldn't just approach you out of the blue, as you'd probably slam the door in his face. So, he came to me for my help. He showed me he'd cleaned up his act, proved that he truly loves you and wants to work things out."

"Don't you understand the concept of divorce, Mother? Or the fact that he cheated on me? I caught him in our bed with Miss Bottle Blonde, and that was the final nail in the coffin. Stanley Mason doesn't know how to keep it in his pants. Goodness only knows how all these women actually find him attractive,

especially with the paunch he had going on towards the end."

"She meant nothing to him. He's only ever loved you. You owe it to yourself to give your marriage another try."

Nix lets out the most exasperated sigh as she runs her hands through her hair.

"This Nathaniel, he's just a phase. Lee cheated, and you feel the need to get back at him. That's all well and good, but you need to walk away now. You need to get back on the right path with Lee."

"The right path with Lee is exactly where I am right now. A place where our paths don't converge. If he'd put half as much effort into our marriage as he did trying to impress those other women—because believe me, Mother, there were more women than just Miss Bottle Blonde, she was only the tip of the iceberg—then maybe we would be on the same path still. But he didn't. That's his fault. I put my all into our marriage and got nothing out of it."

"He holds his hands up to being the one who broke your relationship apart, but he's a changed man. You walking out on him showed him the error of his ways."

A derisive snort leaves Nix as she looks at her mother.

"Leopards do not change their spots. I won't give Lee any more chances, not now, not ever. I'm with Nate now, and you can accept that or not. It's not a call you get to make."

"Jenna Louise Morgan, you are being ridiculous, and I won't hear any more of it. Nathaniel is nothing more than a rebound. You'll see. Maybe not now, but you wait and see, you will open your eyes and see sense."

Nix walks away from her mother, towards the door to the deck in the back garden. I watch her open the door and step out into the fresh air.

Her mother harrumphs and stalks out of the kitchen. She nearly catches me in my hiding place, but I manage to slip back out of sight in time. After placing the crockery on the countertop, I walk out behind Nix and put my arms around her. She sighs and rests her head back against my shoulder. I don't say anything about their argument because if she wants to talk about it she'll broach the subject in her own time.

I know unequivocally that her mother does not like me one tiny bit. That's as clear as crystal, but I'm not walking away from Nix. If she wants out of this relationship, then she can tell me herself. I still haven't told her what I overheard that day, and I resign myself to never telling her. There's no point. It would only serve to hurt her, and I don't want to be the one causing her pain. I want to be the one she feels comfortable with, the one she can open up to, the one who soothes away her pain.

Grabbing my jacket and keys, I head for the car. I told Nix I'd pick her up at nine thirty, and if I don't get a move on I'll be late.

***

After a two-hour drive, we finally pull up outside the building where our magical date is about to take place. I'm excited, nervous as to how she'll react. I want to see the look of pure joy in her eyes as she finds out what we're here to do.

"Where are we?" she asks as I open her car door.

I take her hand and help her to her feet.

"That would be telling."

"The suspense is killing me."

She puts on a fake whiny voice. That doesn't impress me, so I pull my lips into a tight line, refusing to give her any clue whatsoever.

We walk inside the building, a building which is completely unassuming, somewhere that gives no sign as to what's inside.

The reception desk has a sign reading "Lucardo"—the "o" is in the shape of a padlock. The first hint, if you're aware enough to understand its significance.

"What is this place?" Nix asks again.

Still, I don't answer. The fun is in the element of surprise.

***

After completing our escape room, we head back to the car. We're both exhausted, but the sheer magic of the day is etched on Nix's face.

She told me not long after we met that she was a self-confessed geek and a complete and utter Potterhead. She'd proceeded to tell me that she was a Gryffindor and couldn't be in a relationship with someone who was a Slytherin. Honestly, I don't know much about Harry Potter, but I'd been more than willing to experience the Ministry of Magic escape room with her.

And now I can say I am glad that I did. The complete elation I see written on Nix's face tells me it was worth every single second.

We cast spells, made potions—all sorts of weird and wonderful things. The excitement she felt couldn't be contained; it radiated from every pore of her perfect skin.

"I've never done anything like that before," she says from beside me as I drive us home.

"Nor have I. Is it safe to say you had fun?"

"Definitely. I'd do it all over again in a heartbeat."

"So, it was a good date?"

"On a scale of one to ten, I'd give it a"—she pauses for effect—"twelve."

She chatters endlessly about the Harry Potter books and films on our journey, and by the time we get home I feel like I know all I need to. She cries every single time she sees Sirius Black die; she loves Gary Oldman in general, but especially as Sirius. She blubbers like a baby when Albus Dumbledore dies—he's the headmaster at Hogwarts, that much I know now—and when Dobby gets killed, she mourns him like he was a friend.

I'm getting the impression that a Harry Potter marathon is on the cards, so that I get a crash course in all things related to it.

We pull up outside her house, and I walk round to open her car door. She takes my hand and I walk her to the front door.

"Fancy a takeaway? I'm starving. All that magic seems to have worked up an appetite."

Heading inside, she grabs some takeaway menus from a drawer, and we sit in the kitchen, deciding what we fancy.

My phone rings and I nearly ignore it, seeing as though I don't want any interruptions to our evening, but peering at the screen, I see Haven Lodge displayed there.

"Hello."

"Nate, it's Linda. You have to get here immediately."

"What? Why? What's happened?"

My heart thumps against my ribcage and a lump forms in my throat.

"Just get here quickly," she replies in a pained voice.

I hang up and grab my keys from the kitchen island. Nix appears dismayed as she grabs my hand and we run back to my car.

Like I'm driving on autopilot, I'm aware of nothing during the drive, apart from the deafening silence in the car.

We get out of the car and run to the door of the nursing home. There's an ambulance blocking the way, so we scramble around it and head inside.

I'm met with chaos. Gramps is strapped to a stretcher and is being brought through the reception. His complexion is sallow and there's an oxygen mask over his face. There's also an I.V. in place, and my heart drops like a stone.

"What's happening?" I ask one of the paramedics. "I'm his grandson and next of kin."

"He appears to have had a heart attack, sir," he replies hurriedly as they load the stretcher onto the back of the ambulance.

"Can I come with you to the hospital?"

"Yes, but only one of you can come."

"I can drive your car and meet you there, Nate," Nix says.

I throw her my keys and climb into the ambulance. My hands are shaking, my heart is racing, there's a hollow feeling forming in the pit of my stomach as the driver gets in and races in the direction of the hospital.

Holding his hand, I look at my grandfather, my only living relative. He's everything I want to be when I grow up. He always was and always will be. No words are spoken as I watch over him. I can't bring myself to say anything in case the paramedic tells me the worst news. I know in my heart what's coming, but I can't force the words from my lips.

"Hang in there old timer," I whisper as I stroke the pale skin of his hand.

Arriving at the hospital, everything happens in a rush.

It feels like a lifetime—but is probably only minutes—before Nix is at my side, her hand in mine as we wait in the waiting room for someone to come and talk to us.

Chapter Thirteen

Jenna

My heart shatters into a million pieces as I watch Nate fall apart in my arms. It was the longest wait of my life before the doctor came to break the news. His face was solemn as he spoke in a monotone voice, saying things I can't even remember as I hold Nate tightly against me.

His sobs threaten to drown him as he sits on the floor between my legs. I'm sitting on a horrible, hard plastic chair in the waiting room, and Nate is still sitting where he collapsed when the doctor opened his mouth.

The doctor has long since left us, but neither one of us has spoken to the other. I whisper soothingly as I stroke Nate's hair as he lays his head in my lap.

Devastation. The only word I can describe what this moment in time feels like. It feels like it will never pass. Everything is a blur, my eyes misted by my own tears. I haven't the mind to wipe them away.

"Would you like to sit in the relatives' room?" a nurse asks, startling me.

Nate either doesn't hear or doesn't care to answer.

I stand up and offer him my hand. He grasps it tightly and he stands and follows on as the nurse leads us to a quieter room.

The nurse offers us a hot drink and says she'll be back shortly. As the door closes behind her, I sit on the cream sofa. Nate sits next to me with his head in his hands. Uselessly, I stroke my hand up and down his back, as though that could really do anything, but I can't simply sit here and do nothing.

The more I got to know Gramps over the month or so that Nate and I have been dating, the more I loved him like my own grandfather.

Sometimes he remembered us, other times he thought we were his son and daughter in law.

Nate had explained about his dementia and Parkinson's one night back at mine. My heart had felt broken then, but that's not a patch on how it feels now.

Every shard pierces my skin, and I feel hollow inside. He was Nate's only living relative. Now he's utterly alone in this world. First, an orphan when his parents tragically died, then again when his grandma Lillian died, now he no longer has Gramps either.

The nurse places two cups of awful hospital coffee on the table beside me. She offers me a sympathetic smile before retreating from the room.

I encourage Nate to lie down across the sofa, with his head in my lap. I run my hand through his hair as I feel his tears soak through my jeans. The only sound that can be heard is his sobbing. My own tears fall silently as I mourn the loss of a wonderful man. A man that, although I didn't spend much time with, I feel will leave a hole in my life—though undoubtedly not as big a hole as he'll leave in his grandson's heart.

***

Hours passed, and we stayed immobile in that room. Neither one of us spoke. There are no right words when someone loses a loved one. There is nothing that has the power to erase the pain. In time, you embrace the pain and it makes you stronger, even though you still feel the loss as keenly as the moment it happened. There's no magic wand, no spell to be cast. There's just a whole lot of nothing. A vast emptiness inside. The pain carves a hollow in your soul, and there will never be anything that can fill the void.

Eventually, I asked Nate if he wanted to go home. I got a nod in response, so I drove him back to mine. I scrolled through his phone to find Steph's contact details and sent her a text. There were no fancy words to soften the blow, so when she called, I took the call out of the room and told her that Nate would need to cancel his bookings for the next few days at least.

Leaving Nate alone in the living room, I make a cup of coffee for us both, but subsequently, his sits untouched.

I grab a fleece throw from the back of the sofa and drape it over Nate as he sleeps. His tearstained face looks relaxed in sleep, but I know that when he wakes, he will feel like shit. I want him to remain asleep, lost to dreams where reality can't touch him.

Sitting myself at his feet, I pull them up into my lap and take off his shoes and socks. I pull the blanket back to cover him again and sit quietly.

Feeling desolate, I don't switch on the TV; my phone and Nate's are set to silent; my house phone is unplugged. The silence might be deafening, but it's better this way. No distractions.

As Nate sleeps, I cry until I can cry no more. I want him to see me as strong, as someone to lean on, and I feel like I can't do that if I'm a blubbering mess. I allow my tears tall fall unbidden because I'm hoping to get them out of the way, so that, when he wakes, I can be the one to provide him the support he needs.

I can't believe that such a magical day turned to shit in the blink of an eye. I don't know how Nate will recover. But I do know that I'll be there for him every heartbreaking step of the way.

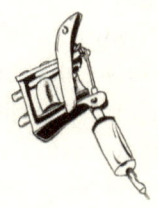

Chapter Fourteen

Nate

The day of the funeral broke me even further inside. Nix held my hand tightly in hers the whole time. She held me as I cried. She drove me home when I drank one too many whiskeys. She covered me with a blanket as I slept on the sofa. There isn't anything she didn't do, whereas all I managed to do was cry and drown my sorrows. Or at least I tried to drown them. I tried to make it so they'd never re-emerge. But that was a fruitless task. I realised that as soon as I woke on the sofa the next morning with a dry mouth.

Nix made me breakfast and sat across the island from me as I pushed my food around my plate. She even sat next to me and rubbed my back as I threw up the little I ate.

When I showered to get rid of the stench of vomit, she climbed in with me and lathered the soap against my skin.

It's safe to say I couldn't have got through those first days without her. She's fast become my everything. And, if I'm honest, that fact alone scares the life out of me.

I haven't worked since Gramps passed away. If I was in my right mind, I might care about cancelling on the clients, but as it is, my mind is as empty as my heart. I feel hollow. There's no other way to describe it. There's this searing pain resonating around in my chest.

Nix has been by my side since that day at the hospital; she won't let me out of her sight. She drove me home to fetch some fresh clothes and then took me back to hers.

She's been nothing but patient as I've refused to eat, refused to even move off the couch at times. Brogan has been covering her shifts at the florist and the pub. She even did the flowers for the funeral, and Nix declined to take any payment from me.

I've been staying in Nix's house, sleeping in her bed, wrapped in her arms day and night. Sometimes we put on a DVD to break the silence in the air, but I never pay any attention to what's on the screen. One thing blurs into the next, one *day* blurs into the next, and I don't even know what day of the week it is.

Nix had to force me to shower and shave the night before the funeral. She had climbed in the shower with me and scrubbed my body clean as I didn't have the inclination to do anything other than stand under the steady jet of hot water. I wanted to turn the temperature up to scalding hot, just to see if I could feel anything, but not wanting to scald Nix, I left it as it was.

I've slept a lot of my time away. In my dreams, Gramps is still with me. While I've slept, Nix has done some of her graphic design work because she has contractual obligations to fulfil, otherwise—she told me in no uncertain terms—she wouldn't have bothered. She hasn't left me, even as I've slept. She's sat on the sofa with her Mac on her lap.

Every day without my wonderful Gramps is hard from the moment I open my eyes to the moment I close them. But Nix wraps herself around me as we sleep, and I feel comforted by her touch. She feels like an anchor in the storm. She's holding me steady while the world around me is swept off its axis.

How do I put one foot in front of the other? Autopilot. That's pretty much how I'm handling everything.

Chapter Fifteen

Jenna

Nate finally returned to work this morning, but only because Steph thought it might distract his mind for a while. He rang me on his lunch break, and he sounded like he had been crying. I sent a text to Steph, and she replied that she'd found him crying in his room between clients. After finding him like that, she sent him home. So, he returned to his house to collect some more clothes.

I'm sitting here waiting for him to return. My mind isn't on my work, but I have to force myself to finish the task. If I didn't have a deadline, I wouldn't even be bothering.

My phone chimes with an incoming text and I retrieve it from the coffee table.

>I'm so sorry Nix, please forgive me, but I can't do this. I need to spend some time alone. You've done so much for me and I am so grateful, words cannot express. But I've realised I need to be able to function on my own again.

My heart drops to my stomach and my eyes water. He's not coming back. I can understand his need to feel like he can function on his own, but it still breaks my heart. He shouldn't have to be alone at a time like this.

I type out a reply and delete it several times before simply replying with just two words:

>>I understand.

I will my phone to ring, for him to tell me he still wants me in his life. Because, to be honest, it doesn't just feel like the end of him staying with me, it feels like the end of us. I can't explain how or why I jump to that conclusion; maybe I'm just fearing the worst.

I want to switch my phone off, to cut myself off from the outside world for a while. But I leave it on in case Nate needs me. I'd hate to turn it off, only to find he needed me and I wasn't there.

Leaving my phone on the coffee table, I go upstairs and grab a towel. I turn on the shower and discard my clothes. Standing under the jets, my tears are lost amongst the scalding water.

One week later

It's been seven long days since I last saw Nate. Seven long days with absolute radio silence. Not a text, not a call, not a smoke signal. I understand on some level because I know how hard Gordon's sudden death hit him. However, understanding it isn't my problem. It's coping with the deafening silence that's crippling me. I want to be there for him. I want to help in any way I can.

Brogan imparted one sage piece of advice—to have me there was like having a crutch. I could hold him up, but when I wasn't there, he would fall. And it's only when you've truly hit rock bottom that you can find your way back up. Some people need a helping hand, others need to find their own way.

In my spare time—of which I seem to have a lot now that Nate isn't around—I find myself thinking things over and possibly overthinking them. We knew Gordon wasn't a well man, but Nate thought he had years left with him. He thought he had time to prepare himself. But the truth is—as I said to him when he stayed over—that you can never truly prepare yourself. Death comes to us all. It's the one and *only* certainty in life. But it doesn't come with a clock. There's no neon warning sign that your time is up.

The fact that Nate wasn't with Gordon when he had his heart attack weighed heavily on his mind in the following days. I tried to placate him, to soothe away his pain, but I failed. I keep telling myself that I did my best, but then I question whether I actually did.

Brogan has tried her best to distract me. She's kept my mind occupied at work in the way only a best friend can. She came to mine for a DVD and takeaway over the weekend—though I didn't really taste the food or pay attention to the film. Everything seems different without Nate around. Food tastes bland like cardboard—when I even bother to eat— sights and sounds seem muted in comparison … everything just seems … lacklustre. I guess that's the word I'm searching for.

I understand Nate's need to find his own way through his grief. I can't do it for him. But I wanted to be there for him, to help him. To be strong for him when he can't be strong for himself. But it's clear I'm not wanted or needed.

Just a simple text would let me know he still wants me in his life. Without that, I have to move on with my life. I'll be there for him when he comes back … *if* he comes back. But I won't wait around forever. I can't put my life on hold in the hopes of him coming to his senses.

I keep that old saying in mind—If you love somebody set them free. If they come back, then it's meant to be. I know that if things are meant to be between me and Nate, then he'll come back. And if he doesn't, then those three little words that I felt but never said, I'll realise it was all one-sided.

***

"Here you go, sweetie," Brogan says as she hands me a Pornstar Martini.

We're sitting in the new cocktail bar that recently opened in a town a few miles from us. It feels like a betrayal not to be drinking in the Siren, but even Riley knows that they aren't a competitor for our business. They cater to a different kind of clientele—or maybe the same people, just when they want something a little classier than their local pub.

I look at my drink and then at Brogan. She smiles and nods her head encouragingly. It was all her idea to come here tonight, to escape my woes. I'm not sure it'll help, but I'm willing to try—even if it is just to appease my best friend. She knows I'm finding it really hard, and she's doing the best she can to make me feel better. Best friends, where would we be without them?

Taking a small sip of my drink, I realise it doesn't taste as bad as I expected. I still don't get why it's served with a shot glass of prosecco on the side, but according to Brogan, some places do the shot and others don't.

"Get a few of those inside you and we'll move on to the club. Dancing is the best medicine. Well, that and alcohol."

"I thought they said laughter was the best medicine?"

"*Some* people say that, but not me. I like to drink, dance and have fun."

"You're young, that's why. I'm too old for clubbing, Brogan. I'm thirty-six, for goodness sake."

"I'm still dragging you with me, even if you're kicking and screaming all the way."

Brogan is more or less half my age. She's twenty. Young, slim, curves in the right places, gorgeous. She's got enough energy for the two of us. I would kill to have half her energy.

Even though she's a fair bit younger than me, the moment we met, we clicked. She has this energy—some might call it her aura—that surrounds her. She's the kind of person that draws people to her. Her personality is eccentric. She sometimes comes across as a bit ditzy, usually when she's had a few drinks, but I know that she's got a bloody good head on her shoulders. Level-headed, mature, studying sociology so that she can become a youth counsellor. Brogan is the brightest person I know. And I know she'll make a good youth worker because two of her best skills are listening, and offering advice and wisdom.

Some people might wonder why I enjoy hanging around with someone younger than me, but to me, our friendship is the most natural thing. We have a connection, the likes of which I've never had with anyone else. She supports me in everything I do. She helps me even without realising it. Sometimes, I'll be in a situation and I'll find myself asking "what would Brogan do?"

It's the fact that she acts more mature than any twenty-year-old I've ever met. She acts more mature than a lot of people *my own* age, let alone younger. She sees the world through open eyes instead of being a narrow-minded kind of person with tunnel vision.

"I'm hardly dressed for clubbing," I add, taking another sip of my cocktail

"Babes, we're going. Like it or lump it."

We stay for another round of drinks before getting a taxi to the club. Molly's is for a younger demographic, like Brogan, but she insists they play the best music. Personally, I'd rather listen to country music or something. I was never one for clubs when I was younger. Sure, I went because friends wanted to, but I was usually pretty drunk, so I didn't mind the crappy music they played.

Maybe I'm just old. That could be the reason why I just don't feel like dancing the night away. Or it could be the utter desolation I'm trying to hide. The feelings that bubble to the surface even though I'm trying my hardest to bury them.

"Ooh, hello handsome," Brogan says, making me follow her line of sight.

Tall, dark hair that's tousled, yet stylish. Smart casual dress sense. Chiselled jaw. Bright blue orbs for eyes. There's no denying he's handsome. But all he does is cause my heart to squeeze in my chest. He reminds me of all the things I loved about Nate.

"Can we leave now?"

Brogan looks at me as if I've grown a second head.

"You don't want to go say hi to the hottie who just walked in?"

"Of course I don't. I'm not on the pull. I'm here to drink and forget."

"I would lay odds that one night with McHottie would make you forget Nate's name."

"Not happening, Brogan. So, we can move on to Molly's, or I can go home while you cop off with McHottie."

She grabs her bag and hops down from the bar stool, wobbling slightly on her skyscraper heels. I was more sensible and wore my lower-heeled Jimmy Choos.

Steadying her with a hand on her elbow, I guide us out of the bar. I pull up the taxi booking app on my phone and quickly book one to take us to Molly's before I can back out. I really don't want to go. But Brogan was right. Dancing, drinking, laughing—it could all serve as a distraction. One can only hope.

***

After drinking her body weight in tequila slammers, Brogan is pretty wasted. I'm more sober, considering every other drink, I had water to rehydrate. One of us has to be the sensible one, and after her first couple of shots, I knew it wasn't going to be Brogan.

Her recently dyed bright pink hair is braided down over one shoulder. She's dressed more fitting for our surroundings than me. In her trusty little black dress, she looks incredible. She took her skyscrapers off a little while ago, complaining they were stopping her dancing. I hold them while she dances with some guy.

"Jenna, this is Josh," she says, slurring her words a little as she introduces me to her new friend.

"Hi Jenna," Josh greets with a warm smile.

"Hello Josh, nice to meet you."

I shake his outstretched hand.

"Tequila!" Brogan shouts as she turns to the bar.

The barman brings a bottle over and pours her a shot. I take it from her, and she mumbles about me being a bitch. Josh laughs and asks the barman for a bottle of water. That's when he's on the receiving end of her sharp tongue.

"I think it's time we got you home, honey. You can come back to mine or go back with Jenna, but I don't think you should go home alone," Josh says.

"Umm … why would she come back to yours? You've only known her for a few minutes. She'll come back with me, thank you."

"She hasn't told you?"

He looks a little puzzled, then turns his gaze to Brogan. She shrugs noncommittally.

"Told me what?"

I give Brogan my famous death stare and she pokes her tongue out at me.

"We've been dating for the last few weeks. Well, since the night of the speed dating event at the Siren," he replies.

"What?"

I have to shout over the song that's just started playing too loudly.

"Yep. He's my boyfriend," Brogan says with a smile.

"Then how come you haven't told me? I'm your best friend. Isn't that the kind of information we share?"

"Normally, yes. But since he's a certain someone's best friend, we agreed not to bring it up yet. Especially now you-know-who is out of the picture."

"But you arrange to meet him here and then ditch me, so you can go home with him?"

I'm actually affronted at the fact she would do that to me.

"No, I didn't know he'd be here."

"You're really *his* best friend?" I direct my question to Josh.

"Yes. Been that way for a few years now. He might be a sullen ass at times, but mostly he's a great guy."

"Why are you defending him against things I haven't even said?"

"Because I know how you feel about him and, in turn, how he feels about you."

I bristle at his succinct assessment.

"I feel nothing for him, so you can get any other notion out of your head, Josh."

"If you say so, Nix."

"*Don't* call me that," I shout.

"See, you still feel something. If you didn't, then the use of a nickname wouldn't bother you so much."

"I don't feel *anything* except pity for his situation. Anything on a romantic level went out of the window when he fell off the face of the planet. I tried to be there for him, and he threw it in my face. As for the nickname"—I pause, taking a deep breath to steady me—"only Nate could get away with calling me that. Now, nobody calls me that. Not you, and especially not *him*."

I turn on my heel and race to the ladies' restroom. Bursting through the door, I find the closest empty cubicle, slam the door behind me and slide to the ground with my back to the door. Tears fall unbidden. Tears of hurt and anger. Tears to mourn a love lost.

I hadn't realised I was so bitter about what happened until I ranted at Josh. It's not his fault, and I shouldn't have shouted at him, but bitterness, regret and anger coursed through me. They still do as I sit here and bawl my eyes out.

A sudden hammering comes from the other side of the door.

"Open the door, Nix."

My blood sears through me in a white-hot flash. What the actual fuck is he doing here? I stay silent, but my breathing is so loud in my own ears that I'm sure he can hear it too.

"Nix, please."

Anger makes my pulse race. How dare he. He falls off the face of planet earth, then turns up here on the same night as us. That's no coincidence. And in this moment, I am laying all the blame on Brogan. She stitched me up like a kipper. Well done, Brogan. If you wanted to hurt your best friend, then you win.

More banging on the door ensues before silence falls.

"Leave her be, Nate." A small voice breaks into the heavy silence.

"I can't, Brogan."

"You can, and you will. You hurt her. Do you really think she'll open the door and fall into your arms like nothing happened? News flash; she won't."

"Nix," he whispers.

The use of his nickname for me prickles across my skin. I stand and straighten myself out before opening the door.

"Oh, Nix," he says softly when he sets eyes on me.

"Fuck you, Nathaniel," I spit and then break into a run.

I don't stop running until I am out of the club and out of breath. I pull my phone out of my pocket and book a taxi. I need to get out of here. I'd be worried about Brogan if I didn't know her boyfriend would see her home safely. I can't believe she's dating *his* best friend.

Hearing the music through the door of the club, I realise they're playing "Broken Strings" by James Morrison and Nelly Furtado. Not a song I'd associate with clubbing—not that all the songs played since we got here were ones I'd normally associate with clubbing either. Maybe clubbing is different now I'm older, but it makes my breath catch in my throat and I can't swallow. There's a lump I can't dislodge.

My taxi pulls up and I yank the door open a little harder than I intended.

"Nix."

His sinfully sexy voice comes from behind me. I climb in the taxi and shut the door, trying to escape the goosebumps that break out on my skin at the sound of his voice.

"Where to?" the driver asks.

"Anywhere, I don't care. Just get me away from here," I say on a sob.

I end up going to my parents' house. It's cloaked in darkness as I arrive, but I pay the driver and walk to the front door. Retrieving the spare key from the top of the doorframe, I slip it in the lock as quietly as I can manage.

I slip quietly into the dark house and turn on the kitchen light. I walk over to the sink, grab myself a glass and use the ice maker in the fridge door before filling it with water.

Tip-toeing my way into the living room, I sit in the armchair my father favours. The scent in the air reminds me of home.

Sure, my parents—or should I say mostly my mother—can be overbearing, but they always did their best by me. Well, their version of it anyway. They thought throwing money at a problem would solve it. But I know that won't happen this time.

My phone rings and I see his stupidly gorgeous face light up my screen. I silence the ringer and sit in the dark. Taking small sips of my water, I feel a little better. I didn't drink much anyway, but now I feel as sober as a judge. At least that's one headache I won't have to deal with in the morning.

"Jenna?"

I startle at the sound of my name. When I see my father in his pyjamas, I settle. He wipes the sleep from his eyes and puts his glasses on.

"Sorry, Daddy, I didn't mean to wake you."

"What are you doing here at this time?"

"I was out with Brogan. It was late, and I realised I didn't have my house key. I must have forgotten it when I switched bags to go out. Sorry, Daddy."

"Don't be sorry, darling. You're always welcome here."

He walks forward and turns the living room light on. It hurts my eyes until they can adjust. My father sits on the sofa, and I look at him. He's a good man, but my mother was so against me and Nate being together that I don't want to tell either of them about what happened. Mother would be happy, which would kill me inside. Not because she's happy, but because I've lost the man I thought stood a chance of being "the one".

"Come here, darling. Come and sit," he says as he pats the space beside him.

I get up and move to sit next to him. He places a warm hand over mine and offers me a smile.

"Baby girl, it seems like there's something on your mind. Do you want to talk?"

"Not really, Daddy."

"Is it a boy?"

I nod. He looks at me sympathetically.

"Did he hurt you?"

Again, I just nod. That's when fresh tears fall. Just when I thought I couldn't cry any more. My head falls to my hands and my father's arm comes around my shoulders. My body shakes with my sobs and my father draws me into his chest.

We sit silently except for the sound of my sobs. He doesn't push me to talk, and I'm grateful.

"What's going on in here?" my mother asks.

A silent exchange must go on between my parents because I hear her footsteps retreat.

I don't know how much time has passed, but my tears have subsided, and exhaustion has crept up on me.

"Your old room has clean bedding. You know your mother, not a mote of dust in sight. Why don't you go and get some sleep, baby girl?"

"Thanks, Daddy."

I lightly kiss his cheek, before standing and making my way to the stairs. I climb the seemingly never-ending staircase and open my old bedroom door. It's exactly like I left it when I moved out. The faces of Brian Littrell and Co. staring at me from their places on my walls. Then there's those eyes that belong to J Brown from 5ive. The cheeky smile on Lee Brennan's face. The memories hit me square in the chest.

Walking over to the dresser against the back wall, I run my fingers over the wooden top. I spent hours sitting here getting ready to go out with friends or boys. My old Walkman is still in the top drawer where I left it. I pull it out and put the headphones on. It starts to blast "Wild Boys". I'm surprised the batteries still work.

Tucking it back into the drawer, I see my old diary. It still has the padlock on it, so I'm assuming my mother never found the hiding place for my key. And she won't unless they pull up the carpet at the corner of my room by the loveseat in the window.

I used to sit there in my window as I confessed my secrets to my trusty diary. It was the only thing I could trust not to tell my mother when I'd had a fight with a friend or if I had a crush on a boy.

Walking to my old bed, I flop down and lie on my back, one arm over my face. I kick my shoes off and throw my bag to the floor. I didn't really forget my house key, I just couldn't face going home alone tonight. Alone to the bed I'd shared with Nate so many times. I couldn't face looking at "his" side of the bed, empty and hollow like my heart.

Chapter Sixteen

Jenna

A month has passed and I'm no less sad. My heart still skips every other beat. The ache in my chest isn't as sharp as it was, but only because I'm refusing to acknowledge it. If I did, I know it would come back with a vengeance. Trying to make myself forget everything I felt might be a foolish endeavour, but it's all I can do.

A whole month of radio silence from Nate. I think he must have got the message that night at Molly's.

Brogan and I have been busy at work. She's also been busy dating *his* best friend. I'd call her a traitor, but she says she hasn't seen anything of Nate, and I want her to be happy, even if it's with Josh. At least I haven't had to see him. She never lets him pick her up from work. And he never comes for a drink in the Siren. I think she's trying her hardest not to rub my nose in it.

I'm happy for my friend, of course I am. She's sickeningly happy, always wearing a goofy smile, and she hums as she works, a new thing for Brogan. I just wish I had the same kind of happiness. Is it wrong to be jealous? That shade of green never really was my favourite colour.

Tonight is the night of my parents' wedding anniversary and I am going solo. My mother wanted to set me up on a date of course. With one of her rich friends' sons. But I emphatically refused. I'd rather be single and independent. It's what I wanted after Lee anyway. So, thanks to Nate, I've got what I wanted all along. Well, what I *thought* I wanted, until I met him.

I'm sitting at my dresser painting my lips red to match the manicure I had earlier. The colour is called "Queen Sinner". I like the name as much as I like the colour; it makes me feel bolder, somehow.

My iPod plays quietly in the background. The opening bars of

"You Could Be Happy" bring tears to my eyes, so I blink back the salty reminder of my heartache. I get up and switch songs for something happier.

Looking at my dress, hanging there on the front of my wardrobe door, I smile. Its burgundy satin fabric wraps around your body, hugging all the right places. The hemline is asymmetrical and falls just a little higher than my knee on the shorter side of it. With only spaghetti straps to hold it on my shoulders, it's the epitome of sexy. I'm pairing it with black strappy heels, my sexiest Louboutins actually, and a little black clutch bag.

My mother will have kittens, seeing me in something so daring. But I couldn't care less what she thinks. I'm dressing for me and nobody else.

I take my dress from its hanger, slip its gorgeous fabric over me and look in my full-length mirror. I barely recognise myself. I wouldn't normally dress in something so sexy—I guess I'm more conservative by nature—but something about it called to me when I saw it in the window of the store.

Perching on the ottoman at the end of my bed, I slide my feet into the killer Louboutins and pick up my clutch. I'm ready to go except for a spritz of perfume. I select one of my favourites, Scandal by Jean-Paul Gaultier.

A knock on my front door tells me my mother's driver is here to take me to the party. I make my way downstairs, lock the front door behind me and get in the sleek black chauffeur-driven limousine. I did tell her I could drive myself, but she refused to hear of it.

She'll be trying to ply me with champagne all night like she usually does—heaven forbid I tell her I actually prefer prosecco to champagne, and that I actually mainly drink cider—but then my father comes to the rescue, ready to drink it for me. She always wonders how he's so tipsy at the end of the party, knowing she's counted how many drinks he's had. I love the fact that my father is a little less "stiff upper lip" than my mother.

Arriving outside their ostentatious home—because mother has to have the best and be the best in her social circle—I exit the limousine and head for the door. The party is already in full swing by the sounds coming from behind the door.

My father greets me with a kiss on the cheek, and then he takes in the sight of what I'm wearing.

"Your mother is going to have a fit," he warns softly.

"I know, Daddy, but do you know what? I don't really care."

"You may live to regret that, darling."

"Jenna, how lovely to—"

She stops mid-sentence as she looks me up and down.

"Hello, Mother," I greet in a falsely cheerful tone.

I reach to embrace her, and she air kisses both cheeks as she always does.

"Couldn't you have worn something a little ... well, a little longer?" she seethes quietly into my ear so nobody else can hear.

"Lovely to see you too, Mother," I respond.

She takes me by the elbow and steers me towards the atrium at the back of the house, where the bar is temporarily set up.

The bar top is lined with crystal champagne flutes and my mother takes two, handing one to me. I always drink the first one she gives me, just to appease her. Even more so tonight, considering her distaste for my choice of clothing.

***

The party is full of prestigious people that my mother calls friends. I'd think of them more as acquaintances, but it's not my place to comment.

The catering has been provided by one of the most elite catering companies in our area. The amuse-bouches were apricot and goat's cheese. Not something I found to be very pleasant, but I ate it under my mother's watchful eye.

She's been eyeing me all night like a hawk. I've felt her eyes burning holes in me, and whenever I've looked at her, she's been looking my way.

The main course of monkfish wrapped in Parma ham with rocket leaves on the side was even less appetising than the amuse-bouches. But I ate every bite because I was so hungry.

To be honest, I'm still hungry. The portion sizes looked like they were made for two-year-olds.

After the dessert of white chocolate panna cotta with stewed strawberries—which was the nicest course of the night—everybody was encouraged to get up and dance to the band my parents had hired.

As the band crooned old songs from my parents' era, I looked to make an escape. I wasn't so lucky. My mother caught hold of me and made me dance with her. She looked a little less disdainfully at me than she did earlier, which was likely due to consumption of champagne.

As I'm sitting at an empty table, I hear a throat clear behind me. Turning around, I lock eyes with none other than Levi Burkhardt. He smiles at me, and my heart plummets to my feet.

Having unceremoniously ditched him for Nate, I feel a pang of guilt. I was meant to go on a second date with him, to give him a chance, but I didn't. I fell hook, line and sinker for the tattoo artist. The bad boy.

Why, oh why, couldn't I have fallen for the lawyer? The one with the sweet smile, the kind manner … the boring, dull-as-dishwater guy.

Excitement. That's why. Nate offered me a thrill that Levi didn't. Nate gave me butterflies. Levi didn't. Just the sound of Nate's name brought a smile to my face and made my heart skip a beat. The sound of Levi's name brought the same boredom as seeing him did.

"Levi, what are you doing here?" I ask as I realise I have been staring at him without actually saying a word.

"I'm your parents' lawyer. I deal with some of their business when they need contracts drawing up, that kind of thing."

"Oh, I didn't know. How did I not know you knew my parents?"

"Probably because we only had one date and never really got to know much about each other."

He takes a seat next to me.

"Well, it's nice to see you, but I really have to get going," I say as I stand.

"Don't rush off. Have a drink with me … please?"

I sigh, feeling sorry for the guy. He's younger than most people here and probably doesn't know anybody other than me. God, how I wish I'd invited Brogan and Josh. Then it would feel a little less awkward. Josh is more Levi's age, and they might have had things to talk about. And having Brogan here definitely would have helped me survive this ordeal.

"Okay, but I really only have time for the one. I have to be up early tomorrow."

He stands and walks to the bar while I sit back down. I sigh in resignation. One drink. I can take his boredom with a side of alcohol … I hope.

In all fairness to the guy, our date had been nice. He'd had good taste in music. But that was about the only thing I could say for him. Nice car, good manners, good job. My mother, no doubt, would think he was the perfect catch. She's always wanted me to date a doctor or a lawyer, someone in a respectful profession. Nate definitely didn't have a respectful career as far as she was concerned.

When she learned that Nate and I had stopped seeing each other, she'd pretended to be upset for me, but I could see her brain ticking, I could hear it chanting in delight.

"Here you go," Levi says as he hands me a dreaded champagne flute.

"Thank you."

He sits down next to me and I'm not one hundred per cent sure it's an accident as his leg brushes against my thigh.

We make idle chit-chat for a while and it's all I can do not to yawn in his face. I wonder if alcohol might help, so I gulp back my champagne. But it doesn't help. I'm still bored out of my skull. I wish I could force myself to like him. He's easy on the eye. But he isn't so easy on the ears.

Looking at my watch, I fake a small yawn, covering my mouth with my hand.

"I'm sorry, Levi. I really should get going. I have to do some design work tomorrow and it's going to be a very early start because of the time difference between me and the client."

"What kind of design work?"

"Rebranding. It's graphic design."

"Oh, that sounds interesting. I thought you just worked at The Siren Song."

"No, I own my own florist shop in town. I work at the Siren because it's fun and earns a bit of extra money. But graphic design was always something I loved doing. I took it up more professionally after my divorce."

"You're divorced?"

God, how did he not know that already? I'm sure I told him on our date.

"Yes. Quite recently."

I really don't want to get into a conversation about Lee or anything else for that matter.

"I'm sorry, Levi, but I really do need to get going."

"Yes, of course. I'm sorry. Let me walk you out."

He stands as I do, and I can see his eyes are on my cleavage. This dress is sexy and, yes, it shows my cleavage a bit, but it gives me the creeps when someone just stares unabashedly at me.

I grab my clutch and make my way to say goodnight to my parents. It would be considered the height of rudeness by my mother if I didn't.

Levi trails after me like a lost dog, and my mother's eyes light up as she sees him by my side.

"Do you have to go so soon, dear?" she asks in her most saccharine voice.

"Sorry. I have an early call in the morning."

"Well, don't forget to call me about our lunch sometime next week, dear."

Lunch? We haven't arranged anything. And I don't want to either. Suffering her for a whole lunch would be like sitting with Satan himself. We never have lunch. I've reached the age of thirty-six without having to suffer lunch with her since I moved out of home.

"Will do, Mother."

She raises an eyebrow slightly at the sarcasm in my voice. She's never liked my sharp wit or the fact that sarcasm is my second language. But that's her tough shit. I've never liked her obstinate nature or the fact that she's always right, even when she's wrong. That's just the way we are with each other.

"I'll walk you out," Levi says, causing me to jump. I'd forgotten he was even there.

"There's no need. I'm good."

Seriously, when will this guy get the message? I'm guessing it'll be around the same time they discover intelligent life forms on Mars.

"I'd like to see you again," Levi says.

"Umm ... I'm sorry Levi, I really am, but I'm not dating right now."

I can't bring myself to say what I want to, which would be along the lines of "I'd rather watch paint dry". Or maybe it's "I'd rather play Russian roulette with a gun with one bullet and five empty chambers". That seems a bit harsh, so I'll go with the paint drying.

"Oh, right. Well, you know, we could just go out as friends. We could see where it goes from there."

"I'm very busy with work, Levi I juggle three jobs, remember?!"

"I'm sorry if this is a personal question, but you said you had an inheritance from your grandmother. So why do you work so many jobs?"

"Mainly because my mother always thought I'd rely on that inheritance and not bother working. So, I've made sure to bust my ass by working and being independent."

"But three jobs? Are you really that desperate to prove your mother wrong?"

"I started working at a florist part-time when I got out of school. I was studying graphic design at college, but I needed some money of my own. My parents made sure I didn't get into debt as a student, but that didn't mean I wanted to live off them. I found I loved floristry so much that I decided on doing that instead, as I knew I could make a living off it. My parents hated the fact I didn't study something they deemed 'serious' at college, so I got Venus in Rhapsody up and running. Graphic design became more of a hobby. Then when Lee and I got married, he wanted me to spend less time on the computer and more time with him. But since our divorce, I've got back into it. It became less of a hobby when I started designing book covers for authors. Then they started asking for logos and other graphics, even rebranding of their websites. So, I branched out to doing it for small businesses.""Sounds like something you enjoy doing."

"I do love it, I really do. But it can be isolating, so I decided to take a few shifts at the Siren because it got me out and meeting people. Lee had cut me off from most people, so I needed to get back out there."

"I'm glad you did, else we might never have met."

Levi opens the front door for me and holds it open as I pass.

"It was good seeing you, Levi, but I really have to get going."

God, is it me or am I just repeating what I've said a million times already?

He walks me to the sleek black chauffeur-driven car I came in, but before I can get in, his hands are on my waist and his lips come crashing down over mine. I can't back away from him because the car is right behind me, but I don't kiss him back. I place my hands on his chest to push him away, but he's stronger than me, like a wall of solid muscle.

I can't speak because his lips are all over mine. I don't know what to do. Do I wait for him to get bored of me not kissing him back? He has to get the message at some point. Doesn't he?

Levi pulls back slightly and looks into my eyes.

"You taste so good, Jenna."

"Levi, I—look, I don't want to be rude, but I really can't date you. I'm in love with somebody else, even though I haven't actually had the guts to say that to his face. I'm sorry Levi, you're a nice guy. But I really need you to see that you and I can't be together."

"You're dating someone?"

"Well, no, we broke up—I think. It's hard to explain. He's dealing with something at the moment, and I don't want to push him. But it doesn't matter whether we're together or not. I still love him. I'm sorry I didn't say anything before. The truth is, because we aren't actually dating at the moment, I find it hard to talk about him."

His face falls and he steps back. I feel nothing but relief as his body moves away from mine.

"I'm sorry, Jenna. If I'd known …" he trails off and rakes a hand through his hair.

"It's fine, Levi. I should have said something. Like I say, it's hard to talk about. It hurts because he won't let me in."

"I'm sorry. I hope you guys manage to sort it out. And—well, I'm sorry for springing that kiss on you."

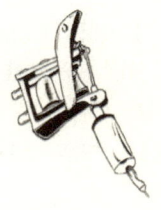

Chapter Seventeen

Nate

Seeing him kiss her, I'd felt a rage rise within me. I wanted to walk over there and pull him off her. Maybe punch his face in, too. But I realised I have no right to do anything of the sort. It didn't stop me wanting to, but I'm not really sure Nix would have appreciated me stepping in.

I mean, we're not exactly dating at the moment, and that's all my fault. But seeing her kiss another man, that was like being sucker-punched. It was like somebody reached inside my chest, tore out my heart, used it as a trampoline and then shoved it back inside my chest cavity battered, bruised, and hardly beating.

They're standing there talking, though I can't hear a word they're saying. Are they dating? She didn't look as into the kiss as he was. Maybe it was their first kiss and she wasn't expecting it.

I can't say I blame her if she's dating someone new. It's not like I deserve her. Not anymore. If I *ever* did. I shut her out and she deserves so much better. She deserves a man who can communicate his feelings. Whereas me, I closed down. I didn't just shut her out. I did the same to Steph. I buried myself in work without coming up for air.

Losing Gramps hit me like a freight train. It gutted me. Turned me upside down and inside out. I didn't know up from down, left from right, and obviously right from wrong.

What was I even thinking coming here tonight? I overheard Brogan in the Siren Song telling her boss, Riley, that Nix was at her parents' house this evening. I'd finished my drink in a hurry and got on my bike. I'd parked up a few houses down, so she didn't hear my bike pull up, then I'd walked up to the bottom of her parents' drive, ready to pull up my big boy pants and go in there, throw myself on her mercy, and beg her to give me another chance. But I'd been stopped in my tracks when I saw someone on the drive. I hid behind a tall hedge to one side and looked up to see it was Nix, with a guy.

He looks familiar. I don't know where I know him from, but I've definitely seen him somewhere.

I'm still standing at the bottom of her parents' drive like a stalker. I watch as she gets into the chauffeur-driven car and I hear the engine start up. She waves to the mystery man and he walks back inside the house, so I hope I'm correct in assuming she's going home alone.

***

I take a deep breath to steady my nerves, then wrap my knuckles on the door. I pulled up a few houses down, like déjà vu from earlier. I didn't want my bike being heard.

A vision in red opens the door. She looks divine. I want to sweep her up in my arms, carry her to bed and spend hours worshipping her body the way I used to.

Her face contorts as she realises it's me. From happy to pissed off in zero point five seconds. Go Nate! I obviously have a way with the female of the species. Especially this one.

"What are you doing here?" she seethes, but her expression doesn't match her tone.

"Nix, please—"

"Don't! You don't get to call me that anymore."

"I'm sorry Jenna. Please, I didn't come here to fight. I came to talk."

"Oh, you've suddenly remembered how to talk?"

Okay, so I asked for that.

"Nix, please … I … please hear me out. If you still want me to go afterwards, I will, and I'll never darken your doorstep again. I swear. Please, just hear me out."

She steps aside and pushes the door further open. I take it as an invitation and thank my lucky stars she didn't just close the door in my face.

I follow Nix into the kitchen, staring at her gorgeous ass all the way. The red satin clings to her curves … is it wrong to be jealous of a dress? If it is, then so be it.

"Coffee?" she asks, without turning to look at me.

She stands at the countertop, fiddling with the coffee machine. I pull two mugs from the cupboard above her and place them on the counter next to her.

"May I sit?" I ask.

Her only reply is a slight shrug of her shoulders. I take that as a yes, so I pull out a stool by the island.

I've rehearsed over and over in my head what I might say if she was willing to hear me out. The only trouble with that is that I've forgotten every damn thing I wanted to say. Seeing her kissing that guy made me lose my mind. Then seeing the way she looks clad in red satin ... the way it's moulded to her perfect breasts, the way the hemline skims above her knee on one side and below the other ... the way it clings to her perfect hourglass figure and highlights every curve of her lithe body ... I've about lost my mind.

I'm trying to remember what I needed to say to her, but those long legs and her shapely ass are distracting me. I need to get my shit together before she turns to face me and I look like a goldfish, just opening and closing my mouth without making a sound.

"Hey, my eyes are up here," she says as she turns and catches me staring.

Her eyes dance, telling me that even though she's mad at me, she likes the way I'm looking at her. I must look like a starving man salivating over a delicious-looking doughnut in a store window.

"So?"

I open my mouth, then close it again.

"What is it you want, Nate? You said you came to talk, so talk."

"I don't know what to say, Jenna. Truth be told, I've rehearsed it so many times, gone over and over what I wanted to say, tried different ways of saying things, written it down and tried to memorise it. But now that I'm here, I'm just ... lost. I know it's been a while—to say the least—and I wanted to apologise for the total silence. The complete and honest truth here is that the more time that went by, the harder it got to start the conversation. That makes me stupid and selfish—weak, even. As much as I wanted to break the silence, it was so hard. I picked up my phone to text you, wrote out a million texts and deleted them all. I hovered over the call button at least a hundred times a day, but never got the courage to press it.

"I lost myself, Nix. I was adrift at sea, and as hard as I pushed myself, as hard as I tried to swim back to shore, I couldn't do it. Every time I thought I'd reached dry land, the horizon moved further away from me. It was all I could do just to stop myself from drowning."

I take a deep breath, feeling again like I've been sucker-punched.

"Losing my parents when I was young felt like I'd lost a part of myself. Then my grandmother died, and another piece went with her. Losing Gramps took what I had left. I didn't have enough left of me to give to you. Or so I thought. I know you were there for me; you were close to Gramps too. I know that you wanted to help me through it, you stood by my side and didn't budge. But as I went through the stages of grief, I could feel myself slowly slipping away. It was gradual at first and then, all of a sudden, I've cut everyone off and I'm alone. And before you point it out, I know that was all my own doing.

Gramps had dementia and Parkinson's—I knew he was on borrowed time, but I thought we had more time together. I know there's no amount of preparation that can actually prepare you for the inevitable. You try to tell yourself there is. You try to persuade yourself that you'll be okay. But then the worst happens and it's like someone ripped the rug out from beneath you. All of a sudden, you're plunged headfirst into the unknown."

The first tear falls, and I try to wipe it away, but all too soon, another replaces it. A sudden cascade of salty water almost drowns me on dry land.

Nix rushes to me and engulfs me in her warm embrace. God, I've missed this. I never thought I'd feel this again. Her warm body, her heart beating against my ear.

What the hell was I doing when I pushed her away? I tried to save her from me. I thought I was doing her a favour. I thought I was doing us both a favour. But all I did was hurt us both. And I will forever be sorry for that. I just hope to god that my Nix will forgive me and allow me the chance to make it up to her.

Whispering soothing words, she strokes my hair as she holds me to her. It calms me like it did in the days after Gramps passed away. How can one simple touch from her ground me?

Something always brings me back to Nix. It doesn't matter what I say or do. I want to lose myself to her, for the rest of my life. I want to drown in her love, never needing to come up for air, because she breathes life into me. She makes me feel truly alive. I thought that without her I could be strong. But it turned out that I needed to lose her in order to find myself. And now I never want to let her go again. When I found myself, I realised that I was only half the man I had been before. Without Nix, I was incomplete. She's the yin to my yang, the light to my dark—she's the missing piece of the jigsaw puzzle. Will she forgive me my sins? Only time will tell.

I need to tell her I love her. My heart has felt it for a long time now, I just didn't have the courage to speak the words. I thought I'd push her away, that it was too soon to say those three little words. Because while the words themselves may only be little, the meaning isn't. There was this one time that I nearly told her, but I chickened out. I said something about those words being said too much when people don't really mean them, and that when we say them, I want to know we both mean them. But I've meant them for a great deal longer than I care to admit.

Does love at first sight exist? Is it truly possible to fall for someone in that instant? Maybe it's more like you start to fall for them slowly, then wake up one day to find that you've fallen hard. And when you look back, trying to pinpoint when you fell, all you can see in your mind is the moment you met. So that's what makes you attribute it to love at first sight.

I've never really known much about love. Lust, yes. But love, that's a different story. In hindsight, I've realised I never loved Nikki. The only true love I've ever known is that for my family. Yet here is a woman I would walk over hot coals for. I'd die a thousand deaths if it meant that she got to live.

"Nix," I whisper.

She pulls back and looks at me.

"I'm so sorry. I never meant to hurt you. I'd never intentionally break your heart. It would be like hurting myself. You're so much a part of me. I see my future in your eyes every time you look at me. You're the best thing about me. You're my gravity.

"I've waited all my life for a woman like you to come along. I didn't know it at the time, and I messed it up. Do you think you could ever forgive me? Is there any hope of us starting again? I know I'm asking a lot of you, but please tell me that there's hope. While there's breath in my body, there's a flicker of hope in my heart. I don't want to extinguish it, but I'd rather do that now than prolong the agony.

"If I've lost you forever, then I understand that it's the consequences of my own actions. I own my mistakes ... Please ... please tell me I haven't lost you."

Her eyes show a myriad of emotions. Each one passing as quickly as the one before it. It's an eternity before she speaks.

"I—"

She puts her finger over my lips, stopping me from saying whatever was coming next.

"I forgive you, Nate. It's going to take time to build the trust back up again, but you haven't lost me. I never turned my back on you. I am partially to blame for the radio silence too. I knew what you were going through, and I didn't pick the phone up to see how you were doing. I guess I justified it by thinking if you wanted me, you'd call. But I could have reached out to you. I should have at least tried. I'm so sorry that I didn't."

A tear forms and I reach to wipe it away with the pad of my thumb. When I go to pull back, she wraps her hand around mine. She leans in to my touch, and I cradle her beautiful face in the palm of my hand. More tears fall, but she doesn't move to wipe them away, and nor do I.

Soon all that can be heard is our breathing. Silent tears fall from my eyes, just as they do hers.

"I love you, Nix."

A short gasp for breath pierces the air around her. She looks into my eyes, and what she sees must confirm my words to be true because she leans in and ghosts a kiss across my lips.

"I love you too, Nate."

My heart is full to bursting. It races in my chest, and I feel it like I haven't felt in so long. It's here in this moment that I realise that my heart didn't beat without her in my life.

Chapter Eighteen

Jenna

It's been a month since I first told Nate I loved him, and I haven't stopped telling him every day since. I couldn't believe it at first when he said those three little words. I knew without a doubt that he wouldn't say something he didn't mean, and one look in his eyes told me he was baring his soul to me for the first time.

I can't say it's been an easy few weeks. We've both been incredibly busy, but we've spent every night together since the night he came to see me. I didn't let him leave that night. Instead, I took him to bed and made love to him with all that I am and all that I have to give. I don't know when I realised it, but he completes me in a way no other person ever has.

We're trying to build something solid and real, and I believe we have a very strong foundation for that.

Nate has spent every day showing me how sorry he is for what happened. I forgave him that night, but he insists on trying to make up for lost time. We talked long into that night before I asked him to stay. He told me how hard it had been since he lost Gordon, and he also opened up to me more about losing his parents. He told me what kind of effect it had on his life. My heart broke for him. For the young boy who became an orphan, who lost the two people closest to him. Then his grandparents took him in and helped him become the man I see before me today. When his grandmother passed away, he felt like it was another arrow through his heart. He never thought his heart would heal. So, losing Gordon had been the final straw. His heart had broken completely, and he didn't know what to do. He wandered around aimlessly for a while before realising that he wasn't alone. He did have someone that cared deeply for him. And he's right, I do. I love him more than I have ever loved another person in my life.

My mother wasn't happy when we got back together; she tried to pretend like she was happy for me, but her expressions, her mannerisms, all gave her away.

My father, however, was happy for me. He told me that all he wanted was to see his little girl happy, and it didn't matter who I was with, as long as he made me happy.

Tonight is yet another family meal—my parents, mainly my father, insisted on getting to know Nate better and, being a good daughter, I agreed—and yet another night I am dreading. My mother is a very good actress; she's good at pretending that she likes Nate, that she's happy with us dating. I know different. I know she's hoping it's only a "phase" between us—she told me as much the first time I told her we were back together. But I know in my heart we'll prove her wrong.

***

I knock on the front door and my father answers. He's all smiles, and I know that, unlike my mother's, they aren't fake. My father has come to know Nate a little better and actually likes him. He thinks he's good for me. I know he's right.

"Daddy." I greet him with a hug and a kiss on his cheek.

"Come in, darling," he says, standing to one side.

Nate and I enter, hand in hand. I squeeze his hand, an affirmation of my affection for him, letting him know that it will be okay, regardless of my mother.

Walking into the dining room, I see the table set for eight. That's weird. I thought it was only the four of us for dinner this evening.

"Ah, here she is," my mother says as she walks through the door leading to the kitchen.

"Good evening, Mother."

She greets me with air kisses to both cheeks and does the same to Nate.

"Good evening, Nathaniel."

She always insists on using his full name instead of his preferred name, and I know she does it to try and gain an edge. To irritate us.

"Good evening, Mrs Morgan."

His response is courteous as he pulls a chair out for me to sit down.

My mother still insists on him calling her Mrs Morgan, rather than

Martha. Another thing she does to be a pain. My father, however, insists Nate calls him Don.

"Who's the table set for, Mother?"

"Oh, we just have a few extra guests tonight, darling," she replies in the saccharine sweet tone she's perfected like an art form.

She didn't used to be so false. There was a time when she had softer edges, was warmer, kinder … but I think those moments ended when I was still a child. I guess they could even be false memories, planted by me over the years, to tell myself that my mother wasn't always this way.

The sound of the doorbell brings a smile to her face. My father's face doesn't mirror hers. For once he looks pissed off with her, and I'm glad to see I'm not the only one.

My father, Don Morgan, is a good guy. He has a good career, earns good money, pays for all the extravagance in my mother's life. He usually agrees with her because it's easier, he says a happy wife is a happy life, but he doesn't always agree with the things she says or does. There are occasions when he stands up for what he believes in or for someone he loves.

I've always been more of a daddy's girl. Sure, he can be "stiff upper lip" just like my mother, but when it's just the two of us, he's a different man, softer. He doesn't always know how to show that he cares, he's not an emotional man by anybody's standards. But he's always got time for me. I'll always be his "little girl".

After answering the door, my mother can be heard laughing in that falsetto tone. It sets me even more on edge than I was before.

"Come in, take a seat. I'll go and get the corkscrew for the bottle," she says as she walks into the dining room ahead of her mystery guests.

She walks through the other door to the kitchen and it's only then that I'm greeted by one familiar face and two other people that I don't know.

"Good evening, Don," he greets my father.

They shake hands, and my father gives him an easy smile, but as soon as his back is turned, he looks to me with sympathy in his eyes.

"Good evening, Jenna. It's nice to see you," he says as he leans in to kiss me on the cheek. "And this must be Nathaniel. Good to meet you."

Nate shakes hands with Levi, and internally I grimace. This evening is going to hell in a handbasket.

"Sorry, where are my manners. Jenna, Nathaniel, this is my mother,

Angelina and my father, Wander," he adds before taking a seat next to me.

The Burkhardt's greet us, all toothy grins and handshakes.

"Don, it's good to see you again," Wander says as he shakes my father's hand.

"You too, Wander. It's been a while."

"I'm sorry, I didn't realise you all knew each other," I butt in.

"We met at a function some time back. Young Levi here was up for an award, and your parents came to the gala evening where it was presented to him," Angelina answers.

She's very pretty. No, more than that, she's striking. Younger than her husband by a good decade or so, by the looks of it. Long blonde hair, beautiful blue eyes, a lithe figure.

"Oh, I see."

I keep my tone polite, but I'm still sitting here wondering what this whole evening is about.

Nate puts his hand on my thigh underneath the table and gives me a quick, reassuring squeeze.

"The table is set for another guest, Daddy. Are we expecting more company?"

"Oh, we were bringing our daughter, Chelsea, but I'm afraid she couldn't make it. I should have phoned ahead, but I didn't think. I'm sorry," Angelina says.

"No problems, Ange. So, how are things?"

My mother comes back in with the now open bottle in her hand. She smiles as she takes in the scene before her.

The parents get into a discussion about work, so I tune out. I turn to Nate and he smiles at me.

"I can fake being ill, if you want to go home," he whispers, so quietly only I can hear.

"No, it's fine. Well, for the moment at least."

He leans in and kisses me on the cheek. I don't miss my mother's disapproving glare. She's as subtle as a sledgehammer.

The conversation soon turns to relationships as we eat our main course.

"You're still single, Levi?" my mother asks.

"Yes, there was this one woman recently, who I thought we could have made a go of things. But she's got a thing for the bad boy type, not stable men such as me."

His reply turns the food sour on my tongue. How could he say that when I am sitting right next to him? And to say it when Nate is present is even more disrespectful. Jesus, I really dodged a bullet when I gave this guy the swerve.

I open my mouth to give him an appropriate response, but my mother's sharp tongue cuts me off.

"She doesn't know what she's missing out on. Why would she choose a fling with a bad boy over a long-term relationship with a guy who could give her the world?"

"Maybe she doesn't want the world. Maybe she's happy with her little slice of it," I seethe.

"Then she's a fool," my mother says, her tone acidic.

I stand and throw my napkin down on the table.

"I am no fool. I have my eyes wide open. I don't want Levi—no offence meant by that, Levi—I want Nate. I *love* Nate. We're together and there's nothing you or anyone else can do about it."

"What is this?" Angelina asks.

"This? Oh, *this* is a setup, Angelina. I'm very sorry if my mother gave you the false impression that her daughter was single or unhappy in her current relationship. Because the truth is, I've never been happier."

I turn on my heel and walk to the dining room door, Nate hot on my heels. I stop short of leaving and turn back to the room.

"Mother, I'm so sorry that *you* are so unhappy with my choice of man. But you know what? I'm not sorry I chose to be with him. I'll never apologise for being with a man I love. As for you, Levi," I say, looking at him sat there looking a little less smug than a moment ago when he was bad-mouthing me, "I hope that one day you find true happiness. You deserve someone with as much sparkling wit as you. And in case you're not smart enough to figure out the subtle meaning of that, I'll let you into the secret—you are as dull as dirty dishwater. You may be handsome-ish, you may have money, but you'll either end up with a gold-digger who won't care about your personality, or you'll end up with a string of women that leave you when they realise that you have the personality of a ventriloquist's dummy, only brought to life when somebody else is making the conversation and pulling the strings."

I walk over to where my father is sitting, speechlessly watching the exchange. Kissing him on the cheek, I whisper a soft "Sorry Daddy," before I turn to leave.

Taking Nate's hand, I don't wait for any comeback. It would take an idiot like him an eternity to come up with a witty response anyway.

His parents sit there, mouths agape in astonishment. I feel sorry for them, well, almost. They didn't need to be here for this sideshow.

My mother didn't really think through the consequences of her actions. If she had, she wouldn't have brought about this debacle. She's embarrassed the Burkhardts.

I might have been the one that said those things, but I wouldn't have felt the need to if my mother hadn't orchestrated this evening, contrived to show me that Levi is better for me than Nate.

Walking hand in hand with the man I love, I leave my parents' house without a backwards glance.

***

"I'm sorry, baby, I didn't know he was going to be there. If I'd known, I would have warned you that we'd been on a date. The truth is, it was before you and I got together. It was just after the speed dating event. I would have told you about him, I just didn't see him as relevant."

"Honestly, Nix, it doesn't matter. He doesn't matter. The only thing that means anything is you, me and our future."

"I ticked two boxes that night, yours and his. We went out once and he seemed nice enough, if a little dull. Then you took me to the theme park, and he was nothing but background noise. I had promised him a second date, but after going out with you, I knew it was you I wanted."

"Nix, seriously, stop explaining. I don't need to hear it."

"We never even kissed. Well, not until—"

I take a deep breath before continuing.

"Not until the night of my parents' anniversary party. He walked me to my car, and he kissed me. I didn't kiss him back, I swear. I pulled away and told him about you. We weren't talking at the time because … well, you know why … but I told him that I was in love with somebody else."

"I know he kissed you that night. I saw."

"You were there?"

"I was. I came to see you, to tell you I'd been a fool and beg forgiveness. But when I got there, I saw you in your red dress, your back to the car, his lips on yours … then I saw you pull away. I couldn't hear what you were saying from my position by the bush at the end of the drive, but his face looked crestfallen, and that was enough to show me that you weren't into him. That's why I didn't bring it up that night when I saw you. And why I haven't brought it up since. He doesn't matter. None of that matters. It's where we go from here that counts."

"Oh Nate …"

I sigh and collapse against his chest. Pulling my feet up underneath me on the sofa, I snuggle into him and he just holds me.

"You are everything I never knew I needed. I was determined never to let another man into my heart after Lee, but fate dealt me an unexpected hand. You were put in my path, and though I tried to fight it, it was futile. I fell head over heels for you before I even knew it."

"You are everything I never knew I needed too. But sometimes, life pushes you in a different direction. All I really know is this; the most beautiful things in the world are never spoken or heard, they're felt. Do you feel this?" he asks as he places my hand over his heart, "It beats for you and you alone."

Chapter Nineteen

Nate

It's been three weeks, and Nix still hasn't spoken to her mother. In all honesty, I don't blame her.

I knew from previous family dinners—and the icy reception I received each time—that Martha didn't like me and doesn't think I'm good enough for her daughter. Her father, Don, is a little warmer than his wife and actually seems to be a decent man. God only knows how he ended up married to someone like Martha.

Nix and I are back on an even keel, even more so since she confessed that night about the kiss. It was something I didn't want to bring up with her because—as Ross would say to Rachel—we were on a break. But with her full and frank confession, I've been able to fully let it go.

I've asked Nix to take some time off work but am refusing to tell her where we're going or what we're doing. All she knows is that she needs her passport.

She's tried to wheedle it out of me, using her feminine wiles on me, but I'm remaining strong.

One of her questions was "but how do you expect me to change my money into the right currency if I don't know where we're going?" to which, I replied a simple "Euros". Then she tried asking how much money she'd need to convert, and I told her just spending money, because I'm paying for everything else. But, being my typical Nix, she fussed over not knowing how much was "enough" spending money.

She also tried promising me sexual favours in return for a few simple hints. I *am* a typical bloke, so I let her do what she wanted to me, to try and get her answers. But she didn't make me promise to give *useful* hints. So, I gave her small hints like "it'll be warm" or "pack suntan lotion" and "pack enough clothes for a week".

Then there was the withholding sexual favours, but she couldn't last. She tried with all her might, but she couldn't resist me in the end.

That's one thing I can say about Nix—she's a nymphomaniac. And she's the best lover I've ever had. I'm not just saying that the way you do when you're dating someone—I mean you aren't really going to say "Oh no, X was better than you in bed" to your partner, are you?—I'm saying it because I mean it. She's spontaneous, adventurous, flexible— very flexible. Sex with her is out of this world. But it's more than just sex. It might sound girly or whatever to say, but there's a difference between sex and making love. And we do a lot of both. The odd quickie in the shower or on the sofa, the marble top of the island in the kitchen … and also the long nights we spend making love into the early hours of the morning. The times we wake spontaneously in the middle of the night and, rather than letting the other one sleep, we rouse them with kisses and touches … It's a good job we both work for ourselves, otherwise our bosses may have sacked us for the times we've turned up late. She's insatiable, and she's all mine. What would any sane man do in my position?

I'm loading the car up when I feel a pair of arms wrap around my waist. Her warm breath ghosts over the back of my neck, making the hairs there stand on end. I turn in her embrace and slant my lips over hers. She brings her arms up around my neck and pulls me closer, deepening the kiss.

"Hey, beautiful," I say as I pull back, a little out of breath.

"Hey, handsome."

"Did you need something?"

"You."

"You're insatiable, you know that?"

Taking me by the hand, Nix leads me upstairs, and it takes all my effort to restrain myself from sweeping her off her feet and carrying her to her room. I nearly trip over my feet as I try to rush up the stairs, so maybe it's a good job I wasn't carrying her.

"It's absolutely huge," she says in a husky voice.

"Well, it's certainly getting there," I reply, wondering how she can tell the size of the bulge in my jeans with her back to me.

"Help me with the zip, will you darling?"

I begin to unzip my jeans, but then I see what it is she's really on about. Her fucking suitcase! Her overloaded, crammed-crap-into-every-nook-and-cranny suitcase on her bed. She's right, it is bloody huge.

Chapter Twenty

Jenna

I didn't get to see the tickets. I didn't hear the tannoy announcement telling us to board our plane—mainly because Nate insisted I listen to an audio book and I got so lost in the narrator making me feel like part of the story. So, I have no idea where we're going. All I know is I hate flying. Flying sucks. You're in a giant tin can in the air. Mid. Freaking. Air. No, in fact it's worse than mid-air, it's thousands of feet up in the air.

I couldn't tell Nate I was nervous of flying. He'd gone to all this effort of taking me on a surprise trip. The very least I could do was turn up. And to turn up, I have to get over my teensy fear of flying. So, I downloaded a few books by my favourite authors, lined up a couple of audio books, made sure my iPod was fully charged. And, when I realised I had a window seat, I got Nate to swap with me and keep the blind closed.

He didn't know my palms were sweating, and he didn't need to know my heart was racing faster than a horse in the Kentucky Derby. I won't let the anxiety conquer me, ruin this holiday for both of us. I simply need a distraction or two.

We're currently watching the in-flight movie, *Bridesmaids*. I've seen this film so many times before, and yet it's still funny as hell. I love Melissa McCarthy, have done since I saw her as Sookie in *Gilmore Girls*. The scene with her and the puppies—it gets me every time. And the bit with the giant cookie. Oh, my god. It's madness. I wish they'd get a wriggle on and make the sequel they talked about.

"Can I get you anything to drink, sir, madam?" the perky flight attendant asks.

"Do you have Somersby cider?" Nate answers, correctly predicting what I want.

"We do. Would you like the original or the new strawberry and rhubarb?"

A shudder runs through me at the mere thought of rhubarb.

"We'll take two of the original please," he replies.

She passes Nate our drinks with an over-the-top smile. She likes what she sees, it's easy to see. She may as well have little cartoony hearts coming out of her eyes or something. I don't blame her one bit. My boyfriend is extremely handsome. In fact, he's more than that. There's something magnetic about him, he just draws you in. Slowly at first, and then all at once.

"Thank you," he replies as he turns away from her and back to the film.

I see the disappointment in her eyes as she walks away, but seriously, she can see he's sitting right next to his girlfriend. Does she think he's going to flirt with her? Does she expect him to ask for her number before he gets off the plane? Just because she's blonde and has breasts the size of beach balls—which I'm hazarding a guess are fake—does that mean he's meant to fall at her feet?

"Are you ever going to tell me where we're going?"

Nate makes a motion of locking his lips and throwing away the key.

"Fine," I huff and fold my arms.

I pout at him and try for the puppy dog eyes, but that doesn't work either, so I go back to the film.

***

Nate insisted I put in my earphones when the captain made the announcement about landing, so I have no clue where we have ended up. Wherever we are is hot and sunny though, so I'm glad he told me what kind of weather to pack for. I sure don't need jumpers and a thick coat here.

We disembarked the plane and went through customs, and now we're out in the sunshine. Nate and the taxi driver are packing our bags into the boot of the car and I'm standing soaking in the rays.

"Where to?" the driver asks, in an accent I'm finding hard to pin down.

"The Grand Hotel Excelsior Vittoria, please."

The scenery out of the window is awe-inspiring. Absolutely picture-postcard perfection.

After a while, we pull up outside the hotel, and I look up at a beautiful building. Its pink and cream walls with green shutters on the windows look so inviting.

Nate pays the driver, and he helps us take our bags to the top of the steps, leaving them just in front of the double doors.

Our room is decorated in creams and golds, a simple colour scheme yet a very opulent room. What you think is a double bed is probably big enough to fit four people. It's so big that it actually has two headboards.

The floor-to-ceiling window has lush cream-coloured curtains hanging, but wide open so we can enjoy the sunshine.

I walk to the window, only to realise it's actually a door and it opens out onto a balcony with a table and chairs set up.

A knock at the door makes me jump, but I walk out onto the balcony as Nate answers the door.

"Would you care for a drink, sweetheart?" he asks from behind me.

I turn and see him holding a bottle and two glasses. The bottle is rose gold and the label reads "Bottega". I've never heard of it before.

"They normally serve champagne, but I know how much you dislike it."

Setting the glasses down, he pops the cork and pours us both a glass. He hands me mine and clinks his glass to it in cheers before taking a sip.

It has a slight pink colour to it; I just hope it isn't flavoured with something I don't like. I don't want to disappoint Nate by not enjoying it.

I taste strawberries and other berries I can't identify, yet something floral to it too. It's delicious.

"Welcome to Sorrento, darling," Nate says as he stands beside me and wraps an arm around my waist as we look out at the view from our balcony.

"It's really beautiful here. Absolutely breath-taking."

"It's not the only thing of beauty to be admired here," he whispers, before placing a soft kiss on my bare shoulder.

"No, there's a gorgeous pool too, by the looks of it."

"That's not what I meant, and you know it," he says as he chuckles at me.

His breath tickles my neck and stirs up a kaleidoscope of butterflies in my stomach.

"What do you say to a walk and then an evening meal in the hotel restaurant? We can go sightseeing tomorrow," he asks.

"I'll grab a shower and then we can head out, if that's okay?"

"Sure. Is there room in the shower for two?"

"What do you say we go and find out?" I ask as I take his hand and lead him back into our room, through to the en suite.

The deep green marble surrounding the double sink is divine. I run my fingers across the smooth surface and sigh in contentment.

Warm hands come up to caress my bare shoulders and I relax against his solid chest behind me. His arms wrap around me and he peppers soft kisses on my skin.

He takes hold of the hemline of my top and slowly inches it up. I raise my arms, so he can slide it off with ease, then he discards the material.

Undoing the zip at the back of my skirt, he slides that to the floor too. If it was any other man, I'd feel exposed, standing here in just my bra and panties, but Nate makes me feel cherished. From the top of my head to the tip of my toes, he worships every inch of me.

Showering me with kisses, he slides my panties over my hips, and they fall to the floor. Then he undoes my bra and I allow the straps to slide down my arms before discarding it.

"It's a little unfair, right now," I whisper.

"What is?"

"That I'm naked and you aren't."

"There's an easy remedy for that."

His voice is a husky whisper, and I'd be lying if I said it didn't turn me on.

Turning slowly, I stand a couple of feet away as Nate strips himself of his t-shirt and jeans, leaving him in just his boxers. I see just how turned on he is, and it excites me.

Closing the distance between us, I slide my hands up and over his sculpted body. I dip one hand to that V that's so prominent. There's something about it that turns me on, sending a delicious shiver right through me, stoking the flickering warmth inside me.

Dipping his head to kiss my shoulder, he trails feather-light kisses up one side of my neck. He trails one hand up the side of my body and goosebumps break out in the wake of his touch. His thumb grazes my nipple and it sends a jolt of pleasure through me.

My pulse races as his kisses graze the hollow of my throat, before his lips come up to claim mine in a passionate kiss.

"How about we forego the shower?" he asks as he breaks the kiss.

My chest is heaving with desire and he doesn't have to ask me twice.

I go to walk around him but end up squealing as he picks me up. His hands grip my bare ass and his erection rubs against my core.

I wrap my arms around his neck as he carries me to the bedroom. He lies me down on the bed, then stands back to remove his boxers.

My mouth waters at the delectable sight of my man in all his naked glory. Waiting for him to touch me feels like an eternity.

His hands trail up my thighs as he stands between my parted legs. His strong grip pulls me further down to the bottom of the bed.

Leaning over me, he claims my lips in a searing kiss. The heat of it sings in my veins, then travels down to my abdomen and stokes the growing warmth pooling there.

The love I feel for him grows exponentially as he touches me with a gentle reverence.

Kneeling between my legs, he trails gentle kisses up my thigh. I quiver under the ticklish sensation. My hands grip the sumptuous sheets below me as he works his way up and up, eventually moving to my clit. Desire is like a lightning bolt as he gently pushes one of his deft fingers inside me. Like a flame to a match, he awakens a myriad of sensations within me.

"I love you, Nix," he whispers as he worships me.

I try to speak, but all that comes out is a breathy moan as he pushes another finger inside, stretching me, hitting the spot that makes everything come to life in glorious technicolour. He takes me to the edge, only to stop. The feeling inside begins to ebb, and he must see some sign of this written on my face as he begins to move again, bringing me back to life.

All too soon I succumb to the need, crying out his name as I fall into the abyss.

I lift my head as I feel Nate moving. He stands between my legs and strokes his erection a few times as his eyes roam over my curves.

I crawl slowly further up the bed and his eyes follow my movement. His salacious grin lights his whole face as he crawls up over me and braces himself, an arm on either side of me, holding him above me.

Craving his touch, I reach out and trace my hands up his biceps. Leaning down, he claims my mouth with his. I pour all the love I feel into the kiss. Sliding my arms up around his neck, I pull him closer, deepening the kiss. Our tongues duel for dominance, and a growl reverberates through his chest.

Aligning his body with mine, he plunges into me without warning. I cry out as he withdraws and repeats the movement. The look in his eyes shows he's struggling to restrain himself, so I slide my hands down to his delectable ass and pull him forward. He pushes into me once more and I cry out again.

I meet his hips thrust for thrust as he builds a steady rhythm. He leans down and draws my nipple into his mouth, biting, then kissing away the slight sting. My body arches off the bed and my hands fall away from him, down to the bed where I grip the sheets as he begins to move faster.

A searing fire begins to burn within me. Nate feeds the flames as he lifts my legs and pushes deeper inside me. His pace quickens, and it's all I can do not to burst into a ball of fire as my climax takes hold of me. I cry out his name like a curse and a prayer into the night.

Nate pushes harder, faster and then his rhythm begins to falter. I grip hold of him by digging my heels into his ass and drag my nails down the muscles in his back.

"Oh shit, Nix …" he whispers hoarsely.

"It's okay … just let go."

He moans long and loud as he ceases movement. His breathing is laboured as he leans down and peppers kisses along my collarbone.

"I love you, baby," I whisper into his ear.

Moving to lie next to me, Nate pulls me into his chest, and I wrap an arm across his torso and a leg over his.

"I love you too, Nix. So very much."

Those were the last words I hear before I fall into a deep, sound sleep.

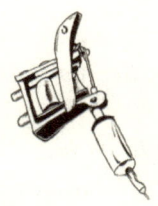

Chapter Twenty-One

Nate

Ristorante La Marinella. Set in a beautiful, idyllic location just off La Marinella beach. It's picture-postcard perfection brought to life.

I want tonight to be perfect. Nix deserves nothing less than absolute perfection. It's our last night here in Sorrento, and I want to end it with a romantic meal and a walk on the beach. I'm an old-fashioned romantic at heart.

The restaurant sits right on the edge of the water, and the table I booked is right on that edge. Our view will be the vast expanse of crystal blue water. Calming and blissful. That's what I'm hoping for. Nix deserves good old-fashioned romance, and that's what I intend to give her.

My gramps brought my grandmother Lillian to this spot many years ago. I doubt the restaurant was built back in those days, but he walked along that very beach and got down on one knee. He said she burst out crying and couldn't answer him right away. He was down on one knee in the sand, his knee was killing him, but he stayed right there until she said yes. When she finally said yes, he stood and picked her up, spinning her around, and she squealed in delight.

It's good to see the place he brought her to. It feels so special here, knowing that I'm walking in his footsteps. I wish I'd told him before he died that I planned to bring Nix here. He would have loved it.

Remembering that first time he met her makes me smile. He'd known before me that she'd be the woman I fell head over heels in love with. He'd told me on a visit that Nix wasn't able to make.

"Look deep into your heart, boy, tell me, who do you see?"

"Stop being mushy, old timer," I reply.

"Stop holding back, Nathaniel. Open your eyes to what your heart is trying

to tell you. Now tell me, who do you see?"

"Jenna," I respond around a lump in my throat.

"Close your eyes and picture her. See her beautiful face, that gorgeous smile ... now tell me what else you see."

My palms feel clammy and my heart begins to race as I close my eyes and picture her. She's so beautiful, gentle, courageous, compassionate ... my heart skips a beat as I see what Gramps means.

"Forever," I whisper hoarsely.

Forever. Such a simple word and yet complicated connotations.

I've never been a forever kind of guy. Have I? My heart disagrees with my head.

My head tells me to fear the unknown, that forever is a long time. But my heart tells me that I can never let her go.

She came into my life at a time when I wasn't looking for anything or anyone. If I'd ever thought I was serious about anyone before, it was Nikki. But she showed me how much a person can hurt the one they claim to love. But I know Nix isn't the same. She cares about me deeply. It's written on her face, clear enough for even a blind man to see. And that's what I've been, blind.

I guess it's true what they say, love comes when you least expect it. Whether it was fate that put her in my path, whether it was written in the stars, I really don't know. All I know is I have to do something about it before I lose her to somebody better than me.

I know she says she cares about me, but she deserves someone who can give her the world. All I can offer her is my small slice of the world. Will that really be enough?

I shake my head to dispel the past. Opening my eyes, I look out over our balcony. The sky is a vibrant blue, not a cloud in sight. The sun shines down on me and I soak in the warmth it offers.

Hearing Nix sing as she showers, I smile to myself. She can't help but sing along to the iPod she has linked to a dock in our hotel room.

I hear her belt out "You Make Me Want To" by Luke Bryan. That girl sure loves her country music. She has the voice of an angel and could have been a country singer herself in another life.

I finish getting ready and pour myself a beer. It isn't a far walk to the restaurant tonight, so I won't be driving the rental I hired for when we got here. Walking over to the balcony, I take a seat outside in the sun.

Thinking about Gramps and Grandma Lillian, I close my eyes and remember the look in his eyes as he talked about her over the years after she passed away. I imagine the same twinkle in my eyes when I talk to Josh about Nix. He's told me a million times how I wear a goofy smile when she's around. Even Brogan has noticed and has stopped giving me such a hard time about when I retreated into myself and didn't let Nix in.

Josh and Brogan make such a cute couple. I know there's a bit of an age gap, and some people might say it won't work because they are at different places in their lives. But I know that's not true. They both want the same things. They want a bright future, a happy home, maybe even a couple of beautiful children. They want the white picket fence, the whole nine yards. And I know they'll have it one day.

I've been thinking of asking Nix to move in with me, but I know she doesn't want to leave her grandmother's home. That was a bit of a sticking point for a while, because I didn't want to give up my gramps's home either. But I found a solution.

Josh is currently renting a place just down the road from me, and I know he'd really rather live somewhere bigger, somewhere he and Brogan can raise a family. So, I told him if Nix is open to me moving in with her, I'll rent Gramps's house to him. That way, it still stays in the family, because I'll still own it and because Josh is more like a brother than a best friend.

"Hey," Nix says from behind me.

I open my eyes and see her in nothing but a towel. My tongue darts out to wet my lips and she gives me that sweet smile, the one that tells me she knows what I'm thinking. But we'd miss our reservation if I had my wicked way with her right now. And as much of an appetite as I have for her, I know we have the rest of our lives for that. Tonight is a one-night-only kind of deal. I won't ruin my plans.

"Hey, gorgeous."

I stand and walk towards her. Her smile widens as I wrap my arms around her waist. Leaning down, I ghost a kiss over her lips before stepping back.

"Hey, no fair," she says as she swats my chest with her palm.

"Sorry, baby, but we really can't afford to be late."

She pouts and turns on the puppy dog eyes. I can't say it has no effect on me, but I won't let amazing sex derail our last night, no matter how much she turns me on.

***

After a short walk from the hotel, we're finally at the restaurant. It's more gorgeous than I imagined, and, though I Googled pictures of it, they didn't do it justice at all. It's simply breathtaking.

Nix looks incredible in a deep purple dress. It's got a sweetheart neckline, and the fabric clings to her curves and dips in at her waist. The clingy material stops just above her knee, but a chiffon sort of material wraps around it all and drops to her ankles at the back, leaving her legs exposed at the front due to it being higher than the back.

The nude colour high-heeled shoes she's wearing serve to make her shapely legs look like they go on forever.

The dress makes her look sexy but refined. It shows some cleavage but not in a trashy way. Her pert breasts are accentuated by the white beading in a floral pattern that goes down to her waist on the left side of the dress.

Her rich chocolate-brown hair falls over one shoulder in a loose braid. Her green eyes look like the most expensive emeralds as they twinkle in the sunlight.

I want to man up and stop thinking of all the little details, but I can't seem to help it. Nix does something to me that makes me see things in a whole new way. She ignites a passion deep inside me, and I know nothing in this world can extinguish the flame.

Not wanting to turn up wearing my typical jeans and t-shirt, I've gone all out in a black suit, crisp white shirt and black pencil tie.

Holding the door to the restaurant open, I gesture for Nix to go first. I don't miss the gasp that comes out of her mouth as she takes in her surroundings. Not that I blame her, because the sea view is spectacular. The sun is just setting on the horizon, casting spectacular hues across the sky.

"If you'll follow me," the waiter says as he walks ahead of us.

We get to our table, and I hold Nix's chair out for her before taking my own.

"This is so beautiful. The view is really something to behold," she says as she looks out over the water.

"As far as I'm concerned, nothing outshines the beauty of the woman I love. All else pales in comparison. But you're right, it's very pretty."

I don't miss the blush that flushes across her chest and cheeks. She's so cute when she blushes.

"You're not so bad yourself. You look especially good in a suit, Mr Peterson."

"Are you saying I don't look good in a tee and jeans?"

I put my hand over my heart, feigning offence at her words.

"I was trying to pay you a compliment. But if you want my honest opinion, your clothes all look better on the bedroom floor."

"Miss Morgan, you are such a naughty little minx."

***

After a fabulous meal, the freshest seafood you could ever ask for, Nix holds her heels in her hand as we walk across the sand. She's walking at the edge of the water, the waves lapping gently at her feet.

"This has been the most amazing holiday. I wish we didn't have to go home."

"I wish we could stay too. Maybe we can come back someday."

"That would be wonderful. I feel like there's so much we have yet to discover."

We walk a little further and I can't keep my secret very much longer.

"My gramps and Grandma Lillian came here, you know. To this very beach. I feel like I'm walking in their footsteps."

"Really? That's so sweet. I can just imagine the pair of them talking a romantic walk on the beach in the moonlight."

"I nearly brought his ashes to scatter here. But I'm not ready to let him go yet. Maybe next year, we could come back and do that."

"Oh, baby," she says as she squeezes my hand.

"It's okay. I'm not sad. I'm actually quite the opposite. I feel close to them both here."

"I would have loved to have known Lillian. I know I didn't know Gordon for long, but I came to love him, you know?!"

"It's impossible not to love the old timer. He was quite the character. I can only imagine what he was like when they were younger. Gramps used to tell me stories about their past. He was an old romantic. He proposed to her here in Sorrento."

"Oh, wow."

When Gramps died, I inherited everything. One of the items of most sentimental value was my grandmother's engagement ring. He'd said when I visited shortly before he died that, when the time came, he wanted me to give it to the woman I wanted to spend forever with.

"I like to think they're both watching over us in their special place."

"I'm sure they are. They're reunited at long last, and their happiness will be eternal."

Her words slice right into my heart.

"I was hoping," I say, pulling us to a stop, "that this could also become *our* special place. I love you, Jenna Morgan. You make me the happiest I've ever been by far. You came into my life like a breath of fresh air. Your smart mouth and your beautiful eyes. You had my heart before I even knew it had happened."

I lean down and claim her lips in a sweet kiss before pulling back to look at her. I'm almost certain she can hear how hard my heart is beating against my ribcage, feeling like it might explode.

"It all started when I walked in for my tattoo. When I walked into the wrong room, you whispered in my ear and caused my whole body to shudder. I hadn't even seen your face, but I was turned on by the timbre of your voice. The entire time you were tattooing me, I wished your hands were touching me all over. I didn't think there was any chance you felt the same … until you kissed me."

"I've never done anything so unprofessional, but it was the best thing I've ever done. If I could go back and do it all over again, I would. But we can't live in the past, so I want to live for the future. *Our* future."

I feel my palms become clammy and my pulse sky rockets.

"Are you cold?" I ask as I see her shiver.

I slip my jacket off and place it around her shoulders.

"Thank you," she says as she leans up to kiss me.

"Jenna, you know I love you, don't you?"

"Of course I do. Why would you even need to ask?"

"And you know that I'll never hurt you. I can't promise you a future without a hitch, because all couples row from time to time. But I'll never intentionally hurt you. I'll always love you. I'll prove it every day for the rest of our lives, as long as you let me. I've told you before that the best things in life are *felt*, and what I feel for you—well, everything else fades into insignificance. There's nothing I want more than to be with you. Well, there is one thing…" I trail off, causing her to look a little puzzled.

"This," I say as I get down on one knee.

Her gasp is the only sound I hear.

"Jenna Morgan, I promise to love you until my dying breath. I promise to cherish you and show you how special you are to me every single day. I promise to never break your heart. I promise to never make you cry, unless they're happy tears. I need to know just one thing; would you do me the honour of being my wife?"

Tears fall silently as she looks down at me. It feels like an eternity passes before she speaks. Gramps would say that's history repeating itself like with him and Lillian all those years ago.

"Yes. Oh, Nate, yes. I would love nothing more."

I slide my grandmother's ring on her finger—whilst silently being grateful to Brogan for borrowing one of Nix's rings for me to get the size right.

As she looks down at her ring, then at me, I hear her choke back a sob.

Standing, I pull her into my arms and claim her lips once more. I can taste the salty tang of her tears.

Her arms come up around the back of my neck and she pulls me closer to her. We're standing so that nothing can come between us—and nothing ever will.

"I love you so much, Mr Peterson," Nix says as she breaks the kiss.

I pepper her face with kisses, trying to kiss away all her tears. She giggles, and it's the sweetest sound. I could listen to her laugh for the rest of my life and I fully intend to.

"I love you too, Mrs Peterson."

She exhales on a dreamy sigh as she hears me call her that. It's like she's been waiting all her life for me to come along and make her this happy.

Chapter Twenty-Two

Jenna

After landing back in the UK, I FaceTimed with Brogan and showed her my ring. I would have done it last night, but I was … otherwise occupied, with my amazing fiancé.

I never thought I'd get married again. I never wanted something to end in disaster like it did with Lee. If I ever lost Nate now, I know it would do irreparable damage to my heart. If there's one thing he's taught me, it's that some people are meant to come into your life for longer than others. Some may be there for a short period of time but make a huge impact, and he's right. Lee is a part of my past I'd rather forget. He made a huge impact on my life though. He taught me he wasn't the one.

Nate says that you experience three loves in your life. One is your first love; whilst it may only be fleeting, it opens your eyes and your heart. The second may also be brief, but it shows you what love isn't meant to be like. It teaches you a very important lesson—what to look for in your one true love. Then the third and final love is the all-consuming, overwhelming, love story to end all love stories. It's what romance novels should be written about.

If, one day, someone was to write about me, they'd know that Nate is my third and final love. They'd know we're going to grow old and grey together.

I'd told Brogan this on the phone, and she had made fake gagging motions, rolled her eyes at me, the usual Brogan behaviour. But I know that, one day, she'll see I'm right.

Arriving back home, I put my key in the lock, and it hits me. One of us is going to have to give up our house. We both own houses that mean so much to us, and I feel a crippling fear run through me. But it passes as briefly as it comes. I know that it doesn't matter where we live, as long as we're there together. Material possessions don't matter, it's the memories we make with the ones we love that mean the most.

Walking into the living room, we're greeted by cheers and the popping of party poppers.

"What the—oh, my god."

I look around at all the smiling faces of our friends and family, noticing my father is present but my mother isn't. In all honesty, it's probably for the best. She'd only ruin the moment for us.

"Congratulations," Brogan says as she comes up to hug me.

She squeezes me tight before pulling back and bringing my hand up for her to inspect my ring.

"It's beautiful," she says in awe.

"It was Nate's grandmother's ring," I reply as the first tear falls.

I promised myself I wouldn't cry, but these are happy tears.

Nate slips an arm around me and hands me a glass.

"Oh Brogan, I do hope this isn't—"

"It's cider," she interrupts me, correctly guessing what I was going to say. "Somersby cider, to be precise. I thought you might like that as opposed to what the other guests are drinking."

I move away from Nate and pull Brogan with me. Motioning her into the empty kitchen, I close the door behind us.

"I can't, Brogan."

"But you've just agreed to marry him. You can't turn him down now."

"I don't mean that, silly. I mean I can't do this," I say, motioning to my glass.

"What?"

Her expression crumples in confusion. Me refusing a drink probably tells her I'm showing signs of brain damage. She knows how much I love my cider.

"I'm late," I whisper.

"You're what?" she asks, rather too loudly.

"Shh!!"

She silences immediately and looks at me with that penetrating stare of hers.

"I haven't even told Nate yet. I only did the test this morning while we were still in Italy. I thought I'd wait until we got home to tell him in case he said something about me not flying in the first trimester. Although, thinking about it, it would have been rather nice to stay there longer—"

Brogan pulls me in for a hug, effectively silencing my rambling.

"And now we're all here and you wanted to tell him in private. I'm so sorry."

"It's okay. I can tell him later once people have left."

"I can't believe I'm the first person to know," she says in shock.

"Well, you wouldn't be—no offence—if it weren't for you handing me alcohol. Now quick, grab me some apple juice out of the fridge and pour it into a champagne flute so he doesn't know the difference."

She does as I ask, and then we return to the party.

***

After everyone has gone home, Brogan says she'll be back to help tidy up in the morning and then leaves us to it.

Now the time is here, I'm nervous. I don't know what to tell Nate. I don't know how to say the words. Will he be mad at me for not telling him the second I did the test?

"Nate ... umm ... we need to talk."

"Uh-oh! Everyone says that's girl-code for 'I'm leaving you'. Is this where you say, 'it's not you, it's me'?"

"No, nothing like that. Now listen," I say as I take a seat on the ottoman at the end of the bed. "I didn't tell you sooner, because I hadn't had time to process it myself. Plus, I wanted to get home and confirm it ... Please don't be mad at me for not saying anything all day ... oh god, I'm rambling, I'm sorry ..."

"Nix, calm down," he says as he kneels between my legs. "Take a deep breath, in then out ... good, now tell me."

I take a couple more breaths before I feel I have enough composure.

"In a few months' time, there's going to be someone else—"

"What?" he asks as he pushes back from me.

"Wait, no, I'm sorry. I'm getting this all wrong. I don't mean someone else as in another man, although, it's a possibility it'll be a boy. But then it might not be."

"Baby, you're rambling again," he says as he takes my hand in his.

Moving my other hand to take his wrist, I look into his eyes as I place his hand over where our baby is growing.

"Nate ..."

"Yes, Nix."

"We're … I mean you're … No, *'we'* was right. We're having a baby."

"Oh my god."

The look of love in his eyes shines so brightly. My fears about us not being ready to be parents are quashed in that instant.

Nate sits stroking my stomach reverently. My heart doubles in size, allowing room for the love I have for him and the love I have for our unborn baby.

Epilogue

Jenna

I'm cooking turkey and all the trimmings, and I have to say, I'm bloody exhausted. I never realised it would be so much more hard work to cook for a family of seven. Why in the ever-loving hell didn't I just let my mum do it like she did last year? Because I'm a glutton for punishment.

Heavily pregnant and cooking for the seven of us—I clearly wasn't in my right mind when I suggested it.

My back aches, the soles of my feet are sore, and I'm working up a serious sweat.

"Wait, Poppy, wait for mummy to come in the living room," I hear Nate say.

Poppy ignores her daddy and comes into the kitchen.

"Are you after scraps, pooch?" I ask as I bend to fuss her behind the ears.

"Sorry, baby. She just wouldn't listen."

"It's okay, I saw her, it's not like I would've tripped over her. And you need to stop talking to her the way you do our daughter. She's a French bulldog, not a human being."

He rolls his eyes at me as he picks Poppy up off the floor and scratches her belly.

"Mumma," I hear Lily say as she toddles into the kitchen.

"Yes, baby," I say as I turn to her.

"Poppy a bad dog."

"Why is she, Lil?"

"She camed in da kitchen when Dadda say no."

Her speech is good for a kid her age and always makes me giggle when she's trying to get Daddy to understand what she's on about.

When Lily came along, Nate was unsurprisingly wonderful with her. He changed nappies, did night feeds, bathed her. Most importantly of all he spent time with her, bonded with her. She's a total daddy's girl because of it. I love watching them together.

"Oh yes, yes she did."

"She go on da nawty step?"

Lily pulls a face as she puts her hands on her hips.

"Definitely her mother's daughter," Nate says as he chuckles and carries Poppy back out of the kitchen.

"She wouldn't stay still on the naughty step, baby girl. But we'll put her in the living room while we eat."

"She no get scwaps?"

"Not right now, no."

I bend down to kiss my beautiful daughter on the top of her head.

"Good. Nawty girls no get any tweats."

"No, you're right, they don't. Now be a good girl and go back in to Grumpy."

"Gwumpy asweep, Mumma."

"Oh, okay, well go back to Dadda then so Mumma can finish our Christmas dinner."

"Okay, Mumma. Me a good girl. I get tweats."

She toddles off to find her dadda before I can get another word in.

I can't believe where the last few years have gone. My mother has finally thawed when it comes to my husband. I didn't really give her any choice in the matter, considering I told her that I was having his baby. She finally realised I was deadly serious about being with him.

It hasn't been an easy ride by any means. She still didn't agree he was good enough for me. But she did do one thing I hadn't expected. She apologised for trying to set me up with Levi. She realised it was a bad idea, made worse by the fact that she did it in front of Nate.

We didn't speak for some time after she did it. I'd only talk to Daddy. But when he told me she wanted to meet up and try and put the past behind us, I did it. Not just for me, but for Daddy, Nate and our unborn daughter.

There were still some awkward family dinners, but my mother finally started talking to Nate like he mattered.

He told me she'd opened up and given him a full and frank apology.

She'd asked if they could speak alone after dinner one night, and they'd gone out on the back deck to talk.

When they came back in, they were both smiling. I thought it was safe to say they'd cleared the air or at least come to a mutual agreement.

Nate later told me that she said she only wanted what was best for her "little girl" and she would always be protective of me. But she knew she should allow me to make my own decisions as an adult now.

I think Daddy told her that he wouldn't put up with her crap on this subject. After all, this is my life, not hers.

Family dinners have been easier since then. And when they learned they were expecting their first grandchild, they were both over the moon. My mother cried upon learning our news. And being a grandma has mellowed her out some.

Of course, she took me baby shopping and totally spoiled me and the baby. We had all we could need for months after her birth.

Nate and I decided on the name Lily, after his grandma, Lillian. I thought it was a fitting tribute.

When she was born, he was the most attentive, most loving partner and father and has been ever since. He loves us with all his heart and soul.

We'd got married before Lily arrived. Not a shotgun wedding because I was pregnant, it was because Nate had already proposed in Sorrento and, when we learned we were expecting, we both wanted to be married before our baby girl was born.

Our wedding day brought us both so much joy. My father had walked me down the aisle with tears in his eyes. Brogan was, of course, maid of honour, and Josh was Nate's best man.

The two of them have since got engaged, and I couldn't be happier that my best friend is happy.

Not long after we got home from that first holiday in Sorrento, Nate moved in with me and let Josh and Brogan move into Gramps's old place, so it stays in the family. It turned out he'd thought it through before even proposing, so I needn't have worried the way I briefly did when we got home.

Our daughter being born was the second best day of my life. Well, second in chronological order, at least. It's actually joint first with my wedding day.

Since then, Lily has brought so much joy into our lives, and now we're going to get to experience that joy all over again when her brother

Daniel is born. We were overjoyed to learn we were having a boy, and I asked Nate if we could call him Daniel, in honour of his father. He cried, and that was all that agreement I needed.

To date, I can name a few times my "bad boy" has cried. And to think he gives off this persona, but underneath it all, he's just a teddy bear.

He cried as he turned to see me at the altar, as our daughter was born, and when our latest scan showed us we'd be completing our family with a little boy and I had suggested his name.

To other people, he may come off as a bad boy. But to me, he's my husband, father of my children, and everything I never knew I needed.

I still find myself wondering how I ever got so lucky. A lot of crap has happened over the years, including my first marriage. But now—now I'm truly, madly, deeply happy.

When I think back to how I felt when I left Lee, I realise I am the embodiment of a phoenix. I was born again from the ashes of my marriage, and I rose out of the flames to become a strong, determined woman. And, just like the mythical creature, my tears have proven to have healing qualities.

The End

About the author

Keren is a bookworm whose bookshelves groan under the weight of her obsession, but she believes there's always room for "one more book."

She lives in the UK with her son and when she isn't reading or writing, she's nurturing the reader and writer in him as he's currently writing his own book.

Keren loves to connect with her readers. You can reach out to her on social media. She loves to talk anything books, movies and TV.

Her other obsessions include Disney, Marvel, and she's a Potterhead for life.

Also by Keren Hughes

Safe
First of The Jagged Scars Duet series

In every way Elise is a survivor.

As a child, she was abused by the first man she trusted completely.

As a teenager, she was manipulated mentally and physically by a man, to the point that she could not see just how bad their relationship was. She ended up too scared to stay, but even more scared to leave.

Having suffered for years at the hands of men she trusted, she met Jensen. Finally, she felt that she had someone good in her life. Their relationship was all too brief, and when it ended she built a wall around her heart. How could she ever trust a man again?

Elise; a single, disabled mum. It was all too clear that men could not see past her disability. Forsaking the love of men, she concentrated on her son, Caleb. It was the one thing she knew she could do right. Her love for Caleb was beyond measure. He was her whole world. However, Elise's best friend Sam had other ideas, and set her up on a blind date with an extremely hot paramedic.

With so much hurt in the past, she was not sure if she was strong enough to face rejection again. Could she truly open her heart again to another? Could Elise finally find her safe haven in his arms, or would he just add another scar to her soul?

Home
Second of The Jagged Scars Duet series

~Home isn't a physical place, it's the place where your heart beats.~

Drew Wright always said he had the "reverse Midas touch"; everything he touched turned to shit instead of gold.

As a child, he was beaten, neglected, and abused by drug addicted parents whose next fix was more important than having food in the cupboard. Plagued by flashbacks of a past that haunts him, he's worked hard to become a paramedic and help others often caught in the grip of the same trauma he experienced.

After being set up on a blind date with the love of his life he thought he'd lost, it seemed his luck was turning and fate was giving him a second chance. Happily married with two children, he has everything he ever dreamed of.

But then one tragic moment throws his world into upheaval and lands Drew in the middle of a battle to hang on to the life he loves.

Can he separate the past from the present and save his future?

Or will the demons that have stalked him his whole life finally devour him?

Secret Santa

Being born and raised in the town of Snowflake has its perks for Aneurin Mackenzie, she's seen it all; businesses booming and the town flourishing. Sadly, she's also seen it torn to shreds by a previous mayor.

Then, in comes cocky, arrogant, filthy rich Preston Wolfric III with his "fresh ideas" to bring business back to this small town. He wants to turn Snowflake around, bringing it to the 21st century.
However, Nye will not let her town be changed without a fight.

He's a big city alpha male, she's a small town girl with no desire to change. She plans to run him out of town but what she doesn't count on is that cocky jerk making his way under her skin, seeping into her veins.

She didn't realise how devastatingly handsome he is. He didn't realise what he needed was right in front of him.
What will happen when Preston and Nye's worlds collide? Will there be sparks or will it become a fire that lays waste to everything they thought they knew?

Do opposites really attract?

More Black Velvet Seductions titles

Their Lady Gloriana by Starla Kaye
Cowboys in Charge by Starla Kaye
Her Cowboy's Way by Starla Kaye
Punished by Richard Savage, Nadia Nautalia & Starla Kaye
Accidental Affair by Leslie McKelvey
Right Place, Right Time by Leslie McKelvey
Her Sister's Keeper by Leslie McKelvey
Playing for Keeps by Glenda Horsfall
Playing By His Rules by Glenda Horsfall
The Stir of Echo by Susan Gabriel
Rally Fever by Crea Jones
Behind The Clouds by Jan Selbourne
Trusting Love Again by Starla Kaye
Runaway Heart by Leslie McKelvey
The Otherling by Heather M. Walker
First Submission - Anthology
These Eyes So Green by Deborah Kelsey
Dark Awakening by Karlene Cameron
The Reclaiming of Charlotte Moss by Heather M. Walker
Ryann's Revenge by Rai Karr & Breanna Hayse
The Postman's Daughter by Sally Anne Palmer
Final Kill by Leslie McKelvey
Killer Secrets by Zia Westfield
Crossover, Texas by Freia Hooper-Bradford
The King's Blade by L.J. Dare
Uniform Desire - Anthology
Safe by Keren Hughes
Finishing the Game by M.K. Smith
Out of the Shadows by Gabriella Hewitt
A Woman's Secret by C.L. Koch
Her Lover's Face by Patricia Elliott

Love Times Infinity by K.L. Ramsey
Naval Maneuvers by Dee S. Knight
Love's Patient Journey by K.L. Ramsey
Perilous Love by Jan Selbourne
Patrick by Callie Carmen
Love's Design by K.L. Ramsey
The Brute and I by Suzanne Smith
Love's Promise by K.L. Ramsey
Home by Keren Hughes
Worth the Wait by K.L. Ramsey
Only A Good Man Will Do by Dee S. Knight
Secret Santa by Keren Hughes
The Christmas Wedding by K.L. Ramsey
Killer Lies by Zia Westfield
A Merman's Choice by Alice Renaud
Theirs to Keep by K.L. Ramsey
Line of Fire by K.L. Ramsey
Theirs to Love by K.L. Ramsey
All She Ever Needed by Lora Logan
Nicolas by Callie Carmen
Torn Devotion by K.L. Ramsey
The Story of JESS & AVER by K.A. Neeson
Theirs to Have by K.L. Ramsey
Paging Dr. Turov by Gibby Campbell
Theirs to Take by K.L. Ramsey

Our back catalog is being released on Kindle Unlimited
You can find us on:
Twitter: BVSBooks
Facebook: Black Velvet Seductions
See our bookshelf on Amazon now! Search "BVS Black Velvet
Seductions Publishing Company"